IT
HAD
TO
BE
YOU

ALSO BY ELIZA JANE BRAZIER

If I Disappear
Good Rich People
Girls and Their Horses

IT

HAD

TO

BE

YOU

ELIZA JANE BRAZIER

BERKLEY
New York

BERKLEY
An imprint of Penguin Random House LLC
penguinrandomhouse.com

Copyright © 2024 by Eliza Jane Brazier
Penguin Random House supports copyright. Copyright fuels creativity, encourages diverse
voices, promotes free speech, and creates a vibrant culture. Thank you for buying an authorized
edition of this book and for complying with copyright laws by not reproducing, scanning,
or distributing any part of it in any form without permission. You are supporting writers
and allowing Penguin Random House to continue to publish books for every reader.

BERKLEY and the BERKLEY & B colophon are registered trademarks of
Penguin Random House LLC.

Library of Congress Cataloging-in-Publication Data

Names: Brazier, Eliza Jane, author.
Title: It had to be you / Eliza Jane Brazier.
Description: New York : Berkley, 2024.
Identifiers: LCCN 2023050025 (print) | LCCN 2023050026 (ebook) |
ISBN 9780593438923 (hardcover) | ISBN 9780593438930 (ebook)
Subjects: LCSH: Assassins--Fiction. | LCGFT: Thrillers. | Novels.
Classification: LCC PS3602.R3985 I8 2024 (print) |
LCC PS3602.R3985 (ebook) | DDC 813/.6--dc23/eng/20231024
LC record available at https://lccn.loc.gov/2023050025
LC ebook record available at https://lccn.loc.gov/2023050026

Printed in the United States of America
1st Printing

Book design by Daniel Brount

I go where they require me
And I fight for those who hire me
I spend my time living on the run
There ain't no girl waiting for me
No one left up in my after-glory
That's the life of a Hired Gun

Sometimes I think I'd like to settle down,
Just to change my ways,
But what's the use in dreaming,
I just drift around
As I move from town to town.

—"HIRED GUN" BY ALAN WASS

IT
HAD
TO
BE
YOU

I

ATTRACTION

1

Eva

I'VE HEARD THAT KILLING SOMEONE IS LIKE FALLING IN LOVE. BUT I wouldn't know. I've never done it. Fall in love, I mean. That's for lunatics.

I see him on the sleeper train from Florence to Paris. He's standing there—now, right now—on the other side of the glass, trying to peer in through the mirrored window, and I think, *I wish we could stay like this forever.*

This is the exact relationship I want. I can see him but he can't see me. He's attractive, but especially attractive is the expression he wears because he thinks nobody can see him. His expression says, *It's the end of the world, this is the worst day of my life and I'm stuck in a sleeper compartment with seven other people.*

Hard same.

I can almost see him debating, *Can I just stand for twelve hours?* Contemplating, *How did I end up here?*

No one takes the sleeper train anymore. I'm here only because it's harder to hide weapons on an international flight. Not impossible, but harder.

I could find all the weapons I want in Paris, but the longer you work this job, the more superstitious you get. I guess everyone gets superstitious when someone dies, especially when you're the one killing them.

He takes a step back. I think he might leave, walk down the aisle, maybe hang in the dining car.

It's actually me who opens the door. Sometimes I do things without thinking. Hazard of a job that's based on instinct. I want. I do. It happens. Just like that.

"Oh, I'm sorry. I didn't see you there." I've been staring at him for the past two minutes, but I'm so convincing that I half believe myself.

His face changes the moment he sees me, like I'm the whole world watching, expecting some kind of performance. Suddenly his expression is bland, almost meek. He's over six feet tall and borderline hulking, but with me in his sights, he's Clark Kent.

"Oh, no, *I'm* sorry. I wasn't sure if there was space in the car." He pushes his glasses up on his nose.

Let it be known that the seats are assigned.

I hold the door open. "We're the first ones here. But I checked the stubs; it's a full car." There are little ticket stubs above every seat, so everyone knows exactly where they belong.

He hesitates, as if caught between his performance of politeness and train angst.

"First time on a sleeper?" I ask.

"It's not that," he says.

"Anything I can help with?" I don't like to pry. It's true. I *love* to pry.

"Probably not." He has a suitcase behind him, so utilitarian that I assume he works in tech and wants people to know it.

I'm very good at reading people. This guy works out—*a lot.* He's wearing a suit he either has borrowed or can't afford to replace; it's loose and tight in all the wrong places. He probably took the train because he's actually broke. Or because he's too broad to fit comfortably in an airplane seat. He's favoring his right shoulder. He keeps his arm slightly cocked, as if bracing for impact.

He's not my usual type, which intrigues me. It's always better to choose a type that isn't yours. Call it an insurance policy.

I step back so he can move past me. He seems to think I'm much bigger than I am, because he hits the doorframe trying to avoid me, then hisses slightly through his teeth. It's obvious he's extremely uncomfortable being a human, which I find attractive.

"Do you want me to help you with your bags?" I ask.

I don't wait for him to answer. I grab the handle of his big wheeled suitcase and start to pull. It doesn't move. It's much heavier than I expected.

"I can get that," he says, but now it's a challenge.

"I got it." I engage my muscles and roll it neatly through the door. "What do you have in there?"

"Uh, computers." Called it.

He frowns at the bag like it's the bane of his existence. I can understand. If I had a bag that heavy, I'd dump it in the Arno.

"You don't want to leave it in the luggage racks?" I left all my bags on the racks—black, nondescript, with nothing in them that ties back to me, unless you recognize the custom satin finish on my Glock.

"No." He stows it neatly under the seats.

"You've done this before."

"I don't like planes," he says, pushing his glasses up again. They keep sliding down. At first I thought it was because he doesn't normally wear them. I thought he was trying to look smarter. But I can see the variation in lens thickness—he's practically blind in his right eye—and then I realize they're falling because they're bent.

"Here." I reach for his glasses, slide them off his nose and

5

quickly adjust them. "Everyone's face is crooked in a slightly different way."

I go to put them back on him but he is completely frozen. I can be too familiar with people sometimes. I know so much about them—heart rates and arteries and pressure points—that I sometimes feel this false sense of intimacy, as if I can wind them up like toys.

"Sorry," I say, handing him the glasses instead of putting them on his nose.

He swallows, seems uncertain. Of what, I don't know. He hesitates before he puts them on. When he does, they're perfect.

"See?" I say, as if that justifies everything.

"Thank you," he says, and then he takes the seat farthest from me. I don't think it's even *his* seat. He surreptitiously takes the tab off and lets it fall into a crack.

It's so weird how total strangers can casually devastate you. Not that I really care. I don't *really* care about anything. It's just easier sometimes to care deeply about things that don't matter.

"I get motion sickness," he says because he knows that I noticed him removing the tab. "I have to be close to the door." And it's suddenly so fucking awkward between us. It's shocking, actually, how awkward interactions with complete strangers can sometimes be.

"I don't care where you sit," I say, which only makes it more awkward. I should reassure him that I like the window. We could smile at each other, delight in our unique preferences, ruminate on our beautiful differences, but instead I just take my seat. Placating people is such a chore.

I look out the window and into the train station. It's eight p.m. and the crowd is starting to thin, get drunk and tired and hopeless. I should've just taken a plane.

"Six more people, huh?" he says. He's pacifying me, trying to smooth things over. Like the world might end if two strangers don't get along.

I sigh. Six more people. The train is almost full. I ran a check before I came to our car. There are open seats scattered here and there, but no real space. It's the law of assassins: Everything that can go wrong will go wrong. Sometimes it's fun. Sometimes it's eight p.m. at the end of a depressing weekend in Florence. Unless.

"You know," I say, "there is something we could try . . ."

He shifts uncomfortably. I'm starting to suspect he really doesn't like me. It's almost like he knows me.

I nearly say *Never mind* to let him off the hook—but why should I? I'm out here solving his problems for fun, and he's looking at me like I'm presumptuous.

"I'm sure it will be fine," he says, saintly in his repaired glasses.

The compartment door slides open. An Italian woman comes in. I'm relieved. Maybe she can break the spell. Maybe this guy and I can both stop trying to be nice to each other now. I thought he was cute at first, but this is getting too messy. I want to hook up with men who worship me completely. Otherwise it's kind of a waste of my time.

Of course this woman is the passenger whose tab he removed. It's fun watching him squirm as she looks at her ticket and the seat number—for so long, the story of it might constitute an epic— while we watch.

"I think I'm . . .," she starts, but drifts off when she looks at him. He has a *drift off* face.

"They always bungle these things, don't they?" he says in perfectly accented Italian. I recognize his strategy immediately— blame *them*, those damn train people.

"They always do!" the woman agrees. "It took me two hours on the phone to arrange my ticket! My granddaughter had to help me! We had a ticket booked for Monday, but I need to be in Paris *by* Monday and I didn't realize I needed to book for the day before. Well, it was such a mess!"

It's a tedious story but we all listen because we're all here together for the next twelve hours. At around ten o'clock we'll pull out the beds and sleep on racks like corpses. Dead bodies are all laid to rest with strangers, too. Life is chance more than anything else. So is death.

"I'm sorry," he says. "That sounds like such a nightmare." He is using his pleasant voice. He didn't use it with me.

The woman has moved on from her problem with the seats. She realizes there is an open seat beside *him*, so maybe it's not all that bad. "I suppose I'll just sit here—what difference does it make?" She takes the seat. He shrinks in a very convincing way to make room. I bet he regrets not sitting next to me now. At least, I hope he does.

I can't help smiling as she slots in beside him, from the bottom of her thigh to the top of her shoulder. So cozy. He catches me smiling. To my surprise, he smiles back.

I feel something catch between my legs, like he's been fishing down there all this time.

He quickly stows his smile away, lest I forget I've decided not to like him.

The other passengers all come at once.

Two young Italian men. An American businessman. An older Englishman. A young Frenchwoman. A partridge in a pear tree. All in this one little train car.

Glasses Guy catches my eyes again. He is now crammed against the wall, looking exceptionally pale and miserable. Still, his eyes are almost hopeful when they meet mine. Like everything that happens from here on out is an inside joke between us. Like we are the only two people in the world who understand the absurdity of this exact circumstance. We were here first. Everyone else is part of *our* story.

It's so weird how certain people in your life just stick out. How you can go for years and years not meeting one. How you can convince yourself they don't exist. That it was something that happened when you were young. That it'll never happen again. That you were made of magic once, but you aren't magic now. And then, suddenly, you look across a train car and see someone sticking out like a page that's misaligned in the book of your life.

An Italian voice comes over the speaker system, telling us the train is about to depart. The lights flicker. There is this dragging sensation beneath our feet. He flinches. The train jerks. It rolls out of the station and into the night.

Our eyes meet every so often. He's super miserable now. He seems like he's in real, physical pain. When the woman beside him jerks with laughter—she's talking on the phone. When the train jolts. Even when the lights flicker. Still, he seems okay with this, like he wants to suffer as much as possible. To get his money's worth.

But eventually he seems overwhelmed. He's pale as paper. His eyelids flutter occasionally. I think he might throw up, which is one way to clear a compartment. I imagine the two of us alone with his vomit. I'd stay. Puke doesn't really bother me. I see it a lot in my line of work.

Eventually he extracts himself from his seat—calmly, efficiently—and walks out the door. The train jolts. He lurches against the doorframe, then catches himself and disappears down the aisle.

2

Jonathan

I AM ALWAYS ATTRACTED TO WOMEN AT THE WORST POSSIBLE times. When they are married, and I am assigned to kill their husbands. Or today, when I have been shot.

My heart is hammering so hard, so fast. Then it stops. That is the worst part.

It hangs its heartstrings up for one . . . two . . . three seconds. I think it is never coming back. My heartbeat, I did not know I loved it so much, and then:

Bam! It starts up again with a stabbing jolt.

I am dying. It is not the first time. In some ways I have learned to enjoy it, the musicality of the world refreshing and receding. The subtle interplay. Life. The absence of it.

There is no afterlife. I know that for certain because I have died before. Four times. I have died and been brought back— always against my will. I black out. I wake up in a hospital. That is all death is. A break between being alive.

Unless you do not come back.

I leave the train car. I stalk down the aisle toward the toilet.

My cheeks are burning up. My hands are numb. My heart is beating too fast, and then *flick*, it stops.

I fall sideways.

Smack!

My temple hits the wall, which brings me around, blinking, heart beating. Alive.

Now on the ground. The train is coursing like blood over the tracks beneath me. I can feel the vibrations all through me. They rattle my teeth.

A woman in red shoes is peering down at me. "Are you all right?" she says in French.

"Yes," I say back in French. "Sorry."

She scowls at me. I apologize again. I drag myself to my feet. I try to look repentant.

I am dying, and I am so goddamn sorry about it.

When I finally make it into the bathroom and shut the door, all my pain and nausea, and frankly, all my disgust with the entire situation, come screaming to the surface. Now that no one is watching, I can really fucking die.

I grip the sink. I want to splash water on my face, but I seem unable to let the sink go. My knuckles are white. My hands are shaking. I cannot even look up. I stare into the small silver bowl.

I will myself not to die. *You can do it. You just have to believe in yourself.*

The train veers left. I fall right.

I *smack* my head on the edge of the toilet.

This truly does not feel good, and possibly I should just let myself die. There are so many problems it would solve: my problems, a lot of people's problems. But the thing about dying is that when push comes to shove, there is a natural override. Your body wants to live. It really does not care at all about your opinions on the matter. Your thoughts. Your needs. Your wants. Your body takes over. It works its magic. It hands your life back to you like a gift.

I have drugs in my pockets. So many drugs. All different colors and flavors. Not for me, but for my job. Drugs to kill you. Drugs to bring you back to life.

I reach into the less lethal pocket and pull out a handful. I try to be organized but I am slipping dangerously close to unconsciousness. I move the pills around with my finger. I try to remember exactly what they are. There has to be something in my hand that can solve being shot.

I do not have time to figure it out. I swallow them all. Downers to stop the pain. Uppers to stop the dying. They catch in my throat.

I climb up and suck water from the sink beneath a sign that says NOT SAFE FOR DRINKING. Let that be the thing that kills me.

I tumble to the floor. I imagine the pill army splitting up inside my vanquished body. Divide. Conquer. Win the battle against death.

I shut my eyes. The train hums under me, sometimes inside me.

I do not die.

In my experience, you rarely die when you think you are going to.

I lean back against the sink, facing the toilet. Above my head, the world steams by through a tiny window and my mind starts to drift . . .

What a beautiful world. What a beautiful life. I am so lucky to be alive right now . . . Wow.

I am pretty sure one of the pills I took was Ecstasy.

My life returns in a cozy drugged fog. I do not have time to enjoy it.

I undo the buttons of the jacket I am wearing. It is not my jacket. I borrowed it from the man who shot me. My jacket was much nicer, before it was stained with my blood.

I unbutton his shirt and examine the dressing. I am very good at dressing wounds. I am actually quite artistic about it. Death and not dying are the great works of my life.

Little puffs of blood are blooming through the gauze but nothing excessive, nothing to justify the way I felt before the drugs started to work their magic.

It is possible I was just having a panic attack. It is possible, even, that she induced it. I often confuse lust for some form of disease. Maybe she made me feel like I was dying. Maybe she stopped my heart.

I let my head fall back. I take a deep, calming breath.

I am not dead yet.

I am on the sleeper train to Paris. I could not take a plane because the bullet under my shoulder blade might be picked up by a metal detector, and I do not want to raise any flags. I am going to see my brother, who is a doctor. There are other doctors I could see, but he is the only one I trust. I am feeling a little fragile because someone shot me.

In most cases it is safer to leave a bullet inside you, but I do not like the location of this one, too close to a main artery, a through line to my heart—whatever is left of it. I also do not like that I keep fainting.

You spend so long defying death, you start to get too comfortable with it. You learn to live with it hovering over your shoulder, whispering the sweetest nothing in your ear. It becomes hard to tell when you are dying from when you are just living.

I run my fingers over my palms over and over. It is a tic I have sometimes, and right now the Ecstasy is not helping. I really know how to make my life interesting. I should not leave the restroom.

13

I should stay here, sleep if I can, ride the train and the situation out.

But when I shut my eyes, I see her. She looks so familiar. It gives me this uncomfortable sensation that I *know* her already. That we were supposed to meet.

Destiny is the easiest way to explain the unexplainable. I like her. I want her. It must be fate. What else could it be?

I close my eyes and try to find where she belongs, to place her on the map of my twisted life. Is she someone I tried to kill? Is she someone who tried to kill me? She does not fit anywhere. And Ecstasy brain tells me it is because she is my destiny, and suddenly my whole life makes sense—as long as I do not think about it too hard. My life is a train steaming toward this eventual stop: her.

I can see her now.

She has wide, round eyes. Thin lips. Messy hair. A cowlick behind her right ear but not her left. A mole on her shoulder. A protruding clavicle. Muscled arms and shoulders but a soft belly. A broken heart.

Some things I remember. Some things I add on.

The train pitches. My eyes click open.

We will be in Paris in eleven hours. I want to see her again.

3

Eva

H E'S GONE FOR SO LONG THAT EVERYONE STARTS TALKING
about him.

"I hope he's okay," the Italian woman says. "He felt
very cold."

He's gone for more than half an hour before I leave, too. Not
to find him, necessarily. It's almost time for the beds to go down.
I want to stretch my legs. I consider walking to the dining car to
get a glass of wine, but I have to be on form tomorrow. I walk to
the car anyway, to smell other people's wine.

Sometimes I like to be around other people, to pretend I'm
one of them. That I'm going to Paris on vacation instead of going
to kill someone.

I buy a bag of Skittles and an orange Fanta. I eat and drink
while I walk up and down the train aisles, watching dark cities go
by. I'm on my way back to our car when I see him coming out of
the restroom up ahead.

He waits for me to catch up.

"Do you want one?" I hold out my bag of Skittles. "They're

tropical. I'm pretty sure they've been discontinued everywhere except this train."

"I better not." The train lurches but he looks less pale. His cheeks are pinkish. His pupils are dilated. He's staring at me a little. A lot.

"Are you feeling all right?" I say. Then I notice two fresh lumps: one on his temple and one on his cheekbone. "Ouch. What happened?"

His fingers fly to the bumps, like he'd forgotten about them. "I hit my head. On the toilet."

"Yikes," I say. "You're not having a good train ride."

"I took a Dramamine. I'm feeling better now," he says, leaning casually against the wall. I can tell. Where before he was tight and uncomfortable, now he's relaxed, almost loose. He's seriously staring right at me. It's a little unsettling. I'm not used to looking at people for long; avoiding eye contact is one of my tricks for staying invisible. But I'm looking at him, and he's looking back. His eyes are blue but the dark kind, so you could easily confuse them for another color. "I thought taking a train would be easier than flying. It's a sleeper train—you just sleep, right? I forgot I don't sleep anywhere. I don't know why I thought it would be different here."

I sigh. "I never sleep either. That's kind of what I like about sleeper trains, though." I nudge my shoulder up against the wall, matching his lean. "It's comforting to know that other people sleep."

"I suppose."

"Maybe not seven other people in one tiny compartment."

He snorts in agreement. He's rubbing his fingers over his palms. I don't think he realizes it. It's like a nervous tic and it doesn't stop. It's a little suspicious. I've never seen someone get high off Dramamine, but I know enough about drugs to know they don't always work the way you plan. I once gave someone an allegedly lethal dose of Seconal but instead of killing them, it gave them super strength. It also made them really, really angry. Which was understandable, given that I was trying to kill them.

He cocks his head. "What were you saying earlier? That there was something we could try?"

"I thought you were gonna be a good boy."

"I don't know why you thought that."

I grin. I'm bubbling over with sunshine. Sometimes it's that easy. Sometimes it's easier with someone you don't know, who doesn't know you, to be happy. I look him dead in the eyes. "Pretend we're married."

"What?" He seems caught off guard, like I just asked to hold his dick.

"That's the plan."

"I don't see how that will help."

"Just follow my lead. If it doesn't work, you can always vomit."

I spin toward the car. I feel him follow behind me. As soon as we're in listening distance I start:

"I can't believe you're doing this *again*! You're ruining our vacation!" I slide the door open with a jerk. I don't lower my voice. "Like you *always* do. Every! Fucking! Time!" He starts to take his seat, but I scold, "What, so you're just gonna sit down?" He freezes. I'm not sure if he's acting or reacting, but either way, it's perfect.

"Are you two together?" the Italian woman asks, clearly uncomfortable.

"I can't believe you're doing this *again*!" I repeat. It has to be cyclical. It has to be inane. It has to be hopeless and unsolvable. That's how you make it feel like a real relationship.

He hovers over his seat, unsure what to do. He doesn't seem to like the attention. Too bad.

"You're seriously not gonna say anything?" I demand.

"Do you want to switch seats?" the woman asks, keen to stop the scolding. "So you can be together?"

"Are you kidding?" I scoff. "I'm not sitting with him."

And I'm just getting warmed up.

The Italian boys drop out first. "I think I saw a pair of seats in the next car," one says to the other.

And then it's like an avalanche. Everyone goes. Pretty soon it's just Glasses Guy, me and the American businessman. When it's clear the latter could not care less about the fighting, I give up. He can stay.

I smile at my partner in crime. "See? I told you. There's nothing worse than two people in a relationship."

"Evidently." He smiles ruefully. "I'm Jonathan, by the way."

"I'm Eva." I'm not, but he doesn't need to know that.

4

Jonathan

THERE IS A REASON I NEVER TAKE DRUGS RECREATIONALLY. I am very sensitive. I have strong feelings.

Right now I have too-strong feelings. Maybe I did die. Maybe the old me is gone. Maybe he left behind this hollow chamber, which is currently filling with lust.

I am supposed to keep myself separate from the world but I do have sex—more often than I like to admit. I promise myself that I will practice containment, but sometimes I want sex so badly that it becomes the greater danger.

Every time, I act surprised to find that fucking leads to more fucking. That sex leads to more sex. That horniness is not a disease that can be cured but rather one that can be cultivated. One that can and will consume me.

All that I can really say in defense of sex is that it is more moral than murder. On the scale of my sins, I tend to avoid guilt for that one.

Unless the guilt gets me off.

Eva is sitting across from me in her assigned seat. She is gazing out the window. Her legs are crossed. Her eyelashes are feathered. My heart is on a chain that is tied around her ankle.

Thank God for our fellow passenger, folded neatly in his seat. He is the only thing keeping me from peaking.

I am fighting the Ecstasy, but it is knocking at the top of my skull, swelling under my skin. I am rubbing my palms so much that I will have an RSI tomorrow.

My eyes keep being dragged in her direction. I force myself to look out the window. To look at the ceiling. To look at the floor. Every time, I drift. Every time, I land on her.

"You feeling okay?" Her eyes are on me now. Her eyes are so wide that they seem to melt, smoky wet, down her face.

"Better," I say. She looks pointedly at my hands. I stuff them into my jacket pockets. "What brings you to Europe?" I ask, trying to take the attention off me and put it on her, where it belongs.

"Vacation." She smiles dreamily.

"How long have you been gone?" I ask.

Her expression punctures a little. "A long time. Too long. What about you? What's your story?"

I open my mouth to answer her; then I shut it quickly. I shut it because I realize I was about to tell her the truth. I was about to tell her everything. Lay it out on the line to a stranger, with a bullet in my chest.

I do not feel the pain of the bullet anymore. I do not even feel alive. I can feel myself sometimes drifting over our heads, like the drugs have made me a Grecian god watching the performance of my own life.

"Same. Vacation," my mouth says.

She sighs and leans back, as if satisfied by this. "I love being an American in Europe. Don't you? It's like living in a fantasy world. Like nothing is real, as long as you never go home."

My heart stops. Or at least it feels like it does. It is like she is speaking words I wrote. "They must hate us," I finally say. "The Europeans."

She moves closer to me. "Of course they do. We forget there are rules and laws and governments here, too. All we see are the Eiffel Tower, the museums and the gardens."

"And McDonald's."

She laughs. "Of course." She reaches up, hooks her hand above her head and talks to the ceiling. "We don't belong here, and there's something absolutely freeing about that, you know?"

"Yes." I cannot stop looking at her, entranced. Sometimes I feel like I have gone my whole life never fully agreeing with anyone. Never fully understanding anyone. And though I tell myself that it is impossible, sometimes I cannot stop myself from believing that a stranger might be the one who finally gets me.

That a stranger might understand something vital about the world that nobody else ever seems to understand: You can do whatever you want. You do not have to play by the rules. You can kill people and drive fast cars and dress in designer clothes and no one will stop you. No one can. You cannot even stop yourself.

My fingers start moving again. I can hear them rustling in my pockets. Rubbing my palms.

"Are you nervous?" she says.

I start to say something but it catches in my throat, so I make a pathetic *nuh* sound. I am actually quite harmless like this. Mostly. "Are you traveling alone?" I ask.

Her face cracks. "What?"

I am not used to having conversations, so I tend to skip the ordinary parts in favor of the important parts. *Are you taken? Good, I will take you.*

"Do you have a partner?"

"Oh." She tilts her head, putting something together lightning quick.

"Is that a yes?"

"No."

"So it is a no?"

"Yes."

"I think you are very pretty," I tell her engagingly. I am so fucking pathetic.

She frowns. "Are you sure you just took a Dramamine?"

I cannot tell her what I really took, so I say, "I think so."

"You're rubbing your legs."

I look down. She is right. My hands have escaped from my pockets and are now rubbing my legs. I break a smile. "I think I might have accidentally taken the wrong pill."

"But you don't feel sick anymore?"

"No."

She smirks. "Then I guess it worked."

5

Eva

HE IS KIND OF CUTE, THE SAD LOST BOY AT THE END OF A night out, confusing Ecstasy for Dramamine. He looks at me for way too long. Again and again and again. He doesn't look away when I catch him looking. There's something safe about his being high, like none of this is real if it isn't real for him.

I can tell he's into me. He's not exactly trying to hide it. He's a stranger on a train. This is a victimless crime. Except for our American businessman.

I look at Jonathan. "Do you want to go for a walk with me?"

"Yes, please." He agrees so quickly, I laugh.

"Okay."

The dining car is closed. The sleeping cars are sleeping. There's a space at the end of our car for the racks of luggage. I guide him there.

I perch on a luggage rack. "Why Paris?" I ask.

"Eiffel Tower. Museums. Gardens. McDonald's. All that." He stands over me. He holds on to a handle to steady himself when the train lists. "What about you?"

"I want to go to Les Puces," I say. "You know, the market? Have you ever been?" The flea market in Paris is one of the largest and the most famous in the world. I've been there dozens of times. I have no plans to go there tomorrow. It's easier to keep your lies straight if you lie about everything.

"No, I haven't," he says.

"You should go. You can buy anything there. Legend has it that if you walk around for long enough, you're bound to find everything you need." I wiggle my eyebrows at him.

"What are you looking for?" he asks, hitching his pants slightly and moving closer.

"I don't know. That's the best way to go in—not knowing what you want, or what you need." I lift my chin. I shut my eyes in demonstration. "You have to make your mind a blank. To be open to anything, you know? And the market will guide you."

He moves even closer. I can feel his heat. "Sounds a little spooky."

"I love spooky things. I get my palm read all the time." I hold my hand up to him, spread my fingers. "They always get it wrong, but I keep going. Sometimes it's nice to be misunderstood."

Trouble passes briefly over his face, then floats away on a drug cloud. He moves a little closer still. "You're very pretty," he says. It has nothing to do with what we're talking about. He has no game whatsoever. Maybe I'm feeling generous because I find it kind of sweet.

"I'm not pretty," I correct him. I'm ordinary, on the outside.

"You're my kind of pretty," he says. I wonder what that means.

I stand up, then swing lightly along the luggage racks until I reach a darker corner. "I'm forgettable," I tell him. "Tomorrow afternoon, you'll think back on this very moment and you won't be able to remember my face. You'll substitute it with some girl you knew in college, your Starbucks barista . . ."

"No. I won't." He grips the handle. "I won't forget you." The train pitches and throws him forward. He hisses, as if in pain. "This train is going to kill me."

"You should sit down."

"I might not be able to get up again," he jokes. "Where are you from?"

I almost tell him the truth. It feels totally safe. We're strangers on a train. We'll probably never meet again. In fact, it might even be appropriate to tell him that I am about to commit murder. There is precedent. Hitchcock did it first.

"All over," I say, which is a real liar's answer. "What about you?"

"I grew up in upstate New York," he says. Then he weaves a story so delightfully dull, so enchantingly mundane. The stakes are so low. The driving forces so weak. "I went to college in Vermont, but then I transferred to Delaware." The places are so boring that they sound made up: Vermont, Delaware. The kind of places you don't want to know anything about. "I did a summer abroad in France and I fell in love with it." He says this so dispassionately, the way people do. *I stubbed my toe and then I fell in love with it.* His voice is so deep; I want him to bore me to death.

There's something comforting about other people's lives. It's like knowing other people sleep without nightmares. It makes me feel like the world is a better place. A place I've never been to, it's true, but possibly one that exists.

I imagine our future together. What else are strange men for but imaginary futures? We would live in Delaware. In a house on stilts or whatever they have there. Pods. We would raise 2.5 children. The littlest would be half a person, but we would never tell them. Jonathan would give up his childish dreams of computers to work in a factory. He would have to. In this day and age, 2.5 children need factory money to survive.

I would resent the hell out of him. I would blame him for

everything that went wrong in my life. The time that guy stole my parking space. That we never went on vacation. That his breath smelled funny in the morning. That we couldn't afford a headboard. I would unleash my resentment every night by fucking his brains out. I would tie him up. I would spank him. I would make him wear an apron and lipstick.

Our life together would be perfect.

"Why are you smiling?" he says.

"Your life is just so interesting," I say. "I want to hear more about Delaware."

He smiles back. "You're teasing me." He takes a step toward me, steadying himself on the bars above our heads.

I gaze up at him. "Have you ever had sex on a train?"

He hisses lightly, then gazes down on me like I've purposefully wounded him. "Now you're really teasing me."

"I'm not teasing," I swear. I'm not. I'm just direct. I have a busy schedule. I don't have time to fuck around, not when it comes to fucking.

And I like him. I like him, but we have only hours together—most of which will be spent asleep. It's nice to think we could just talk all night, but that's unrealistic. I can lie for only so long before I will run out of things to say and start telling the truth. Besides, I'll never see him again. I can't. So we might as well just skip to the inevitable. The *pleasurable.*

I scan the vicinity. The dining car is closed. The sleeping cars are sleeping.

I swing in his direction until I'm standing right in front of him. Our bodies line up. The hot parts radiate heat.

There's something magic about strangers. You know nothing about them, but bodies mostly work the same way. Minds are mostly cast from the same molds. There's a sense of discovery and familiarity, all at the same time.

I reach up. I brush the lump swelling on his temple. I trace the heart-shaped bruise weeping on his cheek. "We can have sex right here. Right now."

He swallows. "Can I keep my jacket on?"

Weird, but I don't have time to unravel his peculiarities. I do have time to fuck him. It might even help me sleep.

"You don't even have to take off your pants," I promise.

6

Jonathan

THERE IS A NEON SIGN INSIDE MY SKULL TELLING ME NOT TO have sex, but the neon sign is not the one whose permission I need.

She said I can keep my jacket on. She will never see the wound. And the bullet has settled, found a quiet place inside me to sleep and dream.

Her hand slips between my legs, and all my blood rushes down, so my head feels mercilessly light. Then I have one last burst of sense: It is probably not a good idea to have sex with a bullet in my chest.

As her fingers cup my balls, as my chest throbs, my voice says, "We probably shouldn't."

"Oh." Her hand is gone so fast, it is like it was never there. "Okay."

She steps back. I step forward.

"Who am I fucking kidding?" I say in my head and out loud. Then I kiss her. It catches us both by surprise.

First kisses are always the best kisses. The ones you remember. The ones you can never re-create, although you *will* try.

I am a horrible person but I can feel love. Maybe that is what makes me horrible.

She kisses me, mouth to mouth but I feel it everywhere. I am treacherously hollow, verging on soulless. When she kisses me, that single drop of lust in an empty shell is everything at once.

I am echoing with desire, bright and swollen, and I kiss her back harder, so hard it is like I am digging down inside her, excavating the tenderness, taking it all for myself. My vacant body. My sunken thoughts. Her bright fireworks of lust, exploding on the blankest canvas.

"Easy, tiger." She presses her hand, all five fingers, like a star, into my chest and pushes me backward, gently. I feel a muted ache in my chest, reminding me that just because I cannot feel the pain does not mean it is not there. I do not want to die—not yet.

I should probably stop, but I find I cannot. And it is not just the drugs, or the train, or the night. It is her.

She kisses me too hard. The way I like it. So hard, I feel a burst of pain crest the ocean of drugs. Fuck. I am going to die, and it is going to feel so fucking good.

She pulls back, looks up at me through hazy eyes.

"Where do you want me?" I ask. I feel this immense gratitude toward her. I will do this however she wants.

"Um . . ." She studies the scene. Stacks of suitcase racks. There is one open shelf, high in the corner, where there is room enough for both of us. "Up there."

"Do you want to be—"

"On top."

"Of course."

The train clatters. I feel it all through me, like it is clattering just for us.

7

Eva

HE DEFINITELY DID SPORTS. HE'S A REAL TEAM PLAYER. HE takes direction like a champ. I point him toward a high rack and he reaches up with one arm—flinching a little—and then swings himself up into the space with a kind of alarming dexterity.

My heart rate jumps. This is really happening. I'm about to have sex with a total stranger on a train. I grin and climb in after him.

There's really not a lot of room. Right away I can feel his warm, minty-fresh breath surround me. He smells slightly astringent.

"I have one request," he says. "You can kiss me, but no touching above the waist. Okay?" His eyes are a little desperate.

"Okay," I say. There's not really time to analyze, but he definitely seems to be favoring his right shoulder. He's clearly nursing some sporty injury.

I don't really care. His dick is below his waist.

I find it, first through his pants, and then inside them.

"Oh God," he says, gratefully arching his back as I draw my

fingers up and down his length. He's pretty well equipped, which doesn't surprise me. He has that energy. *"Fuck."*

He loses himself for a moment, and then he finds me. His fingers do. They start at my shoulders, travel up and down my arms, along my collarbone, between my breasts. They pause briefly over my heart, to feel it beat inside my chest. Then they slip through the collar of my shirt and inside, where they pinch my nipple.

"You are like an angel," he says.

I kiss him. I can't help it. No one has ever called me an angel. Unless you count Angel of Death.

8

Jonathan

I AM NOT EVEN INSIDE HER WHEN I START TO FEEL IT AGAIN: MY encroaching death. Not *la petite mort*. The big one.

But I am in a little bit of a situation. A woman is straddling me, on a luggage shelf, on a fast-moving train.

It is not my first time in a sticky situation. It is not the first time I have had to think fast.

She strokes my dick and I have to decide. And I do.

Go with it.

I have never been a go-with-the-flow guy, but today I am playing against type. It might be the Ecstasy. It might be the woman. It might be my heart, which will not stop stopping. I feel it sink now in my chest, sucking my rib cage down with it, like my whole chest might collapse.

Maybe the bullet moved, drawn like a magnet down toward my dick, where everything else seems to be going: my blood, my nerves, my brain.

I start to lose consciousness. My eyelids flutter.

"Are you okay?" she says.

"Slap me," I say, a little slurred. She looks unsure, then shrugs.

She slaps me with impressive force. I gasp. My heart starts. "Thank you."

"No problem." She smirks. Then she bends forward. Her hair tickles my neck. "Are you sure you can handle this? You seem a little fragile."

Her words spark in my brain. You see, I am a cold-blooded killer, and there is nothing that incites me more than someone calling me chicken.

"I can fuck you as hard as you want," I say. She seems a little taken aback, but then she grins.

She expertly slips on a condom, then takes my dick and guides it inside her. She bends over me again, puts her lips against my ear, tells me, "I want you to fuck me pretty damn hard."

I can feel my consciousness receding again. My heart sinking in my chest. I cannot even feel it beating anymore. It may have stopped when I took all those pills in the bathroom. I might be a chicken with its head cut off. But I said I could fuck her as hard as she wanted.

I grab her waist, wrap my leg around her leg so she stays with me and I flip her on her back.

She seems impressed. "Neat trick."

"I have a few more." I start to move. "Tell me if it's too much."

"Oh, you'll know."

There is an art to thrusting, although it sounds straightforward. The art of thrusting, the art of sex and pleasure and anything that makes you gasp or makes you smile, is in the element of surprise. You want to beat an unusual rhythm—but even more important than that is to tailor your beat to your audience, to your sexual dance partner. You have to make sure they can keep up.

She can, and I feel this immense relief—a pleasure wave all through me—because the thing about sex is, you never know if someone will be good until you try them. And sometimes you try and find you never *stop* trying. And it is an arduous climb to an orgasm. You still feel the satisfaction of the achievement, but there is no joy in the journey. And is that not what life and sex are all about?

Once I have established that my partner can keep up, I have to feel out what she likes. I do this by marking all the moments when she melts like warm wax in my hands.

When I thrust forward.

When I curl left.

When I pull back, as if to leave her, and then when I come back.

You have to know when to stop. Stopping is just as important as going. Patience is the biggest secret to incredible sex.

Patience and pursuit, of every angle, every appendage, every pressure point and type of pressure. Until you know everything about them. All the important things, anyway.

The spectacular thing is, every body is different. A new experience, a different taste. But every body makes you feel the same. Godlike, the way killing sometimes does. Sex feels that way every time.

Eva likes:

When I run my thumb down the base of her skull.

When I suck her tongue.

When I pulsate her clit.

When I call her sexy. "So fucking sexy."

She comes fast, so I know she was already mostly there.

The train shudders with her. She forgets herself and grips my shoulder—the one with a bullet in it. Which is unfortunate for me, but I feel I cannot complain. I cannot stop her. It would not be fair. Her pleasure is more important than my pain.

When she comes around, she notices her hand. "Sorry," she murmurs. "No touching."

"S'okay," I say.

She struggles to find a place to put her hands, then puts them on my face. She pulls it down and kisses my lips. "What do you want me to do?" she says. "I'll do anything—believe me, I mean *anything.*"

I do believe her. I do not usually meet women like this—who am I kidding? I *never* meet women like this. She is so wholly *here;* I wonder how she has survived this long. It is a dangerous world for people without boundaries. I know that better than most.

The promise alone of *anything I want* should be enough to send me over the edge, but it is possible I am too drugged to come. I am not too drugged to feel fucking *fantastic* as I move inside her, which seems a little unfair. I cannot make her work forever.

I am trying to decide just what I want her to do. I wish I had come prepared. I wish I had known this moment would one day come. It seems like an unforgivable blind spot on my part. I have a long list of fetishes, but which is *the most fetish?* Which is the absolute pinnacle?

I have this dream of taking her with me, taking her all across Europe so we can find out, discover the landscape of our mutual pleasure. We could fuck in so many places. I could sneak away in the morning to commit murder, then come home with croissants. We could have breakfast in bed. It is a dream so provincial that I feel almost ordinary.

Abstractly, I am a little surprised by the sudden pivot of my dreams. The thought of seeing someone every day tends to terrify me. At first I think it might be love, but then I remember it is definitely Ecstasy.

I start to come up again. But this time I do not have to fight it. This time I can just let it ride.

I am moving inside her. She is moving with me. The train expands around us, echoing, throbbing, screeching along the tracks.

"You're perfect," I tell her. "You don't have to do anything."

The train seems to move faster, and I move faster with it, until I feel it bleed into my skin, until I am a part of it, this delicious agony machine. She curls beneath me as if she feels it, too.

Darkness snaps over us. Either we are in a tunnel or I have gone blind. I feel every screech of every wheel like a hit of pleasure through my nerves and I am on fire; I am burning up. My heart starts hiccuping in my chest. My chest is as tight as a fist and I am peaking.

Higher and higher until I am so high, there are only two options: come or die.

And I am not even sure which one I choose when I collapse over her. Until waves of pleasure rack through me like electric jolts, like the shudders of the train.

The tunnel opens. The light comes through.

She is stroking the back of my neck. "Damn," she says. "Contact high."

I lie beside her on the luggage rack. She burrows her head into my chest. It hurts, but I cannot stop her. I like her and the pain.

She sighs with a shudder. The lights grow dim.

Then they go out.

9

Eva

THE DREAM ALWAYS BEGINS IN A DIFFERENT WAY. IT COMES IN disguises, so I won't know it's happening until it's too late. The dream always ends the same.

Everyone I love is dying. It's too late to save them. I can hear them all around me, screaming. The worst part is the things they say. The things they said.

I don't want to die.

Help me.

Please, God, someone help!

Then the gun is in my hand.

And everyone is dead.

The smell of blood fills my nostrils.

I wake with a start. His face is there, separated by my dreamy state so I see it in parts: his square jaw, the single dimple on his left side, the flicker of light on his glasses. The lingering dream-world draws halos in his hair.

"Are you okay?" he asks.

"Of course I'm okay." I sit up too fast and hit my head.

He says "Ouch" for me.

Outside the window, the countryside is powering by, like my nightmares might disappear if we move fast enough.

I'm on the sleeper train from Florence to Paris. I've never had a nightmare in front of someone. Even my fiancé—who, in fairness, rarely slept over—never witnessed one.

Seeing my nightmare reflected in Jonathan's face makes me feel exposed, like my soul is transparent and now the whole world knows I used to be a part of it but I lost it.

"Why wouldn't I be okay?" I ask.

"You were making noises." He's too nice to say I was crying.

"What kind of noises?"

"I don't know . . ." Jonathan says.

"Sorry. Did I wake you up?"

"I was already awake." He told me he never slept. I said I didn't either. I lied. What I meant to say was *I don't sleep; I dream.*

I pull my legs in. "Well, I'm sorry I disturbed you."

"I wasn't disturbed," he says.

I knew it would come to this eventually. It always does. I'm too fucked-up to do anything but fuck. But I wish it didn't have to come this fast. We could've had a moment. One, two, three nights in Paris. I'm way better at sex when I have room to move. And now he'll never know.

I climb out of the luggage rack. "We should go back to our car. The beds are probably more comfortable. *Probably,*" I joke, trying to keep things light.

He stays frozen on the luggage rack.

"Okay, well," I say, "that was fun. Thanks." I'm pushing him away a little. I know this. He seems to know it, too. But I'm not sure if he knows I want him to pull me back.

"I'll see you back there," he says. He doesn't move.

"Okay," I say, forcing myself away from him. "I'll see you back at the car."

10

Jonathan

BLOOD HAS SOAKED THROUGH THE GAUZE, THROUGH THE shirt, through the jacket. It even soaked into her shirt as she thrashed through her nightmare. This is not a good sign. It means the bullet has relocated to a place where it could do more damage.

I need to get to the restroom. I need to inspect the wound, but she is right there, watching me with her sad, scared eyes.

I consider telling her I have been shot, but I have a feeling that might scare her more. It might be a hint that I am disturbed—that I was willing to risk death for a fuck.

It is better if I wait. I will let her go ahead. I will go to the bathroom. I will stop the bleeding; then I will come back and make it up to her. I will be normal just for her. For the next nine hours. For as long as I can be.

"I'll see you back at the car," she says. She even makes this hopeless little wave. My heart breaks a little. This is another reason I avoid drugs. Coming down, I am soaked with the sadness of the whole damn world.

As soon as she is gone, I climb out of the rack. I land hard on my feet and stagger sideways.

My head feels dislocated. My body tingles with numbness. I grip the metal bars. I stare at the floor. I am about to pass out. Shit. This is not good.

I force my body toward the restroom. I swing unsteadily from one rack to the next, gripping the poles so I do not collapse. The train wobbles sickeningly beneath me.

My body is so relieved when I shut the door that it collapses. I grab for something to keep me from hitting the floor too hard but find only the toilet paper roll, which noisily unfurls.

I hit the floor with a resounding *smack!* It wakes me up a little.

I force my eyes open. I have to stay awake. I have to stay alive. I cannot leave her now. She will take it the wrong way. She will internalize it. She will think there is something wrong with her, when as far as I can tell she is perfect. I have to stay awake. I have to stay alive.

I take a big, gulping breath. Then another one. But it is like grasping at straws.

I need to examine the wound. I need to extract the bullet. Maybe I do not need Mas. Maybe I can do it myself.

I force myself to sit up, clawing at the walls. They tilt, or something inside my brain does. The room spins. Fuck.

I take a deep breath. I touch my shoulder. The wetness shocks me. It is far more blood than I expected. Fuck, fuck, fuck.

I can do this. *Calm. Stay calm.*

I lean forward. I start to take off my jacket.

Something happens. I lose time. When I come around, I am on the floor again. The toilet is rattling above me. The floor is still vibrating. The train is still moving. I can still find her. I just have to stay alive. I just have to wake up.

I reach for something. I find nothing.

Sounds feel far away. My body feels far away. I have to get back to it. I am dying. Again.

11

Eva

JONATHAN DOESN'T FOLLOW ME. NICE. REAL NICE.

We had sex, I had a nightmare and he doesn't follow me. This is what I love about men. Really, truly, madly, deeply. They always exceed your worst expectations.

When I get back to our car, all the beds have been pulled down. I find mine. I lie flat on my back with my eyes on the ceiling. I can still feel the shape of him inside me. I'll probably feel it for days. It sucks. I knew it had to end, but I wanted to be the one to end it.

The hours pass. He doesn't come back. Maybe he fell asleep. Maybe he felt sick again. But probably—no, *definitely*—he could sense it. That's the problem with trauma: It fucks you up. It changes you, and when you let people get close it scares them away. I should have seen it coming. I did. He's from upstate. I'm from Hell. It never would've worked.

Eventually I fall asleep. I have another nightmare—I never should've risked a sleeper train—but this time when I wake up, Jonathan isn't there. The American businessman is dead asleep below me. I appreciate it more than I can possibly say.

He's up before me the next morning, neatly packing his bed away.

Outside the window, I can see Paris giddily building itself up from the châteaus and the green fields.

I sigh. Jonathan isn't here. Jonathan never came back. How can everyone be so fucking predictable?

I climb out of my bed. As I land on the floor, my fellow passenger starts. He looks curiously at me. He points at his shoulder. "Are you okay?" he says.

I look down, and then I see it. Dried blood on my shirt, the size of a hand, the shape of a wobbly heart.

"Oh!" I exclaim. "I'm fine. Sorry." I'm not sure what I'm apologizing for.

I search my body, trying to figure out where the blood's coming from. I don't feel any pain. At least not the physical kind.

Oh. It didn't come from me. It came from Jonathan.

Did I hurt him accidentally? Did I stab him with the knife I keep on my ankle? But the blood is near my shoulder.

Maybe the blood has nothing to do with me. He did seem sick. And he had that no-touching rule, and that question: *Can I keep my jacket on?*

Maybe he was injured. I really can't blame him for not wanting me to know. In fact, I can relate. I'm always hiding my wounds from people—the physical ones and the emotional ones.

I'm actually relieved. Maybe he didn't ghost me. Maybe he had to go to the medic. Maybe he's still on the luggage rack. Maybe I should look for him.

I quickly leave the car. I check the luggage rack, but it's empty. The food car is deserted. There's a line for the bathroom. Jonathan is gone.

I return to the car. The train is pulling into the station. The American is reading *Le Monde*. That's when I notice it: Jonathan's suitcase. He hasn't come back for it.

"You know the guy I was with? Did he come back at all while I was asleep?" I ask. I point at the suitcase.

My fellow passenger shakes his head. "Not that I saw."

I want to open it. I have this funny feeling—a dark feeling I get sometimes—that *anything* could be in there.

"He left his bag," I say. "Maybe there's something in here that can help." *Help with what?* I don't say. I don't care.

Soon everyone will be disembarking. Soon the train people will come through. Soon it'll be too late. I'm more than a little impulsive.

I drag the heavy suitcase to the middle of the compartment. The other passenger moves forward as if to stop me. I just move faster. There's a pretty sizeable lock. I break the zipper. The businessman moves closer. I pull the two sides apart. I lift the flap. The man steps back.

Jonathan's suitcase is not filled with computers. It's filled with weapons. Antique weapons, the kinds you just know somebody had a little too much fun making: jagged saws, curved blades, jeweled inlays. Packed with care.

Maybe he's an antiques dealer, a pretty serious one. I know a lot about weapons, and a few of these are illegal. It's understandable that he wouldn't want to tell me that he was carrying a load of weapons. But the bleeding is a little suspicious.

I consider whether this chance meeting could have something to do with me. When you kill people for a living, you tend to assume the worst. But it's not like he tried to kill me. If anything, he's the one who's dying.

The train jerks to a stop, throwing me forward.

I reattach the zipper and close the suitcase, then haul it up. "I better hang on to this," I tell my fellow passenger. "Until I can give it back."

II

—

LOSS, PART 1

12

Jonathan

I WAKE UP ON THE FLOOR OF THE RESTROOM. SOMEONE KICKED me. I can feel the echo of pain in my gut.

"Get up," a man says in French. He is standing over me, dressed in a neat uniform. He is a cop. Fuck.

I sit up way too fast. "Hello," I say in French. "Are we in, uh . . ." Where am I supposed to be? "Paris?"

"Yes. The train is finished." He scowls at me. He clearly thinks I am on drugs. I am so incensed that I almost forget that I am.

"Yes, sir," I say, dragging myself up. I can feel blood creeping down my armpit. "Thank you. Very much."

The train is completely empty. She is gone. I cannot even go back for my suitcase. Someone will have taken it. They might have seen what is inside. More than a few items are not strictly legal.

At least I am not dead. What a wonderful goddamn world.

I feel an intense, almost burning malaise. Perhaps it is because the last of the Ecstasy is leaving my system. Perhaps it is because of Paris.

Everything is gray in Paris, but somehow, after an hour or two,

I know the city will convince me that there is no better color—not one stronger or more meaningful or beautiful. Paris is a city of brooding and pretention. It is probably the city that is most like me, which is why I always feel a certain loathing of it.

Mas doesn't have any idea I am coming, of course. If he did, he might try to avoid me—bullet in the chest and all. Mas is a doctor, so he is always giving himself medical advice. I am bad for his mental health.

I procure a cab. I arrive at Mas's private hospital in Pigalle—the coolest little clinic in Paris. It is probably for the best that I lost my suitcase. Mas hates when I bring weapons to his office.

The front-desk assistant does not recognize me. I do not recognize her. It has been over a year since I have been to the office. Mas has renovated—probably more than once. His office is currently black—black walls with a sandy finish, black marble floors—with taupe accents. It is almost offensively chic, which is so fucking Mas.

That is one of the few traits Mas and I share: the masochistic tendency to blow through money like we are trying to patch over our past with all the finer things in life. Mas is one of the best surgeons in Paris, so he can afford it.

"Hello," I say to the front-desk associate in French. She is a hip, young Parisian woman with heavy chains around her neck and little eyeliner darts protruding from her eyes. "I'm here to see Dr. Ahmed." Ahmed is not the last name we shared. Mas went back to his birth name while I was in prison—possibly to put some distance between us. Mas was adopted right before I was born. I sometimes wonder, if I had not been born, would Mas's life have been worse or better?

"Do you have an appointment?" the woman says. Her eyes narrow on my shoulder, which is now caked in dried blood.

"Mas knows I'm coming," I lie. "Tell him it's Abraham." That is not my real name, but it is the one I give every time I show up like this. Once, it was because I was poisoned. Last time, I was bitten by a security dog because I did not want to hurt it. Once, I came just to say hi. Mas asked me not to do that again.

She calls him. I can hear him grumble over the phone, but I know part of him is curious. What will it be this time?

"Dr. Ahmed can see you now," she says.

"Thank you." I rap her desk, then hurry through the waiting room. I am feeling a little giddy. It might be from knowing this is almost over. Mas will take out the bullet; I will live to die another day. It might be because of something else, but I have trained myself never to question anything that tastes like happiness.

I start to strip as soon as I get into the hall. It feels phenomenal to take off my jacket and my shirt, to undress my wound.

I rip off the bandage as I enter the exam room. Mas is waiting, already pale. He sees me. He goes paler.

"Oh my God." He makes a face.

I shut the door, then lock it behind me. "I thought you were supposed to be a surgeon."

"I haven't seen something that grisly since Afghanistan," he jokes. Mas did three tours of duty. People handle trauma differently. Some become saints. Some become sinners.

"You're hurting my feelings." I grin.

"Are you high?"

"No, but as my doctor you should know I took approximately six hundred milligrams of Vicodin, two hundred milligrams of Ritalin and a tab of Ecstasy."

"That could kill you."

"So could getting shot."

He sighs and walks to his cabinets. "Do you want me to take the bullet out?"

"If it's not too much trouble." I hop onto the exam table. This room has not been renovated to match the waiting room. Or else it has been renovated more recently, and the waiting room has not been renovated to match it. The walls are the color of sand. The floors are sky blue.

"Your office is trippy," I say.

"That might be because of all the drugs you took." He pulls on a pair of gloves with a satisfying *snap*. "I would offer you something for the pain, but at this point that would probably put you into cardiac arrest."

I am about to make a smart-ass comment when he sticks his fingers inside me. "Holy fuck!" My muscles spasm. It is involuntary. He is up to his knuckles in my shoulder cavity.

"Stay still." He fishes around, unnecessarily aggressive, if you ask me. "It's almost like you don't appreciate what I'm doing for you."

I grit my teeth. "You're the best brother ever."

He twists his fingers. Tears spill down my cheeks. Blood seeps down my chest. I want to cry out. I want to complain. I want to leave him a terrible review.

"If you keep doing things like this . . . ," Mas says. His fingers close around the bullet. He pulls it out and drops it neatly onto a metal tray. It clangs. So small. So painful. "You're really going to kill yourself." That is a little the point.

"Thank you, Brother."

"You're welcome, Brother. Now"—he switches out his bloody gloves—"I suppose you want me to sew you up."

"If you would. Don't do too good a job, though. I want to leave a scar."

He rolls his eyes and gets to work.

13

Eva

I STOLE JONATHAN'S SUITCASE. I MEAN, WHY NOT? I PLAN TO return it, if I can. If I can't, I'm doing Jonathan and the French police a favor. All these illegal weapons could incite a manhunt.

Once I am safely inside my hotel room, I remove all the weapons from the suitcase. I spread them everywhere, across the desk and the bed and floor. There are more than meet the eye, dozens of weapons all stowed in customized compartments. I have to think he can't be selling them.

He must be a collector, but someone so strong with so many weapons? A person's mind starts to wonder, especially when that person is an assassin.

You can learn a lot about someone by looking at their weapons.

Me, I'm a simple girl. Give me a Glock and a prayer; that's all I need. Jonathan's *array* is excessive—so excessive and so spotless that I have to think he *can't* be using them. A professional would know to keep things streamlined. Which means he must be playing with them. Maybe he thinks they're cool. Maybe they make him feel powerful.

I search the suitcase, looking for a clue that will reveal his identity, but there isn't one. It's smart, I have to admit. If the police had picked this up, they never would've tied it back to him. That's exactly what I do with my weapons.

But it leaves me holding the bag, literally. All of these weapons, some illegal, are now in my possession. I should get rid of them. But part of me hopes that one day I really will be able to return them to him.

I don't have time to think about that now. I have a man to kill. And to do that, I need a shower, a blow-dry and a lethal amount of makeup.

14

Jonathan

I FEEL AS GOOD AS NEW. BETTER. I ALWAYS FEEL BETTER WHEN I see Mas.

He does not invite me over. He lives in an impossibly chic apartment in Pigalle. His wife, Giselle, is the head of cybersecurity for the EU. She does not like me. She does not know that I am a contract killer; she does not like me because of how I affect Mas. I cannot blame her. Mas and I are tied together by shared trauma, and neither of us can be around the other very long without remembering exactly what ruined us.

I am walking along the cobblestone path beside the Seine, enjoying the feeling of not having a bullet in my chest. The Louvre is to my right; the Eiffel Tower is far ahead of me.

People walk past, but no one is in a rush. We are below street level. We do not come down here to hurry or cut corners. We come down here, mostly, to brood. There are dazed tourists here; we are all lost in a collective dream of Paris. I look out onto the water, where Monet has painted flecks of light.

A woman in a trench coat leans against the railing and gazes over the water. Up ahead, an old man shares a bottle of wine with himself.

I think about Eva. I do not know exactly what it is about her, but she has a quality of sticking in my mind. She was funny. She was up for anything. I find myself imagining what she would do if she were here. What she would say. Which is a strange and, frankly, ridiculous way to feel about a stranger. But maybe it is easier to feel that way about strangers.

Even if I never see her again, if I never find her, I can imagine for us a whole life together. I can place her on a pedestal, and every time that something goes wrong, from now until eternity, I can trace the source back to this very day—the day I lost her. *Things would have been better. You could have had everything. If only* . . .

God, I am so fucking depressing sometimes. I do it to myself, so quickly and so convincingly that I sometimes do not catch it until it is too late.

It is not the end. Yes, I should have asked Eva what hotel she was staying at. Asked for her number. Honestly, it was very short-sighted of me not to; I always suspected I would live. But I know that I can find her. It might even be fun. But first, I have to check in with my handler.

Thomas knows I was shot. I tried to convince him it was nothing, but he tends not to trust me when it comes to anything but murder.

He is especially mistrustful because of what happened the last time I was injured. A dog nearly tore my arm off, and I lied about the seriousness of the situation. I did not want to get the dog in trouble. I took another job where I had a Fail to Kill. My first one. I got my mark a week later, but by then I had been taken off the job, so there was less celebration, more *yikes.*

I have more kills than anyone else in the network, and yet all

I ever hear from my handler is *Could you take it down a few notches? You're kind of freaking people out.*

I call him as I pass through a tunnel. The shade is crawling with tourists boldly drinking red wine and daring the sun to follow them under the bridge.

"I made it to Paris," I say. "I found a surgeon to remove the bullet. It was nothing. I probably could have done it myself." I did try, but in my delirium I only lodged the bullet deeper. Getting a bullet out of your chest is like scratching your back or jerking off: It is better if someone else does it for you.

"We don't have anything for you right now," Thomas says.

"Are you joking? You told me once that the network ran half a dozen jobs a week."

"We don't have anything *for you* right now." Like I did not catch his meaning the first time. "You were supposed to seek medical attention in Florence," he scolds me. "We had a doctor waiting for you. Instead, you jumped a train with a bullet in your chest, passed out in the loo and—"

"How do you know that?" I tug at my collar, scan the periphery.

"The same way I know everything." Thomas would like me to believe that I am being watched all the time. I know this is not strictly true. I have done a few tests to confirm it—breaking rules to see if I would be chastised—but I still stick up my middle finger, just for the hell of it. "Is someone watching me now?"

"You can assume someone is watching you *every time* you do something you are not supposed to do." I wonder if the network was watching me have sex with Eva. I hope not.

I hunch against the tunnel wall. I am still feeling a little vulnerable. Nearly dying will do that to a person. "I'm sorry."

"You're sloppy."

"Excuse me?" I practically vault off the wall. "Sloppy" is the worst thing you can call a control freak.

"You need to prove that you can hold it together a bit better."

I laugh in surprise, maybe a little in bravado. "Are you kidding me? I just did a triple in Florence. Who else can do that?"

"It's not just about kills."

"Really? *What's it all about, Thomas?*"

I hear his hiss of surprise.

He lowers his voice like he does not want to be found, even though I know exactly where he is.

Thomas works from home, in a cottage in the Cotswolds, in England. His office is on the ground floor. His window faces the street. He has a wife, Laura. His name is not Thomas; it is Alfie—as in *"What's it all about, Alfie?"* And now he maybe knows that I know that.

"Listen, *mate*," he says. It is almost always a bad thing when an English person calls you "mate." Trust me on this. "You want me to be honest? You work for a firm. You work *for* them.

"People like you come into this job thinking: *I can be my own boss. I can make my own hours. I'm my own man.* Right? *Wrong.* You are not your own boss. You don't make your own hours. You are not your own man. In fact, you would have more freedom working the checkout counter at Marks and Sparks. Do you understand?"

I know where Thomas lives. I know he oversees the IT department at a UK grocery store. I know his routine and his friends and his family. What I do not know is who *we* work for. He calls them the network. He says they are everywhere, claims they have a hand in everything, but I do not believe that. Nobody controls the world.

Still, it drives me a little crazy that I do not know who they are. Years ago, I tried to find out. I reconned Thomas. As far as I could tell, he lived a totally ordinary life. He woke up every morning and drank tea with his wife. Then they both went into their separate home offices. They spent the workday on their computers. Every night at six, Thomas went to the pub for three hours, where he talked about football and the terrible fates of all the boys he went to school with.

He did not meet with strangers in dark alleyways. He did not have suspicious telephone calls—except when I called him. One night I broke into his office. I tried to search his computer, but I could not find anything revealing.

Thomas's life was so normal that I considered that this whole operation might be a sham. That he might be sending me out to kill people at random. That nothing was real except the money. And then I considered, maybe the money was the only thing that needed to be real.

Maybe it was better that I did not know. Because I knew I did not want it to stop. So I let it go. It still eats me up sometimes, but then, so does everything.

"Yes . . . *sir*," I add for good measure. I need Thomas. I need to work. I need to kill people, and to do that, I really need to keep it together.

He sighs. "You know I like you. I do. You're a sort of charming psychopath. And certainly there have been times when I've wished for a bit of your . . . *verve*. But the problem with you is, you don't think about anyone else. When you're out there running your jobs willy-nilly, with your signature style and your antique weaponry, you are putting dozens of people behind the scenes—with families and loved ones and all the things that you don't want—"

"Cannot have," I remind him, even though we both know I use the job as an excuse.

"—at risk. You put them at risk. And no amount of kills is going to make that worthwhile to the people who want to live."

I say nothing. He interprets my silence as mollification. Maybe it is.

"You are one of the best," he says. "Your record is exemplary, but you were shot less than twenty-four hours ago. You're probably still in shock. Just take a month, one month off."

"A week."

"Three weeks."

"One."

"Start with one. Then we'll revisit." He is about to end the call.

"Thomas?"

He waits.

"I just wanted to say that you are an excellent handler."

He offers a strangled groan and ends the call.

Dusk is approaching. When the world gets dark, I sometimes feel personally responsible, as if I am the cause of all darkness.

I almost wish I had died. I should have considered that option more seriously. When you are dying, it is only natural to try to live. I should have taken the unnatural route. It would have been more my style.

I could kill myself now. I have sewn into the lining of my pants a concoction that would see me dead in three minutes, but for all I know, I would survive that, too. I seem to survive everything. I would probably survive, only with permanent brain damage or shattered nerves or auditory hallucinations.

Death is another one of those things that is better if someone else does it.

In some ways, this job is like suicide by cop. I cannot kill myself, but maybe someday, if I am lucky, I will find the right person. The person who can kill me.

The man with the wine bottle is watching me. I meet his eyes. He pulls his bottle closer, like I might ask him for it. Like we are that close.

I walk toward the Seine. I stand at the edge of the path, lean over the wall. The water is too slow and too shallow and too filthy to kill me. Maybe today is not my day for dying.

I still have to find Eva, to make sure she knows I did not abandon her on purpose.

I turn away from the river. I walk toward the nearest stairwell.

I start toward Les Puces, the flea market. She said it was magical. She said I would find everything I need.

I need her.

15

THE MARKET STARTS ON THE STREETS, WITH A FLOOD OF PEO-
ple selling stolen goods. The fringe market. They sell bright
red steaks. Used appliances that will either work perfectly
or electrocute you—there is no in-between. T-shirts for date-
specific events that no one cares to remember: the 135th anniversary of the establishment of a vineyard in Languedoc, the '98
World Series. Candles that will burn your house down. Haunted
children's toys. Everything you could never want. Everything you
could never need.

All the sellers look stunned, like they have been through wars.
Like they have fought their way through an odyssey to wind up
here, selling steak on the street. The terrible thing is, they probably have.

A market is a place where you realize you cannot save everyone. Not all the time. Not even close.

I keep walking until I reach the more official market: great big
networks of market stalls and warehouses and shops. This is
where they sell the junk they *used* to make—which is so much

better than the junk they make now: tin boxes, carved canes, miniature mechanical birds.

I am pulled in by a little shop selling antique weapons. They are my signature, and I just lost most of my collection on the train. Maybe that is contributing to this horrible feeling I have. Maybe I just miss my swords.

I wear gloves when I kill someone, of course, but I like to think that antiques wreak havoc with DNA. Plus, they just look fucking cool. I buy them on the dark web or through untraceable networks, not live and in person. This is unfortunate, because this shop has an emerald-encrusted rapier that I would really love to kill someone with.

Eva was right; I *need* this. The market wants me to have it.

"You like it?" the shopkeeper says in French.

"Fuck yes," I say, also in French.

He takes it off the wall and holds it out to me. "Feel how light."

He is right. It is incredibly light. It is probably made for fencing, not murder, but I test the bend in the blade and it is solid. I could make it work.

"Do you offer shipping?" I ask.

"Unfortunately, no. This is a weapon," he adds like I might not know. "I would need to see your passport." I have seven.

"Maybe I'll come back later." I am supposed to be finding Eva—which is seeming more unlikely. The market is bigger than the world. In a way, it is more impenetrable. Out there, there are clear lines and divisions. Here, there is chaos.

The shopkeeper takes the blade back, with the special scowl reserved for people who promise to come back later.

I keep walking, through a broken chain of market stalls and market streets and warehouses. I can see why this is one of the biggest markets in the world. It has no clear delineations. You think you have reached the end only to find yourself in a different iteration. Everything is still for sale. For all I know, all of Paris might be Les Puces.

I have no other plans in Paris now that I have been operated on. Were it not for Eva, I would leave right now. Give myself an arbitrary place, an arbitrary task. Something to do.

Climb Mount Everest.

Cross the Sahara.

Sail to Antarctica.

Anything. I would do anything to keep from doing nothing.

I keep searching well past dark. Past when the market is shut. There is no way she is there. But sometimes I cannot stop myself.

I pass by the same market stalls and shops, now dark, now locked. I pass by the shop with the emerald rapier and I have a thought: *If I steal it, there is no chance of anyone tracing it.*

It is ridiculously easy, the kind of small-time crime that warms your heart. Disable the security system. Disarm the cameras. Break a small pane of glass. Let myself in. The shop reeks of antiques, like they procreate at night. Rusting and fucking.

The rapier is there on the wall, where the shopkeeper left it. I take it down. The shopkeeper was right: It is so very light. I leave cash payment in the register, enough to cover the window, too. I do not haggle.

I keep walking, mapping out the market until it is tattooed inside my head. Laid out like a body under the stars.

16

Eva

I SPEND TWO HOURS BUILDING THE PERFECT FACE. I'M OBSESSED with makeup. I have more makeup and wigs in my suitcase than weaponry. In my free time, I watch makeup tutorials. I check for makeup drops multiple times a day. For me, makeup is fun. It's a way to disguise myself, true, but it's also a way to revitalize myself, to recover.

With all that Jonathan business on the train, I haven't really had time to process Florence. I was there because of my fiancé, Andrew—my *late* fiancé. It was the second anniversary of his death, and my first time back in Florence. I've been running for two years.

I went back to bury his ashes. I should've done it a long time ago. I knew Andrew wasn't on good terms with his family, but I guess I hoped that if I left his ashes at the mortuary, someone might forgive him and pick them up. No one did. They were still there two years later, now with a pricey holding fee.

I buried the ashes in a cute little cemetery overlooking the Arno. On the way to the train station the next morning, I passed by Andrew's old apartment and was surprised to see his curtains still hanging crookedly over the window. I realized that not only had no one picked up his ashes, but no one had cleared out his apartment either. His landlord might not even realize he was dead. Like me, Andrew traveled a lot. Like me, he paid his rent in advance, in cash, to avoid background checks.

The responsible part of me said to skip the train, stay in Florence and iron everything out, but that seemed a little risky. My job basically requires me to avoid anything that involves paperwork, and death involves a *lot* of paperwork. So I didn't stop. I jumped the train. I pushed Andrew out of my mind in favor of fucking the bulky weapons enthusiast. I like to think Andrew would have understood. He always hated paperwork, too.

I didn't love Andrew the way you're supposed to, the way that love is described, but I do miss him sometimes. He made me feel like less of a weirdo, which is kind of the nicest thing a person can do for you.

I force myself to stop thinking about him. I have a job to do.

I sit in front of my mirror and I watch my face transform. My past and my trauma disappear under layers and layers of smooth, flawless makeup.

Normally it's my job to be forgettable. It's easy. I was born forgettable: the girl whose name you can't remember, whose face you can't quite place. Who looks oh so familiar but it could just be that she looks like someone else. That's me.

But not tonight. Tonight I have to be gorgeous, the kind of woman you would follow to the edge of the earth, or at least to your death.

Men don't know the difference between makeup and reality; it's one of their biggest blind spots. Another woman would see a cake face, but men see what they want to see. They appreciate the nod to the unattainable beauty standards they created.

I pull up reference points on my phone. Dove Cameron. Brigitte Bardot. Hitchcock blondes and femmes fatales. I mean, this is France after all.

Tonight's kill should be an easy one, because it's a Fall Guy Kill, which means someone will get blamed. Not me, of course, but murder is so much easier when you don't have to make it look like an accident or an act of God.

The agency I work for kills the bad guys. The dangerous, the wicked, the truly unforgivable. There are a lot of them out there. It's my job to take them down.

The agency is based out of London, as is my handler, Sherri. According to Sherri, the agency has been around since time immemorial, making the world a safer place one murder at a time.

I trust Sherri. I have to. My life is basically in her hands.

Sherri also happens to be my best friend. She took the Eurostar down from London this morning to help with the recon for this job. We're meeting for drinks tomorrow, at around ten a.m. We always drink during the day. It prevents hangovers.

Sherri has been my handler since day one. Long enough that I can't say she has never steered me wrong. We all make mistakes, but the great thing about her is that when things go wrong, she still has jokes. I almost die and we laugh about it. That's true friendship.

Sherri has assured me that the man on the menu tonight is really, really bad. Bad to women. Bad to children. The worst kind. It's easy for me to get fired up about people like this. On a subconscious level, I'm killing the people who killed my parents. Again.

I used to believe that I *could* not let what happened to me when I was a child affect my life. That I had a choice. Growing up, I'd been determined to be like any other girl: pretty, sweet, lovable. And I was, for a very long time. Makeup helped. It wasn't until I met Andrew—and Sherri—that I realized something was missing. I was pretty, sweet and lovable, but I wasn't me.

I was running away from my trauma. I was hiding my true self, but not anymore.

Now I'm preventing the tragedy of a kid like me. And I'm looking damn good while doing it.

I purse my lips at the new face in the mirror. I don't smile—she wouldn't, this character I have created to do the killing for me.

She has epically long white-blond hair, pale skin, wide-set eyes. Only her lips are red. She wears a long black dress and long black gloves to hide any bloodstains. She carries a silver purse, and a Glock, and a prayer.

17

THE KILL IS SET FOR TWELVE TWENTY-THREE AT A NIGHTCLUB
in Pigalle. We choose odd times to make the death feel or-
ganic. If you killed someone at the stroke of midnight, the
police might start searching for Cinderella.

We also choose edgy locations. If someone is stabbed in a
nightclub or shot at a drug den, people tend to assume they were
up to no good—not that the police ever seem to look too deeply
into any of my murders.

I wonder sometimes if they're in on the hits, or paid off. But
even if they are, the police need you to make it easy for them to
look the other way. If you kill a man while he's at home with his
family, or in a church, or at an ice-cream shop, people might ask
questions.

When I arrive at the location, I realize it's a nightclub that's
too shy to say what it really is: a sex club.

Chandeliers and naked women hang from the ceiling. The
wallpaper is animal fur. There's this pressure to be horny that I
find so cringey. Everyone in here deserves to die. Except the
women hanging from the ceiling; I'll cut them some slack.

All my reconnaissance for this job was done by Sherri. For tough jobs, I do most of the work myself. You have to really trust someone to let them do recon for you, because if they don't do it right, there can be lethal surprises. A gun safe you didn't know about. A panic button you didn't see. A camera you didn't switch off.

Sherri has done excellent work here. She found a back entrance. She will take down the Wi-Fi that the security system runs on for exactly seven minutes—hopefully short enough to go unnoticed.

She left photographs of the mark in my hotel room. I studied them while I waved my hair. Sherri even included a shot of his dick. The agency is nothing if not thorough.

I find him immediately. He's in one of those too-tight, too-short suits "fashionable" men sometimes wear, displaying his silk socks, his Cartier watch. He's laughing. Good for him. This might be the best night of his life, for the next seven minutes.

He's at a VIP table surrounded by his sleazy-looking friends. I also spot his brother, slinging shots of Jägermeister. It's probably a good thing he's getting drunk. He's the fall guy, and just as evil as my mark. This might be his last night out for a while.

I prepare for my approach. I need to charm my mark while remaining forgettable to everyone else. To do that, I need to separate him from his wolf pack. I need to do it fast, before anyone else really notices me or talks to me.

Luckily, I'm pretty well versed in what sleazy men want.

As I start toward the table, Jonathan crosses my mind. He's the last thing I want to think about now. His rejection still stings. It makes me doubt myself. I feel my steps start to slow. I catch my reflection in the mirror and I think: *You're not pretty enough to murder this man.*

I stop in my tracks.

This is what I hate most about men, the power they have over us. Totally undeserved. Completely unearned.

A stranger ghosted me and now it's interfering with my *work*.

Fuck Jonathan. I'm not going to let him do this to me, with his antique weapons and his bent glasses and his motion sickness. I don't need him. What I need is to kill this man, go back to the hotel, take a nice long bath and binge-watch Bravo.

I cross quickly around the table. I keep my head down so no one sees me until I want to be seen.

I approach his ear. I gird my loins. I lean forward and I say, in French, "I bet I can make you come in nineteen seconds." I can't, but he'll be dead before he finds out.

He smiles in surprise. "Are you a hooker?" That's a compliment where he comes from.

"This one's on the house." He starts to look around. I stop him with my hand, force his cheeks in my direction.

He doesn't seem to mind. "What's in it for you?"

"I'm just a bored little housewife. My husband keeps me locked in a tower, and every night he lets me out. I have to make five men come before he'll let me back in the house."

"Jesus Christ."

"You're number three."

He licks his lips. "Can I watch the others?"

"Of course." I slip my fingers down his sweaty neck, along his shoulder and down his arm until I lace them in his clammy hand. "But we have to hurry."

It's enough. He follows me. I never should have worried. Men are incredibly easy to manipulate. Most men.

I take him to the "office"—code for the place where the manager does coke. I lock the door.

He leers at me. "When does the clock start?"

I smile back. I'm used to smiling when men leer. I lead him to a black office chair. It squeaks as I sit him down in front of me.

He gazes up at me with an expression between awe and orgasm. It's kind of sweet.

"Do you want to count?" I ask. "Or do you want me to?"

I straddle him on the chair. I chose a dress with a high cut to make this easier. The knife I was given for the job is attached to my thigh. I'd rather shoot him, but this knife belongs to his brother. It's a cheesy replica that Sherri sharpened to a deadly point.

The mark's sweaty hands run over me. His belly pushes against me. He tilts his face up at me and I kiss him. I guess I'm curious. I want to know what he tastes like right before he dies. But he tastes like they all do: like cheap champagne, fuzzy teeth and sweat.

He kisses me back and I slit his throat.

I kiss him until he loses consciousness. One thing I've learned on this job is that everyone dies differently. Some people die fast and some people die slowly. I used to think the story of Rasputin's death was ridiculous, but now I know it's totally possible that one could poison, shoot and drown someone before they actually died. Some people are just really hard to kill.

I've learned to be careful. One of the worst things that can happen on this job is for a mark to realize you're trying to kill them. They tend to get really, really pissed.

I keep him distracted with the kiss as he gasps and sputters. As the seconds slowly pass. He's in shock. Most people go into shock right before they die. They do the strangest things. This guy keeps kissing me. You wouldn't think that he would, but my lips are so insistent, and the idea that I would stab him is so ludicrous, and his life is spilling out of him.

Then he jerks back. His eyes fly open. I can see it dawning on him, the realization. I don't really know of what. That he's dying?

That I killed him? Or something deeper. Something more. Maybe he's seeing angels. Maybe he's seeing Heaven. I mean, probably he's seeing Hell. He is a bad guy after all.

He stiffens, stunned by this mysterious realization, and then he goes limp. I shepherd him to the ground.

I leave the knife behind, saturated in his brother's DNA. I text his brother from his phone: We need to talk. Meet me in the back office.

He'll be the one to find the body. Maybe he'll even touch things.

I wipe the blood from my skin. I tuck the wipes in my purse and leave the club.

I walk back to my hotel, through the city in the dark. It's safer than calling a car. I stick to alleyways and courtyards, all the quiet places Sherri mapped out in advance.

Paris is perfection after dark. The smoky lights. The gray tint. It's so romantic.

Now that my job is done, I let myself think about Jonathan. It's stupid, I know. But I liked him. I liked his big body and his small glasses and the way he looked at me like I was something I always wanted to be: okay.

I remember what he said to me: *You're perfect. You don't have to do anything.*

Look, I know it was bullshit. He just wanted to sleep with me. But nobody had ever said those words to me. No one had ever lied to me like that.

It's my job to be forgettable, to be invisible, to disappear.

It was just nice to be seen.

When I've gotten back to the hotel that night, after I take a shower and crawl into bed and shut my eyes, I see him looking at me.

With his blue-velvet eyes. His rustling hands. Like I'm someone to run toward and not away from.

18

Jonathan

I HAVE A VERY DANGEROUS OBSESSION WITH MY OWN MISERY. IF left to my own devices, I will create a life of such despair that it would shock any other human being. To combat this, I do two things: I buy things and I kill people. I buy a lot of things and I kill a lot of people.

After I leave Les Puces, I check into the Ritz because it is the most expensive hotel I can think of on short notice.

"I would like to book a suite," I tell the front desk clerk. I was paid on completion for the triple in Florence. I have more money than I have ever had at once, and I need to spend it as quickly as possible.

I order everything I can think of online, to be delivered tomorrow, or in five minutes if possible. Artesian water, a medical-grade first aid kit, all the toiletries Tom Ford sells. I order a new suit, and someone to tailor it. And then I order three more suits. Six pairs of shoes. Socks. Underwear. Eight phones.

Then I start making orders through the dark web: designer drugs and designer weapons and designer information.

Nowadays, the internet is a much better place to find people than the out-of-doors. I use the hackers at my disposal to procure a passenger list—all 471 people on our train. I search for "Eva." Her name is not on the list. Strange.

As the sun comes up, I call the train station in Paris. "I'm trying to track down a woman from my car. She left behind her phone . . ."

I call the train station in Florence. "If you could just help me . . ."

I call the train company.

I am just about to start calling the other passengers—I tracked them down, no problem—when I get a text.

Coffee?

I hang tough for a while, knowing that this will turn out the way it always does—badly for both of us—but also knowing I will go. I will try and keep trying. I cannot help it. That is what love does.

WE MEET AT A COFFEE SHOP IN PIGALLE, NEXT TO WHERE MAS LIVES, next to where he works. He fell in love and his world got incredibly small. His entire existence narrowed to a point: her.

He has chosen a chic coffee shop to go with his chic life. He sits on a traditional red bistro chair under an awning, hemmed by scraggly Parisian trees. He is wearing a French suit and French shoes and a French expression of distaste. He looks like he belongs. He looks like a normal human being. I do not understand it.

"Hey," he says as I approach. He has already ordered coffee for me: black, like my heart. "You caught me off guard yesterday," he says as I take the seat across from him. "It's not that I don't want to see you." I know. It goes much deeper than that.

"Never mind," I say. Sometimes I miss him. But whenever I am around him, I feel this phenomenal sense of shame—my wrongness in the world. I feel it now, creeping up on me.

"So," he says, "how are you doing?" I can see how much he does not want to ask, does not want to know. Even though I never tell him the full truth. He does not want the truth. Neither do I. No one wants the truth.

"Yeah. Great."

"You look really . . . I mean, considering you were just shot. You look better than I would expect." I have the money to thank for that. With enough money, you can look *phenomenal* no matter how dark you go.

"You look well, too," I say. He looks a different kind of good than I do. I look flash and expensive and fit. He looks content. You cannot buy that look with money.

We are quiet for far longer than is comfortable. Neither of us knows what to say. Mas does not want to ask about my life. I should ask about his, but I cannot pull the words together.

I sip my coffee to pass the time, hunched forward like I am chained to the table. When we have stayed silent for so long that neither of us can move, neither of us can breathe, I force myself to say something. Anything.

"I met someone." I do not know why I said that.

"What?" His expression is not what I expected—in place of pleasure is something more purely like terror. "What do you mean?"

I do not know what I mean. I did not *meet* someone. I had sex with someone on a train, then fainted. I have now failed to track this someone down. I will probably never see her again. I actually feel bad for Eva, bad for using her for this twisted purpose: to try to make my brother think I am all right.

"I just mean, on the train. I don't know. She was . . ." She was what? Up for sex? Smart? Funny? The truth is, I know nothing about her. Not her phone number. Not her last name. I am not even sure if she gave me her real first name; it was not on the passenger list. Maybe she snuck onto the train. She could be anyone. She could even be no one—did anyone else talk to her? Did I dream her up? Is all of my life building up to the pathetic last-minute twist of an unreliable narrator?

Mas is looking down at my hands. I am doing that thing I do, my nervous tic. Rubbing my fingers across my palm over and over. My hands are still only when they are holding weapons.

Mas sighs. "You need therapy."

"I had therapy," I remind him.

I had years of therapy in prison, although I was not exactly forthcoming with my counselor. I sometimes wished that he could help me, but the risk was too great: that he would see me, that he would say, *This thing cannot get out.*

If I could have faked it I would have, but I never really mastered the art of convincing people that I am normal. Instead, I chose to be invisible. I developed a negative charisma. I taught myself to disappear inside a room.

I returned to therapy, at Mas's request, after I was released. Without the threat of continued incarceration hanging over my head, I floated a little of the truth to my new therapist. The results were unexpected.

"You're so big and you're so intimidating and you've already committed murder. You don't realize," he told me, "what you have is a gift."

Mas feels differently. Hell, so do I.

It was this therapist who introduced me to Thomas—another of his patients, who had been suffering from severe anxiety ever since he had gotten into the murder-for-hire business. He brought us together in exchange for a fee. If he had been really good at his job, he would have asked for a percentage.

Mas knows all this and seems unwilling to argue with me. It is clear that our meeting is rapidly unraveling. We both know exactly how it will descend, all the way down to the moment I killed for him.

Mas sees this ending, too, and it is his turn to try to derail it. "So. I wanted to . . . The reason I asked you here . . ." Mas hedges, which is not like him.

"Spit it out," I say.

"Giselle is pregnant," he says.

I choke on my coffee. "Oh . . . Congratulations." He does not look impressed by my tone. My tone was not intentional.

He sits back in his chair and narrows his eyes at me. "I can't decide if I want you to see the baby. Sometimes I think I do. Then I remember reality, and I don't."

"Goddamn reality," I say wryly. I cannot believe she is pregnant. I cannot believe he is doing this.

"You can't just be happy," he complains.

"Exactly. That is exactly it," I say. I toy with the buttons of my new suit. Tom Ford brought it over this morning. "The thing is, Mas, you don't understand me. And I'm glad you don't. I envy you for not understanding."

He makes a face. He hates when I do this. It is as if he finds my misery competitive. As if he has to win at that, too. "I understand more than you think," he says. "I joined the army."

"To be a surgeon."

"I understand more than you think," he repeats. His eyes are intense. I look away. I hate it when he really looks at me, like I am terrified that he really sees me.

When he looks at me like this, I wish I could go back to when we were children. To when he looked at me in a completely different way. When I was his savior. When I was his hero. When I was the one protecting him.

"No, you don't." I subtly rebutton my coat. If he understood, he would not be settled. If he was really like me, he could not be happy. I do not blame him, but I also cannot be around him for long. "I have to go."

I stand and start to walk away.

"Ethan," he says. Ethan is my real name. It is close to my fake name because that makes it easier to respond to.

I turn back to face him. "Can you please not say that?" I ask him in an undertone, scanning the crowds. I do not think I am really being watched all the time—especially not now, when I am "off sick"—but I do not want to chance anything. Mas knows better than to use my real name in public. We should not even be meeting out in the open like this. Mas knows that, too. His text was a challenge in a way. It said that he was the one trying, that I was the problem. I am.

I start walking again, before he can take any more risks. "We're moving," he says. That stops me. "I'm not telling you where, and I'm not telling you when. You'll have to find another doctor."

It has been a year since we last saw each other—at least since he saw me. I have seen him, here and there. Checked up on him.

The truth is, he could not escape me if he wanted to. But another truth is, I need to let him go.

"Good call," I say.

It is better for everybody. It is the right thing to do. I can do the right thing once.

19

Eva

SHERRI IS ALREADY TIPSY WHEN I GET TO THE BISTRO THE NEXT morning. The champagne is chilling in one of those cute ice buckets. The sun is barely up, winking at the pink Parisian clouds.

"Sorry!" Sherri lifts her second glass, to toast my sitting down, I guess. "I couldn't wait."

"You never do," I say. Sherri has been working for the agency for years. She always complains about it, but she used to be a madam and she's said that was worse. She can sleep at night now, she says.

"Right." She fills my glass and refills hers. "I don't want to talk about last night except to say I think congratulations are in order." She lifts her glass for a toast. "Happy thirtieth."

We clink glasses and I take a sip. The bubbles tickle my nose. I'm not a huge fan of champagne, but I won't give up on it.

"Actually, it's my thirty-third." She's forgetting the kills I had before I started with the agency.

She grimaces. She knows my history, but she tends to forget it. Lucky her.

"Well, whatever the count is, I wanted to tell you that the agency is very happy with you. You're organized and efficient and reliable. You do the jobs exactly as we tell you to. You'd be surprised how hard it is to find employees like that." That's because all their other assassins are men. This industry is really tough for women to get into, even tougher for them to be taken seriously in. I like to think I'm breaking the glass ceiling, one murder at a time.

"Thank you," I say. "I really appreciate the positive feedback. This job is very important to me. It's nice to know I'm doing well."

Sherri's glass wobbles as she brings it to her lips. I don't think she can tell if I'm serious or not. But I am serious. This is the first time in my life I've ever been really good at something. I've finally found my thing. Too bad it had to be murder.

"There's a lot of goodwill for you in the agency," Sherri continues. "Which means bigger jobs. And bigger paydays."

"Excellent." I raise my glass to her again. Why not? The champagne is popping through my brain, deepening my rose-colored glasses. *La vie en rose.*

"But let's not talk about work," Sherri says. "Let's talk about nice things. Life." I feel attacked.

The thing is, in this line of work—especially for a woman—it's better not to form attachments. I did with Andrew. He was an assassin, too. He was actually the one who got me into the business.

When I first started dating Andrew, I was working at a real estate office in Rome. I hated my job. I smoked cigarettes, drank red wine, snorted bad coke on the weekends. I was just like everyone else. I stayed out too late clubbing. I bitched about the cost of Ubers. I tried to keep up with politics.

Andrew claimed he was a bouncer but I suspected he was dealing drugs. He kept weird hours, went away on random trips and came home jumpy and rattled. We were dating for six months before he turned to me in bed one night and said, "Don't take this the wrong way, but I think you would make an excellent assassin." I laughed. I thought it was a joke until he told me more. Until he told me everything.

"This is my work phone," he said, taking out an old-school burner phone that just screamed "drug dealer." He scrolled through all his texts, showing me how to find the codes inside what looked like error messages. "2F04" means "red," means "stop." "022F02" means "green," means "go."

I thought he was crazy. I thought he was making it up.

"It's okay if you're a drug dealer," I reassured him. "I mean, it's kind of cringey, but you don't have to lie about it." It was a little weird that he seemed to think being an assassin was more acceptable, but it was definitely cooler.

Then Andrew got out of bed and walked over to his safe. He had told me it was his dad's and that he used it to store his watch collection. I had never seen inside before. I didn't really care about watches.

He carefully worked the lock. I sat up in bed. He opened the safe and revealed eighteen guns, twenty-two knives, forty-seven types of poison. Give or take.

"Oh," I said. "Shit."

He got slightly giddy then. I know now it was because of the euphoria of just being honest with someone. Of telling someone the truth. Of not hiding.

He explained how he got his start. Told me his kill number.

"Remember when I went back to England last month?" he said, bouncing with excitement. "I wasn't home. I was in London, killing a fella in Camden." He held up his hand. "That's how I broke my thumb. I cracked it on my mark's nose."

I didn't immediately buy it—I mean, who would? I treated it like an unfortunate glitch in his character: *My boyfriend farts in front of me, he never puts the seat down and he thinks he's an assassin. You know how it is with the men!*

Then he let me listen in on a call. Then he let me come with him on a job.

"I *really* shouldn't be doing this," he kept repeating. We were sitting in a busted Fiat around the corner from the Parliament offices in Rome at eleven thirty at night.

He did it. I watched him kill a man. I kept the engine running as he shot a man point-blank. He jumped into the front seat and leapt across the console to kiss me. I had to push him off.

"We're going to get caught if you start doing all that," I said professionally, zooming away from the scene.

He was shocked by my cool head. Honestly, so was I.

But I had seen murder close-up before. I had killed. Watching an organized execution seemed almost civilized by comparison. It felt almost *normal*. Like I expected it. Because what had happened to me when I was a child had fucked me up. Being surrounded by death made me feel normal.

I don't know if I even realized it at the time. I told myself it was fun and exciting. Heroic. Cinematic. Badass.

Andrew started training me every day when I got home from work. He taught me how to fight, how to stab, how to shoot and poison and how to kill. When he went away on jobs, I studied by myself. I went to big Italian libraries and read the classics—the Italians were pretty damn expert at killing. I became infatuated, obsessed. I stopped going out, stopped drinking and doing coke and being like everyone else. I started being like me.

Then Andrew introduced me to Sherri.

We flew to London to meet her in person. It was important, he said, that she meet me. "Then she'll know. She'll see what I mean."

It was a bizarrely normal meetup at a nightclub in Chelsea.

We were in a back room drinking champagne. We even danced a little.

When it was so late that we couldn't leave without seeing sun, we sat down in a private booth and had one of those intense bonding conversations reserved for the very intoxicated.

I told her all about my childhood: the real story. I pulled no punches, too drunk to edit. I gave her the kind of dirty details that I usually regret sharing the next day. Then I jumped to my life after: the girls' home, college, how studying abroad led me to Italy, and to Andrew.

Sherri pulled back to consider, with drunken enlightenment, all the things I had told her. "It's incredible, really, how you've managed to pull your life together from such tragedy. You graduated from college. You have a good job."

"I didn't have a choice," I confessed, speaking words I had considered many times before. "A man with my backstory would be a tragic hero. I was a freak. There was no place for my story, so I buried it."

She took my hand. I used to jump when people touched me. "Thank you for trusting me." She took a deep breath. She shook her head. "I've never been through anything like that, but in a way, I know what you mean. I used to be a dominatrix, and then I was a madam. My husband doesn't even know that."

"Weirdly, I think your backstory might be even *less* accepted by society," I told her.

She shrugged limply, not disagreeing. "There is no place in this world for a woman who sins."

I thought she was right, and yet: There we were. The two of us together, two women who had sinned. We had a place with each other.

She squeezed my hand. "I like you. And more than that, I *want* you to succeed. We need more women in the field." She sat back, patted my hand. "Let me run this up the flagpole. See if we can get you something easy to start."

Andrew walked over, hearing that last bit. "We could do something together," he suggested.

But Sherri was adamant: "No. We don't run jobs like that. Every assassin is independent." I was actually relieved. I wanted to prove myself. I wanted to do it on my own.

My first kill was easy. So easy, it felt like destiny. It felt *good*.

I had killed the bad guys once, but I had killed them too late. And I think it was almost therapeutic killing them on schedule.

I loved the approval, the praise I got from Sherri and Andrew for every kill. The truth is, I sometimes felt bad about my past. I sometimes felt guilty and weird and fucked-up. So being congratulated on a kill felt like someone saying I was okay. And "okay" is a powerful drug.

The thing about Andrew was, it was never really love. Not for either of us. It was *honesty*. In some ways, that felt more important. It was acceptance. Acceptance that we would never find another person who would accept what we did for a living. Andrew wasn't a very good liar, and I wasn't very good at being alone, and there was a kind of intimacy in the truth, at least. In being able to tell each other, *I killed someone today*. People build relationships on way less.

I miss him. For real. Sometimes I wish I could just go home and tell someone about my day. That's it. That's all I want. To wash the blood off with someone watching. But that's impossible. I know from experience—it only ends in tragedy.

I can't even talk to Sherri about my work life. Even though she's a part of it, she doesn't have the stomach for it. All she wants to talk about is *everything else*. All the things I don't have. All the things I can't have.

Right now, she's just waiting for me to give her something. She needs me to reassure her that I'm not some subhuman murderess. That I have thoughts and interests and hopes. That I have a life that's not just taking lives.

I want to give her that. She's my friend, so I want to lie for her.

"I met someone on the train," I find myself saying.

She squirms with excitement. "Tell me more."

"We had sex," I say. She groans with pleasure. She's seriously so relieved. "On the luggage rack."

"Christ on a cracker!" She slaps me, but she's grinning. She's so happy. And then I'm so happy, too.

I tell her about his glasses and his jaw and his single dimple. I conjure him up like he's more than a man. Like he's a solution. The life I'm missing. Because everyone knows relationships are what make you *human*, what make you one of the everyone.

It's what every mother asks. What every friend checks up on. It's the thing that carries the *most* premium in society, the most meaning. *Yes, you are thriving! Yes, you are rich! But what are you doing, really, if you're not fucking someone on the reg?* All the world pities and fears you if you aren't fucking someone. It's a pretty ridiculous but undeniable fact.

My love story is giving this meetup meaning. It's making the sky brighter, the birds more singing. It's making the champagne sweeter. Then I get to the sad part: "I went back to our compartment, and he never came back." I leave out the part where he left behind a suitcase filled with weapons. That doesn't really scream "romantic hero."

I'm worried that the ghosting will devastate Sherri, who is clinging to this story like it's a lifeline, but she surprises me.

"Ohh! Noo!" She calls the waiter. She waves frantically, like this is an emergency. "We need another bottle of champagne," she says in French. "Quick!"

She practically leaps across the table to clasp my hand. "He's such an asshole! What a fuckwit! Absolute tosser!"

That's when I realize she loves this part, too. Maybe even more than the sex part. The ghosting.

Sherri and I spend actual *hours* giddily berating Jonathan, dismembering all the parts of him we recently loved, until he is a regular swarm of inefficiencies.

He has bad eyesight!

A horrible constitution!

He'd probably get motion sickness in bed!

He is not going to solve you, but somebody will. Don't worry! Don't lose faith! Somewhere out there is a man who will solve y-o-u! You just have to keep looking. You just can't give up!

A strong woman like you needs someone really, really special.

I'm seriously so jazzed when our meetup is over. I'm ready to have sex again. Or go shopping. Or kill someone.

When we part, we're both so drunk that we can barely walk to our separate cabs. We exchange air-kisses—three, like true friends do.

I ask Sherri to get me another job as soon as possible. I don't want to hang around in Paris. I don't want to risk running into Jonathan. He's nothing to me. He couldn't be anything, even if I wanted him to.

All he could ever be is another person to lie to, another person to pretend for.

Another person to break my heart.

20

Jonathan

THE PROBLEM WITH GRANTING ME SICK LEAVE IS THAT I AM really, really sick. And if I cannot get it out of me one way, I will immediately find another.

I track every person in our train compartment. The Italian woman to her daughter's apartment, the Italian boys to their hostel in Montmartre, the Frenchwoman to Burgundy, the Englishman to Marseilles and the American to a penthouse near Les Puces, and then to his private gym, which I join.

I have to prove something to myself. That Eva existed, maybe. That I can find her.

It is clear she lied to me about everything. It is no wonder I liked her.

Normally I have a mark, a goal I can fix my lethal focus on, but now I have only her.

I have been at the gym for six hours. I am practically sweating blood, but I do not want to leave. It is only noon—the worst time of the day: the afternoon and then the evening, the time when people come together, especially in France.

They sit outside sprawling cafés and drink coffees and cocktails and they talk and they laugh and they do all the human things I am excluded from. That I have excluded myself from.

I cannot lift anymore and I cannot run anymore. My muscles are twitching in this mildly electric, painful way. There is a point at which exercise is just damage, and I am past that point but I do not want to leave. I cannot sleep and I have no one to kill and my life is a meaningless expanse, so I wander the floors of the gym looking for ways to die.

That is when I finally see him: the American from the train. He greets all the staff as he enters the gym, carrying a fencing bag. He walks toward one of the side rooms. A fencing class is starting in ten minutes.

I wander in his direction, planning our spontaneous meeting. Eva must have gone back to our compartment. He might have spoken to her. She might have given him clues to her identity, even her location.

I am not sure if he will recognize me, but his face lights up when he sees me. He drops his fencing bag and strides over.

"The weapons guy!" he says, catching me off guard. I am not sure how to proceed. "Did that woman ever return your suitcase?"

"Oh . . . No." Eva opened my suitcase. Eva *took* my suitcase. Another reason I need to find her. The good thing about her stealing my weapons is that I have an excuse to question the American directly. "Did you speak to her at all? Do you have any idea where she might be?"

"No, I was asleep, and then in the morning she opened the suitcase. She said she would return it to you. I assumed you knew each other."

"She didn't say anything else?"

"No. I'm sorry I can't be more help. It must hurt to lose a collection like that." He studies me. "Do you know how to use those things?" This is spoken like a challenge. I can see him sizing me up, trying to determine whether he can kill me. It is a thing men do sometimes.

"A little," I say.

"I'm teaching a class in five minutes." He starts to open his bag. "If you want to join"—he removes his sword—"I'd love to see your style. You don't look like a . . . *traditional*." Comments like that set my teeth on edge.

I do not know if it is entirely fair for me to join, but I convince myself that if I use my nondominant hand I can participate. I can play well with others. "Sure."

We wear masks. It is all so very innocent.

I try to hang back, to not draw too much attention to myself, but the instructor wanders into my orbit. He calls out exercises and watches as I execute them.

"That's a very interesting technique," he says, now in French. "Where did you study?" He probably studied fencing in private school. I first learned to fence in prison—they did not offer classes. I had a cellmate who could make a shiv out of anything and would try to stab me at odd moments—to break up the boredom, I guess. So I taught myself to parry; I taught myself to riposte; I taught myself to flèche.

"I just learned things here and there," I answer the instructor in French.

He tilts his head, watching me. "Why don't you pair off with me for this next part?" He licks his lips.

I can tell he wants to fight me. Almost every man wants to fight me. That is what happens when you are in peak physical condition. Other men see you and want to kill you. They cannot help themselves. It is a natural instinct. Survival of the fittest.

I know that Thomas would not like this. He does not like me to even train in public, because it draws too much attention. I am supposed to be invisible. I am supposed to not exist. Most of the time I am fine with that. Before I took this job, I was already mostly gone.

But today I am on sick leave.

"All right, everyone," the instructor says. "Let's pair off for this next section. Try to find someone with a similar skill level." A man and woman pair up and he separates them. "No, no, men with men and women with women." I cannot wait to pretend to kill him.

He oversees every pairing until he thinks we are all evenly matched. He is wrong.

"All right. Now." He passes up and down the rows, waving his sword. "We will fight in turns so I can observe your technique. But first you will watch us." He gestures between me and him. "What is your name?" he asks me.

"Frank."

"Okay, Frank. Now. You will see Frank—he fights with a different style. He's very sloppy." Again? What is it with people lately? He takes his place across from me. "Go ahead, Frank."

"Go ahead with what?" I ask.

He laughs. "I want you to fight me. Don't you know how to start a fight?"

"I know how to finish one," I say under my breath.

He salutes me with an air of condescension. I advance toward him and he stops me with a hand. "Wait. You have to salute me back. Have you never learned the rules?"

I have learned the rules—seven years ago, when I first moved to France—but I am a little rusty. I do not salute someone before I take their life.

"Sorry," I say. I return to my mark. I salute him back.

"Go!" he says in French.

He did ask. I am using my nondominant hand. I have been working out for six hours. I cannot get fairer than that.

I lunge so fast that he stumbles back. I stab him right in the heart, or pretend to. He seems surprised, and a little annoyed.

"Oh. Okay. Wow." He walks in a circle, shakes out his hands. "Let's try that again."

I go back to my spot. I salute him.

He takes a deep breath, finds his place. "Why don't you give me the right-of-way this time?" he asks.

I shrug.

He salutes me. He says, "Go," a little less forcefully.

He starts it. I finish it. My sword is at his throat.

My classmates look nervous, shifting from foot to foot. There is a palpable tension in the room. A sense that something could go mortally wrong, and I bring it. I always bring it. It is hardwired into my DNA, this ability to turn the world upside down. To scare people.

"Okay," my instructor says. "That's not—I think maybe you don't know the rules very well." He delicately removes the blade from his neck. "You're off target. You are only allowed the area from shoulder to groin."

"Sorry." I shake my head. He is right. What am I doing? I know better than that, and maybe this is not such a good idea after all. Pretending to kill someone is a little too much like actually killing someone. My blood is pumping. My heart is hammering. I keep noticing little things about him—his bad knee and his crooked hips and the blind spot on his left side. His weaknesses light up like targets. I do not want to hurt him accidentally. Or on purpose.

"Maybe we should stop," I say.

"No," he refuses. "You just need to follow the rules." He sounds just like Thomas. He sounds just like everyone. "I can beat you, if you play fair." Okay, now he just sounds crazy.

I try not to laugh. I try not to be a dick—I really do, most of the time.

"You have no technique," he tells me, avoiding his mark so we cannot start. "You don't know what you're doing." He cannot beat me with a sword, so he is trying to beat me with words. I wait for him to take his mark. I force myself not to talk back. I try to stop myself from thinking of ways that I could really kill him. "You're like an animal," he tells me. "You have no grace."

Before I found the job—when I was a kid, and then when I was in prison—I used to love a fight. Fighting makes things so simple. It distracts you from the weight and the ick and the pain of life. I was a bad kid, from a bad house, in a pretty bad town. This is not the first time I have been called an animal. And I am sure it will not be the last.

I want to walk away. I almost do, but then he salutes me, and—before I can stop myself—I salute him back.

"Go!" he says, and this time he moves first.

He comes flying at me with all the dignity of pure fury. The audience gasps. I parry him. He swings wildly. He wants to hit any part of me. He wants to kill me. I know. In my line of work, I see it all the time.

I could kill him. It would be so easy. But it is not my job.

His blade swipes my neck. I feel the cut, feel my own blood wet my collar.

"I got you!" he squeals, victorious, forgetting his own rules. "You're dead!"

I press my palm against my neck to quell the bleeding.

"Congratulations," I say through gritted teeth. "You won."

I FINALLY LEAVE THE GYM. SO IN A WAY WE BOTH WIN. I WALK THROUGH Paris in the afternoon and the streets are a sea of air kisses, of coffee and wine. I have this horrible feeling that everyone else is ordinary, everyone is normal, everyone is happy, except for me.

The world would have you believe that it is good to be unique. It is good to be special. It is good to be different. But the truth is, it is lonely. The reality is, it is alienating. To be the only one in a sea of everyone. The killer in a world of lovers.

Paris is the City of Love. Sometimes I forget that, and every time I remember, I die a little more.

I want to leave Paris, but she keeps me hanging on. I want her full name. I want her number. I want to know why she looked familiar. I want to know who she is so I can discount her, convince myself that she is one of the everyone. That she cannot save me.

She said I would not be able to remember her face, but I remember everything. I remember her elbow, the swell of her bones. I remember her left ear being a hair lower than her right. I remember the little gold line beneath her pupil. I could draw a map, a diagram, even. I can imagine the parts I did not see.

I think about her so much, every detail, that I think I must have made her up. I picture her, surrounded by my weapons, waiting for me to find her. I almost wish I had hallucinated her, because then I might stand more of a chance of bringing her back: cold lips, soft eyes, cowlick.

I am generally too busy to notice that I am alone. I work. Roll over. Work some more.

But right now I do not have work. I walk through the market every day, sometimes three times a day. I find myself selecting her favorite places, as if she told me, as if she is with me, holding my hand.

I am really in a dangerous position. Not because of her but because of me.

I buy everything in Paris. And when I run out of things to buy, I give things away. I drive to the market fringes in my new Porsche and I hand out Tom Ford candles, Italian loafers, all the cash in my pockets.

I want to kill myself. I even know what color my death would be: blue. Which sounds obvious, but you would be surprised how many deaths are red and yellow.

By the time Thomas calls me to check in at the end of the week, I am pleading: *Give me a job. Please. My brain needs a job or its job will be me.*

III

RETURN

Six Months Later

21

Eva

THE FIRST TIME I SEE HIM AGAIN, HE'S IN THE GALLERY. HE'S studying a painting. Not like he's judging it, but like it might be judging him. He's dressed in a Tom Ford suit, like the one he wore in the pictures Sherri slid toward me in a dark bar in Dublin. He's got a new pair of glasses. These ones aren't crooked but they have the same uneven lenses. He's still half-blind.

I keep waiting for him to see me, like I think he'll be able to sense me.

My heart is beating so hard.

The walls of the palace practically throb with it as I follow him down the hall. Past the King's Suite, past the State Apartments, into the Hall of Mirrors, where I see him over and over. His image echoes in my eyes.

I'm following Jonathan through the Palace of Versailles because he's my next assignment, my mark. He's been classified as extremely lethal.

"I don't want you to kill him yet, you understand?" Sherri told me on the phone. "This is reconnaissance. We need to come up with a plan. This guy is beyond dangerous."

Jonathan from the train, with the bent glasses and the motion sickness, is the most dangerous mark I've ever been given.

I want to prove myself, as a woman in a man's world. I want to show the agency that I can take this job. And then I see him again and I think: *It's Jonathan from the train. My Jonathan.*

With the pale skin and the stiff shoulders, the way his blue eyes hooked on mine. The way they said to me: *Everything that happens now is just between us.*

Everything.

This is going to be really, really hard.

22

Jonathan

I FEEL SO MUCH BETTER NOW. I HAVE KILLED SEVENTEEN PEOPLE. I am a little on fire. I hardly even think about Eva, or getting shot, or Mas.

It is a dreary day in France and I am taking a walking tour through the Palace of Versailles. It is part of my self-improvement journey, my deal with Thomas. Ever since that triple in Florence, he has been after me about every little thing.

He has been calling me all morning. I know he wants to talk about my last job. You kill someone, and everyone has an opinion about it.

He calls me now and I answer to gauge how angry he is.

"You fucking—" Fairly angry.

"Sorry, I can't talk right now. I'm in a museum." I hang up before he can catch his breath.

To prove that I am fully—mostly—sane, I am focusing on my work–life balance. I needed more culture; that was what was killing me. I needed museums and monuments and works of art. I needed to know that everyone was fucked and had been since forever. That murder was historical and tragedy was average and everything was going to be as okay as it had always been. No worse. No better.

It is not good to form obsessions with people; it is even worse to form attachments. In a way, I dodged a bullet by fainting on that train. I do not need Eva.

I need history. As I pass by paintings of soldiers and battles and suffering, I feel a keen sense of belonging. I would have made sense back then. I wonder what happened to all the people like me throughout history. The people who killed. I assume they were killed back.

I am in such a state of thrall to history that the first time I see her, I doubt myself.

I am in the Hall of Mirrors, surrounded by my face. I am trying to avoid my eyes when I find hers. Not once, but an infinite number of times.

The sunlight breaks through the clouds. Light sears the room. I cock my head. She smiles, an infinite number of smiles.

IV

FLIRTATION

23

Eva

H E SMILES AT ME ACROSS THE HALL OF MIRRORS. I LOOK both ways—*You mean me?*—then march directly to him.

"What are the odds?" I ask. A lot higher than he might think.

Up close, I notice that his suit is perfectly tailored. I'm guessing his sense of style is part of what makes him lethal.

"You look less pukey," I say.

"Yes." He adjusts his suit but it's already perfect. It falls perfectly. "Sorry about that. Bad time to meet someone." I can think of a worse one.

"You never came back . . ." I try to sound like I don't care, but all that comes out is the trying.

"I'm so sorry." His intensity catches me off guard. We've met in the middle of the hall. People have to walk around us. He doesn't even seem to notice, he's looking so directly at me.

Not to state the obvious, but he has no idea why I'm here. To him, this is probably fate. He has no idea that the agency has been searching for him for days, that I've been sitting around in my hotel room waiting for their call. Painting my toenails, experimenting with makeup, taking long, creamy baths. I was actually in the middle of a makeup tutorial when Sherri called me and asked, "How fast can you get to Versailles?" Which is why I look like a neon starlet right now.

He swallows. "I passed out in the WC. Literally fainted. I didn't wake up until long after the train had stopped."

"Oh." It's a pretty good excuse, but I've been mad at him for so long that it's too late to undo.

And anyway, for all I know, he's lying now. I definitely can't trust him. Not only did he ghost me, but he's been classified as extremely lethal.

"Totally cool," I say. "I didn't even notice." He gives me a look. I really didn't pull that line off.

"I regretted not asking for your number," he says. "Or your full name."

"I think we're blocking the path," I say, because I'm not touching *that*.

"Of course," he says. "Should we go out to the gardens?"

"Sure," I say. "Why not?" He can tell I'm annoyed. He seems a little sad about it.

He's different than I remember. I surreptitiously study him as we wind quickly through the crowds. He feels more present, for one thing. He was big on the train, but he seems bigger. He seems sharper, too, like nothing escapes his attention. And faster, lither. I'm not sure if I'm giving him these predatory traits because I've been told he's a predator, but he seems more dangerous, more intimidating and, honestly, kind of hotter.

"I'm really so very sorry," he says once we're outside, standing beside a fountain filled with vomiting frogs. They're gold, so it's classy.

"It's really not a problem," I say.

His Adam's apple throbs. He's staring at me, like he did on the train. "I've thought about you. A lot. I liked you." If he wasn't my job, I would probably find a way to run from this feeling—this good and painful feeling.

"I liked you, too."

His mouth turns up a little, like he's relieved. "I was face down on the floor, thinking, *If I could just get up . . .*" He's lying. He has to be. But what if he's not? What then?

I force myself to break eye contact. To look out at the beautiful bushes or whatever. The fountains and the statues and all that historical crap.

I have to keep my head on straight. I have to focus on the job. This isn't real life. This is work life.

My mission is to find his weaknesses. Everyone has them. In this job, any predictable habits can be weaknesses. *He always shoots from the hip. He loves to gamble. He brushes his teeth in the shower.* Even strengths can be weaknesses, from the right angle. Everything is usable as long as it's predictable. The enemy of murder is surprise.

To find out his weaknesses, I need to spend time with him. As much time as possible, in as many ordinary situations as I can. We need to hang. We need to be friends. We need to trust and reveal our most sacred selves. Or at least our most intimate ones.

I'm going to have to put aside my feelings. *All* of them.

I was offered the job over champagne with Sherri. We were celebrating my thirty-third (really my thirty-sixth) when she told me the agency had a special job, just for me. The kind of job I'd always dreamed of: high profile, high paying.

"Remember, you don't have to take it," she said, reaching into her purse.

"Why wouldn't I want to take it?" I asked. We were drinking black velvets in a private booth in a dark corner of a bar in Dublin.

"He's been classified as extremely lethal."

"Why?"

"Apparently he's very good with a sword. And a gun. And pretty much anything." She slid me the first photo. I flipped it over, then dropped it immediately. "Handsome little fucker, isn't he?" she said.

"It's not that." I could feel my face go white, the blood draining. Sherri registered my shock. She tilted her head. "What is it?"

"It's Jonathan. *My* Jonathan." I felt a peculiar ping, like he belonged to me because I said it. "That's the guy from the sleeper train."

She hissed through her teeth, stretched back in surprise. "The guy you—"

"Yes." It had been months since I'd seen him, but probably hours since I'd thought of him. Every time I saw a train go by, or someone wearing glasses or carrying luggage. My mind could really *reach*, apply him to any situation. See him everywhere, as if the whole world were just echoes of him. "He had all those weapons," I remembered. It added up, that he would be good with pretty much anything. He had *everything* in that suitcase, which was now sitting in a storage facility in Paris. "Who is he?"

"He's essentially a henchman for a very dangerous man," Sherri says. "He travels around Europe killing people. He's completely psychotic. Soulless. Deranged." But he seemed so nice.

Still, there were many things I overlooked: the weapons, the blood. Maybe because I liked him. Maybe because I'm a little dark, too. Did I really think he was one of the good guys?

"You don't have to take the job." Sherri reached across the table and squeezed my hand.

I wanted to reassure her that I would. I loved Sherri.

We were two dark girls in a too-dark world. I texted her sometimes at three o'clock in the morning, after a particularly brutal nightmare, and not only did she answer me at that time, but she

106

called me back. She walked me through the bad dreams, assuring me over and over that it wasn't too late to talk. We had weekly watch parties for all our favorite reality shows where we savaged all the men and made every excuse for the women, to redress the societal imbalance. We exchanged holiday and birthday and thinking-of-you gifts. Sherri was the perfect gift giver, always managing to buy me the exact thing I had always dreamed of having but would never feel worthy to buy for myself. I tried to do the same for her.

She was my ride-or-die, and when you work as an assassin, that's pretty fucking serious.

But our friendship was also a little tangled up in this job—this weird and dangerous job. It brought us closer, but it also kept us apart. Sherri was my handler. It was her job to *handle* me. Even if she was also my friend.

Right then in the bar, I wanted to tell her what she wanted to hear, but first I wanted another drink, and then another one, and another. Within hours, we were both drunk. And then I assured her, "Of course I want the job. I can do it! He's a bad guy, right?" I also wanted to see him again, which was possibly the worst reason to agree to a hit.

"It might be a good thing," Sherri said, a little wobbly. "Therapeutic. He practically ghosted you. This could be your revenge!" An odd look crossed her face, and then she burst out laughing. "It's perfect! You can kill your ghost!"

I started laughing, too, slightly hysterical.

"It's what he deserves for not asking for your number!" Sherri said.

"I'm doing it for women everywhere!" I declared.

It seemed hilarious then, but now it seems like it was delirium, maybe even a little fear. Isn't that the word for when you have a crush on someone?

Looking at Jonathan now, I try to see the person Sherri said he was. Psychotic. Soulless. Deranged. I can see how other people might think he could fit into that mold—physically, at least, he's intense. But he was so sweet on the train. Possibly because he was drugged. Possibly because he was ill.

I take a deep breath. I remind myself that he's the bad guy. I remind myself of what it felt like when he ghosted me. I have a job to do. I'm going to crush it.

"And now here we are in Versailles," I tell him. "Here's to second chances."

He nods slowly, as if uncertain. "Have you eaten? There's a restaurant, uh, near here. Farm-to-table. No one knows about it. Can I make it up to you?"

I cock my head. I doubt upper-level management expected this. He wants to take me to a restaurant, alone, that no one knows about. It's like he's setting me up to murder him.

I smile. "Sounds perfect."

24

H E LEADS ME DOWN THE STREET TO WHERE HIS CAR IS parked. I really think he's at his most attractive when he's doing mundane things.

Right now, he can't find his car. He's peering this way and that, shielding his glasses with his hand to block the sun. He seems flustered. It's kind of adorable.

"Sorry. I thought it was down here. I didn't expect to see you," he adds like the two things are related.

"It's fine. We don't have to go farm-to-table. There was a café in the garden at Versailles. We could hide behind a hedge. Eat apple slices."

He looks at me, blinking, like I've said something shocking.

"What?" I ask.

"I just think you're cute. That's all." He's killed me. I'm dead. His eyes drift until they land on what we're looking for. "Oh, thank God! There's the car. Sorry." He shakes his head. "I'm not usually like this."

"What are you usually like?"

"Worse." He hurries me to the car. He seems rushed, like he can't wait to spirit me away. I need to stay on guard. You can't trust anyone, especially not someone you're supposed to kill.

A man in a neat suit and a black hat is waiting in the driver's seat, reading *Le Monde*.

"Change of plans," Jonathan says to him in Persian. "There's a little restaurant, east of Plaisir—" He pauses, turns to me. "It's twenty minutes away. Is that all right? You don't have plans?" He *is* my plans.

"Nothing important."

"Near the Sainte-Apolline Forest," he says to the driver. "I'll direct you." He opens the door for me. "I better call ahead."

I climb into his fancy car and chalk up another difference. Jonathan-on-the-train wore an ill-fitted suit and crooked glasses. This Jonathan is dressed flawlessly and has a driver. This Jonathan has *money*.

As I fasten my seat belt, I remember his suitcase. Those weapons weren't cheap. I decide it's better not to bring that up. Arming my mark is not a good way to kill him.

He slides into the seat beside me. He smiles a little awkwardly, then shifts like he's not sure how close he should sit.

As we wind along the French roads toward the restaurant, Jonathan gets on the phone. He spends the full twenty-minute drive convincing the owner of the restaurant to open on a weekday, just for us. He doesn't back down, even though they seem pretty firmly against it at first. It's patently impressive.

He starts with compliments.

He's been to the restaurant *many* times. Over years. Before everyone else knew about it. It's the experience of a lifetime. *How is Renaud?*

Jonathan has a very special woman he's trying to impress

(that's me). He knows this is short notice, but he met her on the sleeper train from Florence to Paris, and he was too ill to get her number, but now he has run into her again—*quelle chance!*—in Versailles, of all places.

"I saw her in the Hall of Mirrors," he says. "Imagine. You are looking for a woman for months. Dreaming of finding her, and then you see her a million times at once."

He says all this in French. I don't think he realizes that I can understand it.

He would be more than happy to pay double the market value for our meal—which he knows is at least double what they charge (which sounds like a lot).

This is where I see his first real weakness—and it's a big one. I'm a trained assassin on a reconnaissance, remember? And I'm very good at my job.

He's determined to pay too much, and that, my friends, is a sign of a guilty conscience. As he insists on paying double—no, triple!—what they normally ask, he rubs his palm with his fingers. I remember this move from the train. His tic.

He doesn't just want to take me to lunch. He wants it to hurt. He wants to punish himself for the pleasure of my company.

The owner agrees, of course. They're French after all. They understand that pleasure and pain pair perfectly.

When Jonathan gets off the phone he has a slight sheen. His sweat smells like Tom Ford.

"You're going to love this place," he assures me. "It's really special."

"That's really super of you," I say. "To care so much." He takes a deep breath. I brush his wrist. Then I lean in. "But you don't have to go to so much trouble . . ." He might be dangerous, psychotic, deranged. But he's also a man, and sex is the easiest entry point for murder. I'm not saying I'm going to sleep with him again, but it's not bad if he thinks I am. "I'm gonna fuck you anyway."

He inhales sharply. His hand closes around mine. And his fingers are so thick. His grip is so strong. I realize he could crush me.

I wonder what that would feel like.

25

JONATHAN LEADS ME DOWN THE ROAD TO A LITTLE RESTAURANT across from a wooded park. It reminds me of Marie Antoinette and her goats. The little cottage tucked away in the garden of Versailles where she pretended to be like everyone else.

Jonathan warns me that the meal will take hours. "Is that all right?"

"I'm on vacation," I remind him. "I have all the time in the world."

His face falls. "You've been on vacation for six months?" he says. I've made my first mistake.

Fuck. I've never done this before. Not since I started my job. I have never met the same guy twice. I'm honestly not sure I can even remember the things I told Jonathan, the blur of my fake life on a train overnight. I take some comfort in knowing he was lying to me, too.

"I'm finding myself," I say. "That kind of thing takes time. Especially if you're lost. Have you ever found yourself?"

"I know myself pretty well. Unfortunately."

He likes to make these doomed statements. *I'm usually worse.*

I know myself, unfortunately. This is another weakness, a pretty common one. He's not a fan of himself.

I feel a pull, like I want to reassure him. *But you're so handsome. But you're so smart. But you're so nice.*

But you're so lethal, Jonathan. There's just so much to love about you.

26

THE RESTAURANT IS RUN BY A MARRIED COUPLE, LOUISA AND Gestalt. They welcome us and guide us to our table.

I take in our surroundings. The restaurant is very cute. In America things are made to look old. In Europe they actually are. Antique farm equipment hangs from the ceiling over our heads: wheelbarrows, scythes, troughs and rakes.

So many weapons at my disposal. Practically no witnesses. I could kill Jonathan between the first and second courses. Delaying is only going to make it harder. But I'm not supposed to kill him. That's not the job. Not yet. That's not what has gotten me here, to bigger jobs and bigger paydays and bigger sacrifices.

Sherri says it all the time: *They like you. You listen.* Basically, *You're easy to control.*

I even agreed to walk into this job unarmed. It's something I would normally never do, but Sherri told me it was for the best. "He can't suspect you're an assassin. It actually works in our favor that he already knows you. You can't be armed. In fact, it might be a good idea to play clumsy, act a bit dim." I had to draw the line at that. I refuse to play dumb, even to commit murder.

Gestalt and Louisa explain how the meal will go. Every day the menu is different. It depends on what they find in the garden, in the local market, on their travels.

"Louisa is the artist; I am her hands," Gestalt says. It's chillingly tender. Jonathan seems a little anxious about having brought me somewhere so romantic.

Gestalt and Louisa wander off to select the wine.

"I hope this is okay," Jonathan says. He's sitting across from me, beneath a scythe—I'm not kidding, so on the nose—with this heartbreakingly earnest expression. I don't get it. I don't get him. How is he lethal? Do you pity him to death?

"Totally okay," I say. "I like all the weapons—I mean, farm shit." *Oops. Maybe I shouldn't talk.*

The first thing Gestalt's hands bring is a bottle of Bordeaux and a plate of escargots. He leaves them on the table and proceeds to forget about us, like the best waiters.

"Have you ever had snails?" Jonathan asks.

"I know you have."

He wields the little pincher thing with predictable dexterity. "How do you know that?"

"You look like a snail person."

"What does a snail person look like?"

"Tom Ford suit. Italian shoes. Patek Philippe watch."

"God, you're right." He pops one into his mouth. "I am a snail person."

"You seem different than you were on the train."

"So do you," he points out. This surprises me.

"How?"

He draws a line over his eye. I'm wearing neon pink eye shadow.

"It's called eye shadow." I grin. I don't know what it is, but when you like someone, everything they say is ten times more

116

charming. Funnier. Like you never laughed until now. Not that I like him. Much.

There's always a smile circling my lips when he's around. I wonder how that will work when I kill him. I wonder how I will kill him, but that's a problem for future me. Me *now* is on reconnaissance. Me now is looking for weaknesses, chinks in his armor.

He glances down at his snails, then up at me with hazy eyes. "I thought about you so much. I built you up in my mind. I honestly thought . . ." He gathers his breath. "I honestly thought if I ever saw you again I'd be disappointed. But I'm not. You're even better than I remembered."

I shake my head. "You don't know me." I'm slightly breaking character here but I can't help it. He can't just say things like that. Things that can't possibly be true. It's manipulative. It's mean. To act like you're in love with someone you don't even know.

He drops his chin. "You're right. I don't. I'm sorry."

I need to get us back on track. "And I don't know you." I need to know him better. I want to figure out if the past he shared was true. How much he can remember. "How's the family back home?"

He seems startled. ". . . Fine."

"Do you have any siblings?"

"No." He's studying me. I don't know why. Maybe because he knows I'm quizzing him. He was on a cheap train in an ill-fitted suit and suddenly he has a driver; he's suddenly wearing Tom Ford. I'm not the only one who's been on vacation for six months. "Your snails are getting cold," he says.

I pop one into my mouth.

"I have a confession to make," he says. His eyes are on me, gauging me.

"What's that?"

"I'm not here on vacation."

I stiffen. Is he about to tell me the truth? Confess that he's an evil henchman? "Why did you lie?" I try to keep my voice first-date playful.

He leans forward even though Louisa and Gestalt haven't been seen in the vicinity in eons. "Because there are people out there who want me dead." I knew that. "I work in illegal-weapons trafficking. It's a very dangerous job."

"Oh." That would explain the suitcase. Perfectly.

I know he must be lying, but it still unnerves me a little. I've never done independent research on my marks. The system has served me. I have trusted the people around me. I trusted Andrew. I trust Sherri. But what if they're wrong? What if Jonathan's not really a villain? Or worse, what if I'm coming up with excuses not to kill him?

"I actually . . ." He hesitates, sitting back as if unsure. "I left a rather large suitcase of weapons I'd confiscated on that train. I don't know if you might know what happened to it?"

"No idea," I say. We're both lying to each other; it's almost like a real first date. "Why didn't you tell me this on the train?"

He shifts in his seat. He keeps looking at me. It's a consequence of our being the only two people in this restaurant. The only two people left in the world, for all I know. And suddenly, I can feel the train underneath us, feel the throb of the ground beneath the tracks, beneath the wheels. Suddenly, it's like we never left.

"I was concerned about your safety. You see . . . ," he says. He shifts away from me, curls slightly like a snake. He's not stiff anymore. He's not nauseated or uncomfortable or sick. "The reason I didn't come back . . ." He's unbuttoning his shirt. Seems a little premature, but I'm comfortable on my toes. Or on my back. He tugs at the collar of his shirt until I can see it: a scar shaped like a snarl. "I'd been shot."

"Oh. That's a pretty good reason." Honestly, I feel a little annoyed with myself. I'm a trained assassin. How could I not notice that the guy I was crushing on had just been shot? In my defense, I knew he was hurt. I just didn't know how.

Even I have a few bullet fragments scattered here and there. They're like really shitty piercings.

I see all his symptoms in a new light: his stiffness, how he avoided me in the doorway. How he took a seat by the window, then disappeared to the bathroom. How he dropped Ecstasy—maybe not the best choice, but definitely self-medicating. His rules about the jacket and no touching above the waist. I thought he was sweet and sensitive; turns out, he was just shot.

"I was going to see a doctor in Paris," he continues. "People in Florence were hunting me. I couldn't risk going to a hospital there. And I couldn't get through a metal detector to take a plane."

I feel deflated. He's definitely lying. His story doesn't make sense. Why would illegal weapons that he'd confiscated have their own neat compartments in his luggage? Why would he be alone? Why would he have been shot? And what happened to the people who shot him?

I hate that he's lying to me, even though I'm lying to him, too. Even though I know strangers lie to one another all the time. It's how every relationship starts, with the presentation of the false self, the most likable version of y-o-u. The one you trade in, the one you sell.

They fall for the good guy.

Six months down the line, they're dating the antihero.

Two years in, they say "I do" to the villain.

"That's quite the story," I say. He seems to sense my disbelief. I want him to. If I am going to find his weaknesses, I'm going to need to guide him toward the truth. But I need to be patient. Careful. "So you don't really have motion sickness?"

He shakes his head. "No." I'm weirdly disappointed. His weaknesses were kind of endearing.

When I first met Jonathan on the train, I thought he was the safe bet. I thought I could take him to my hotel and have good, clean sex. That he would be a cozy little break from my high-octane life. We could lie in bed together in a postcoital glow and talk about Delaware. It would be easy. It would be breezy. I could walk away feeling accomplished because for three or four hours I'd fucked like everyone else.

Instead, there's someone treacherous sitting in the chair across from me. Someone who can flirt with a bullet in his chest.

What if it was another assassin who shot him in Florence? What if others have tried and failed? What if I'm the last resort? Or worse, expendable. *Send the girl; we can afford to lose her.*

It's a lot to take in.

"You still could have asked for my number," I say.

He laughs in surprise.

27

Jonathan

I DO NOT LIKE LYING TO EVA BUT I ALSO DO NOT REALLY HAVE A choice. It makes me feel disgusting—more disgusting than usual. But it would not be safe to tell her the truth, and it would also probably be a turnoff.

I told her about the bullet because she is going to see the scar. I mean, I *hope* she is going to see the scar. But I painted myself as the good guy because I do not want to scare her away.

I just want to have sex with her. Just one more time. Then my head will be clear. Then my obsession will end. It is what everyone needs. What the whole world needs. For us to have sex.

I should do it as quickly as possible but I stupidly brought her to the most epic of restaurants. We are strung now somewhere between the fourth and fifth course, in an almost meditative state. There is farm equipment hanging from the ceiling and every so often her eyes drift up, as if she senses that it might come tumbling down over our heads.

"This was a bad idea," I say. It has been hours. Hours in this restaurant, and I wonder if I did it because I wanted to mimic those hours on the train, as if I wanted to bring us back to the moment when I fucked it up, so I could fix it.

She told me in the car that she was going to sleep with me anyway. I appreciate her directness. But now we are both stranded here, trapped inside my plans, as ancient wheels creak overhead.

"What was?" she says.

"This," I gesture to the empty restaurant. "I should have just brought you to my hotel. I should have just taken care of you."

"Where are you staying?"

"Paris. Currently." I am keeping an eye on Mas. He has bought a house outside Bordeaux with a faulty foundation. He will need to tear down significant portions of the property to repair it, and the permit process is holding him up. I have made myself a promise that I will not follow him, but that does not mean I cannot watch him go. "What about you?" I ask her. "Where have you been?"

She gazes up at the ceiling as she lists countries. "Ireland, Germany, Greece, Portugal . . ." She looks holy when she is looking up, like an icon. A saint. I want to beg her to forgive me. For what? For what I am about to do.

"Can you come sit here, please?" I ask.

We are seated across from each other now. She on a chair. I on a bench that was wrenched from some chapel.

She smiles. "Why?"

"Because I want to touch you." God bless being direct.

She lifts herself languidly from her chair. She is a little fearless—a little too fearless. She sits herself right down on my bench, so close that I am the one who moves away.

I want to touch her but not so much, not all at once. It is overwhelming. I have been cooking her for so long that she burns. I need to take her in slowly. Blow on her first.

I reach out and brush her hair behind her shoulder. I start to take my hand back but find that I cannot. Instead, I wind the rope of her hair around my fist and tug once, lightly.

"I thought about you a lot," I say again. That is an understatement.

"I thought about you, too," she says. I flinch. I mean, God forbid that she should actually like me. That is the last thing either of us needs.

"I looked for you," I say. "In the market." I do not tell her I was there almost every day for weeks, months. Sometimes more than once a day. I do not tell her that I was obsessed, magnetized, dangerously in lust. That I would jerk off thinking about her, waiting for it to stop working, for her to leave my system. She never did. She was like a charm. She worked every time.

"I guess you don't really need me," she says. "If you didn't find me."

"Were you ever there?"

"No. I had to leave."

"To go where?"

"Anywhere. I had to find a place where no one knew me. Where I could be a tourist again." Her words tighten my jaw. "It wasn't about a destination; it was about *going*. And about *not* going. Not going home." It is like she is reading from my script. "Do you know what I mean?"

I know exactly what she means, but I find that I cannot admit it. It is a simple answer. All I have to say is yes.

I cannot say it.

Instead, I run my fingers now lightly along her neck, over her collarbone. I can see her blood pumping in her carotid artery. I can feel exactly how nervous she is: not nervous enough.

"I want to be honest with you," I say. "I think we should have sex again, and then separate. I don't want to lead you on. Or trick you. Or . . ." I drift off, like my mind cannot tell my mouth what else.

She looks unhappy—of course she does—and I want to tell her I do not mean it. I want to promise her I cannot help it, that I am trying to protect her, to save her from me. But then she does the unexpected: She smirks.

"I can make you come in nineteen seconds."

I laugh. "Why would you want to?"

She kisses me first. It scares me. I do not like not to shoot first. But her mouth over mine is so overwhelmingly pleasant, so perfect, so pure, that I forget all that for a moment. I let all that go.

There is nothing as exquisite as finding the thing you were looking for: your lost sunglasses, your car keys. Anything you ever thought you had lost, thought was gone, now suddenly back, now in your hands. Now *real* again. When you had made up your mind that you would never see it, would live the rest of your crushing life without it. Would never taste it in your mouth, feel its breath against your tongue, suck its neck, bite its earlobe.

"The fifth course."

We fumble apart. Gestalt is standing over us, perfectly French in his being unbothered as he lowers the next course onto our table.

He smiles mysteriously, as if he is the hands for us, too, guiding us along on this mystical journey called a meal.

"Salad," Eva says. She is right. Thinly sliced vegetables. Bright green lettuce.

"How many more courses do we have?" I say after Gestalt has vanished again.

"I think two? The cheese and then the dessert."

"I don't think I can make it. Can you?"

She sighs deep in her belly. Then takes up her fork and her knife. "We have to. This is France."

WE MAKE IT TO THE END OF THE MEAL. WE SURVIVE. ALL WE HAVE TO do is make it back to Paris, but there is a problem. I do not want to go back to Paris. I do not want her anywhere near Mas. I have this ridiculous fear that we will run into him, as if Paris is a small town. And he will see on my face how much I like her. And I will quietly die.

"I was thinking," I say as we leave the restaurant, "we could get a hotel room somewhere nearby . . ." I know she said in the car that she would fuck me, but I hope I am not being presumptuous.

"Sure," she says. "I'm up for an adventure— Wait." She suddenly grabs my hand. It disarms me how she does it—so thoughtlessly, like we have been holding hands off and on our whole lives. "We should go back to Versailles."

"Sorry?" I think it is closed now. I think everything is closed now.

"Bet you we could get in there—the gardens, at least. I think the French are very laissez-faire about security. Wouldn't it be cool to come inside the Hall of Mirrors?"

"I think the last people who came there lost their heads."

"Exactly. *Sexy.*" Her fingers are threaded through mine. Her hands are warm. Her smile enigmatic.

Who the fuck is this girl? I know she is not "Eva," although we never touched on *that* in our conversation. I was not about to admit how much I worked to track her down. Besides, we are just going to have sex and then separate. I do not need to know her life story.

She is obviously someone who sneaks onto trains and into palaces.

28

Eva

HERE'S THE THING ABOUT GREAT SEX: IT'S ABOUT SO MUCH more than just the fucking.

People forget about production value. You have to set the stage. You have to light the lights. Like with an opera, you have to build to a crescendo.

I know sleeping with Jonathan is probably a bad idea, but I can't back down when someone throws down like that:

I think we should have sex again, and then separate.

Is he fucking kidding me? He thinks he can walk away from me without a bullet in his chest? He really doesn't know what he's getting into. But he's about to find out.

I have an extensive knowledge of the male anatomy, especially when it comes to arousal, which is the easiest access point for murder.

If I had to make a list of all the most important parts of a man when it comes to arousal, number one would be his brain. People think that's reserved for women. *Women think with their heads; men think with their dicks.* Bullshit. Men can disconnect from their heads, sure. They do it all the time, to keep themselves from falling in love. The trick is not to let them. If you can do that, a man will become attached way more quickly than any woman.

Jonathan wears expensive suits and goes to fancy restaurants. He took a tour of Versailles by himself, for fun. He values the appearances of things. He's superficial. He's also pretentious and secretly kind of nerdy.

It's not enough just to fuck him in a luggage rack, or at a fancy hotel. I have to fuck him somewhere unforgettable, somewhere with real cultural significance. I have to fuck him in Versailles.

I know it sounds like overkill, but when you're trying to kill the unkillable, overkill is the only way to go.

I EXCUSE MYSELF AFTER THE LAST COURSE. "I HAVE TO CALL MY friend and let her know I won't be back tonight. And probably reassure her that you're not going to murder me." I'm teasing, but the look that passes over his face is not lost on me. *God.* When did things get so treacherous?

I exit the restaurant, cross the street and walk into the Sainte-Apolline Forest. The park is that perfect mix of trash, graffiti and antiquity. I find a quiet place in a shelter of trees and call my handler.

Sherri picks up on the first ring.

"Is everything all right?" She sounds anxious. I feel a shot of uneasiness.

"Everything's fine," I say. "We just finished lunch. And dinner."

"Are you on a date?" she jokes.

I lower my voice, even though I have no reason to. "I told you. It's the guy from the train."

"I know," Sherri says. "I thought we agreed that was a good thing."

"It is and it isn't. Are you sure he's really . . ." I hesitate. Am

I really going to question her intel? Trust is a pretty integral part of our relationship—both personal and professional. I exhale. "He just seems nice," I admit, even though I feel a little pathetic. Maybe I want him to be nice. Maybe I can't see the real him because I kind of like him.

"Remember, someone's threat level is not based only on a physical metric," Sherri says. "There's a mental component, and an emotional one. Sometimes those can be the *most* dangerous." Her voice gets this cool professionalism when she instructs me, like she has separate personalities: one that is my friend and one that is my boss. "You can do this," she says, sensing my unease. Sherri knows me better than anyone else. Sometimes that feels like a good thing; sometimes it doesn't. "You're the bravest, strongest person I've ever met. I believe in you."

I take a deep breath, pulling myself back together. She's right. I can do this. I *have* to do this. "There's one teeny, tiny thing I need your help with. I want to break in to Versailles."

"Beg your pardon?"

"It's work related."

"*Eva.*" She sounds a little scoldy, which annoys me. I'm a little on edge, just overall.

"I'm doing the job that no one wants, right? This guy is extremely dangerous, right?"

"So you need to break in to a national monument?" I can sense her smile coming on. This is why we make a good team. We both like to have fun, even when we're committing murder.

"Yes." Short, sweet and to the point. Sherri doesn't need details, especially ones she might try to derail.

Part of me knows this is really, really stupid. Having sex with this guy might create intimacy. It might get him to reveal his weaknesses, or at least his come face, but it's definitely going to make killing him a lot more emotionally complicated.

But a much bigger, much more reckless and convincing part of me thinks, *Well, hell. It might help. I mean, isn't it kind of worth a shot?*

"What is it that you want to do in Versailles?" Sherri asks.

"My job. Find out his weaknesses."

"And how is that going so far?"

"Guilt. That's his weakness." I start carving into a tree with my fingernail. "He's done something he feels bad about."

"Probably more than one thing."

"Probably." Haven't we all?

"I don't think that's enough," she says.

"Neither do I. Hence Versailles." I stand back to admire the "J" I've carved into the tree. Oops.

I hear Sherri typing. "You're in luck. There's a hotel on the grounds. I can book you a room."

"Perfect. And from there, the Hall of Mirrors."

"Eva," she says again.

"*Sherri.*" I can use names, too. "This is the biggest job we've ever done, right?"

"Right," she agrees begrudgingly.

"The biggest payday?"

". . . Yes."

"The biggest challenge?"

"Yes."

I gaze across the road, toward the restaurant where Jonathan is waiting. "So we need to pull out the biggest guns."

29

Jonathan

THOMAS CALLS ME AGAIN WHILE EVA IS OUT. I ANSWER TO DIS-tract myself. I should have known better.

"Do you have a death wish?" he demands. Shit.

I keep my eyes on the path Eva disappeared down. I lower my voice, even though I am alone in the restaurant. Louisa and Gestalt could be back with the bill anytime. "That's kind of a personal question, don't you think?"

"Do you think this is funny?" I am not laughing.

"I'm going to need you to elaborate," I say tersely.

"You were supposed to kill the man in his office," Thomas says. "That was the job."

"It felt a little stale—"

"What. The. Fuck."

"'Arc de Triomphe' is short for 'Triumphal Arch of the Star.' It's a metaphor."

"Murder is not a metaphor."

Gestalt reappears with the bill. "Can we talk about this later?" I ask Thomas. "I'm at a restaurant."

Thomas ignores my request. "You do realize that if you get

caught, the whole network could collapse and you would be out of a job."

"I was careful," I say. That is not true. I was not careful; I was compelled. I was compulsive and out of control and I could not stop myself.

"They're not gonna pay you for this," Thomas says as I am handing Gestalt my credit card.

"Now, hold on—that's not fair."

"Tell that to the guy scraping a body off of your metaphor," he says. I flinch.

Gestalt is hovering over me. "Do you need anything else?"

"No, thank you," I answer in French. "Everything was perfect." I smile persistently at him until he disappears into the back of the restaurant to run my card. Then I return to Thomas, dropping my voice to a hiss. "Do you have any idea how hard it is to convince a complete stranger to drive you to a busy intersection at five in the morning?"

It was actually not that hard. I knew the mark was a coke addict, so I showed up at his office and pretended I was there to supply his business partner, who I knew would not be there. The mark offered to call him, but I said this was a drug deal and I did not want to leave a paper trail. The easiest way to cover a crime is with another crime. I said it was too bad; it was really good coke, but I needed someone to drive me and pay the dealer. The mark volunteered. Most drugs users are as addicted to the danger and chaos of scoring as they are to the actual drug.

As we were approaching that most hazardous intersection, I told him, "It'll be over quick. You'll be gone before you even feel pain."

He started to say, "What?" I unfastened his seat belt, stepped over the console and onto the gas pedal, and when we hit, I helped him into the window.

"The Arc de Triomphe is one of the most treacherous inter-sections in Europe," I tell Thomas now. "You have to pay extra for car insurance to cover you in just that single location. No one is going to ask questions."

"You were spotted fleeing the scene," Thomas says.

"I didn't flee; I walked. Do you think someone is going to iden-tify me? I don't have an identity," I say. "Besides, I wasn't driving the car. I'm a victim, if anything. No one will care."

Through the restaurant windows, I see Eva exit the park. She waits to cross the street.

"It's not your job to construct the hit," Thomas reminds me.

"I went above and beyond. They ought to pay me extra."

"That's not how it works."

She starts to cross the street.

"Thomas, I'm going to have to let you go. I'm on a date."

"You had better be jok—"

I hang up the phone. The last thing I need right now is for my handler to get into my head.

I do not think about murders after I commit them. If I did, I would not be able to keep killing. If I stopped, if I slowed down, I could drown in all the terrible things I have done.

Tonight, I have better things to do.

30

Eva

YOU'D THINK HISTORIC BUILDINGS WOULD BE HEAVILY GUARDED. They are in movies. With lasers and cameras and security guards willing to die for their minimum-wage jobs. But in my experience, they're really just not. That's how people storm the Capitol, steal *The Scream*, grease van Gogh.

The truth is, most people aren't watching. The fact is, most people don't care. Especially not when you're paying a couple thousand euros a night for a hotel room.

I don't tell Jonathan there's a hotel until we arrive. We pull into the porte cochere and he gives me a look like I have earned all the points.

"You're very clever," he says.

"Just you wait," I say.

He doesn't let go of my hand as we leave the car, as we check into our room, as we walk down the hall and through the door. You would think it would feel awkward, but it doesn't. It feels natural. Like our hands have always been attached.

We cross into our hotel room.

"There's a lot happening in here," Jonathan notes of the decor. It's eighteenth century. There's a shit ton happening.

I lead him to the bed. I sit him down. He gazes up at me, a little impatiently.

"Now," I say, "I'm going to give you options, because there's a chance we might get arrested and I think you're altogether too sensitive for prison."

"You are correct."

"We can fuck here, or we can try for the Hall of Mirrors. I had a look at the doors earlier, and the locks are period accurate. Translation: Modern tools can crack them." A fancy multitool is currently en route to the hotel, courtesy of Sherri. It's perfect for window-shopping.

"There are cameras everywhere in there," he says.

"Are you shy?"

"What makes you think the guards won't stop us?" He's smirking slightly, so I know he admires my gumption. And my absurdity.

"Isn't 'voyeur' a French word?" I ask. He gives me a look. "Kidding. I'll work it out with the guards. Let's rendezvous in the southwest elevator shaft in twenty minutes." I start toward the door.

His fingers close around my wrist, pull me gently to a stop. "Who are you, really?"

I take a step toward him. I look him dead in the eyes, like I'm lining up a shot. "I'm whoever you want me to be."

He drops my hand.

31

Jonathan

I AM GOING TO DIE. SHE IS GOING TO KILL ME. I KIND OF WANT her to.

She leaves me in the hotel room. She is off to bribe the guards or tell them to make popcorn.

I am in way over my head; that much is clear. I want her so bad, my whole jaw aches. She has me right where she wants me, sitting on the end of a bed like an ape in an eighteenth-century floral orgasm.

I cannot even move, except to check my watch. It has been approximately seven seconds.

My ears are fuzzy. My throat is dry. My heart is hammering.

I am pathetic. I am so wholly fucking pathetic, like a heart with an arrow through it.

I should go. Now.

That would be the strong thing to do. The real-man thing to do. I should walk away. Save myself. I wanted to fuck her once, but in the Hall of Mirrors I will fuck her an infinite number of times. I might never stop. She is making it too good: the mirrors, the glass, the gold, the historical significance. I am about to be fucked where World War I ended. It is all too much. I have to have limits.

She offered to make me come in nineteen seconds. I could be home now, washing my hands. Brushing my teeth. Crawling into bed.

Instead, I am stapled to a floral bedspread, eyes on the floral wallpaper, designing plans to avoid premature ejaculation.

I need to forget the mirrors and the glass and the gold and the historical significance. I need to focus on something unhorny, un-fuckable, whatever the word is: *un-come-able.*

There has to be something that can slow this train down. And there is. I have thoughts at my disposal that could stop any train, but the trouble is, I do not want to use them.

I have such a compelling reason not to.

Just one night. Just one fucking night.

One fucking night fucking.

I want to be like everyone else. I want to be happy.

Not forever. Not always. I know I cannot be cured.

But for the next few hours I want to be just another guy, fucking a girl in the Palace of Versailles.

32

Eva

WE'RE WALKING DOWN A HALLWAY, FINGERS ENTWINED. I should wait to touch him. That would be the more professional choice—to hold off, to draw him out—but our hands found each other when neither of us was looking.

"I don't understand how you convinced them to do this," he says. I killed the guard. Kidding.

I did it the same way I do everything: by telling the truth and by lying. I had Sherri do some recon on the man behind the cameras. I found out his wife died last year. Tragic for him, yes. Kind of perfect for me. I told him about Andrew—the truth is always the most dangerous weapon. I told him that I thought I'd never meet someone again and then, by chance, on a train . . .

I don't know if he believed me, but I gave him hope—which is more important.

"I could get fired for this," he told me.

That's when I paid him off. Money is a close second to truth as a weapon.

"All I can do is turn off the security system," he said. "Don't let anyone see you. Don't be too loud."

"Of course," I assured him. Then I mused, "How loud is too loud?"

Luckily, there's some kind of event going on in the gardens. Something with galaxy lights and fireworks. As we walk down the hallway, we get glimpses through the windows. Fountains lit like casinos. Couples kissing in the dark. Statues frozen in the middle of doing something awesome, never to do better, never to move on.

I can see that the production value is paying off. I have read my mark correctly. Emotionally, Jonathan is very easy to read. The facts are a little hazy, but his heart is on his sleeve.

He gazes up at the ceiling, enraptured by the sconces.

"How many people do you think have died here?" he says. *Oh. Maybe his thoughts run a little darker.*

"*Le vrai mort ou le petite mort?*" I ask.

"Both." His fingers thread deeper through mine.

We reach the door. There's no going back now.

There's a legend about the Hall of Mirrors. It's a little hokey, but I love hokey things. Legend has it that every time you visit, you see your past self—the last you that came there—reflected in the mirrors. As if every time you visit, you leave a version of yourself there.

If you let yourself believe it, you can see it. It can take your breath away.

Jonathan sighs at our reflections, a little forcefully, like he's trying to keep his mind from dreaming. "How much time do we have?"

"Nineteen seconds," I joke.

I take him to the center of the hall. He seems the type to appreciate symmetry. I turn to face him. I catch our reflections. I get dizzy, as if I forget which ones are the real us.

He steadies me. "I feel it, too."

I don't know what he means. Feels what? What do I feel? Hazy? Lusty? Uncertain. Undone.

I open my mouth to say something smart but nothing comes out. I start to feel a little scared. That I'm losing control of my plans already.

Then he moves over me. He puts his mouth over mine as if he's picking up my slack.

We kiss. We both peek at our reflections at the same time. We laugh.

"I'm going to take off my clothes," I say. "Will you help me?"

"Mmm," he tells my neck. He takes my shirt off a little quickly, and then he apologizes: "Sorry. I need to calm down."

I reach up and brush the ends of his hair. He unfastens my bra, slips it neatly off my shoulders; then, keeping his eyes on me, he travels down, fastens his lips to my nipples and sucks.

A wave of intense feeling washes over me. It's seriously like a reverberation of the day I was created. Torn from that heaven, placed in this hell, only to remember that supernal ecstasy when someone sucks my tits.

My pants hit the floor. I didn't feel him take them off.

He's taking control. That was not the plan.

He starts to go down.

"Wait." Even though this feels really, really great and I'm sure it will continue to do so, this is so not the way to assure his undying devotion. I'm not going to make him want me by allowing him to eat my pussy. I have to eat his pussy, metaphorically speaking.

"I have a feeling," I say, delicately running my fingers along his shoulder blades, "that you're the type that likes to control everything." He chose the restaurant. He moved his seat on the train. He panicked when I adjusted his glasses. "But I don't think that's really working out for you."

This is what I mean by starting with the head. Every human being is pretty much the same. We're all miserable. We don't know why. We're drawn to people who promise us the reason.

I run my fingers down his jacket lapel. "I want you to let me take control of your life. Just for a moment. Just right now. Nothing is your decision. Nothing is your fault." Guilt is his weakness. I see it spark in his eyes. It's so fucking easy. It's so fucking dangerous. "I want you to put your life in my hands."

I can see him resisting. I can see him receding. His blue eyes drawing a blank. Until I put his life in my hands, literally. The wave of feeling catches in his throat.

"Don't you trust me?" I say, with my hands on his dick.

He inhales slowly—maybe a little fearfully—and then he kisses me: meekly, worshipfully, like a good boy.

I'm not going to make him get naked in Versailles. I feel like that would run a little too exhibitionist for his tastes.

Instead, I lay him down, very carefully, very thoughtfully, at the apex of the mirrors, and I give him a blow job, an infinite number of times.

I do it with precision and musicality. I start off slow. I draw him out. Then I tantalize. I tease. I wreck him.

I have a vast understanding of the human body. I can light it up like a pinball machine. Sex is a little like murder. There are certain things that kill everyone, every time.

But the secret to good sex is that it should be a little embarrassing. That's how you know you've truly lost control. You should drool. You should feel brain-dead. You should beg for something you don't have words for.

When we've hit all those little achievements, then and only then do I mount him. He said he wanted to have sex once, but in the mirrors, we have sex so many times.

"Fuck!" he says, and then he comes, a little begrudgingly. I can see the expression on his face as it spools out of him, like he wants to spool it back in. "Fuck."

I dismount him.

"Fuck. Me," he says.

I put my clothes back on. He rolls over, gazes at me with hazy, lust-soaked eyes. Outside there are fireworks. My timing was a little off, but no one's perfect.

He takes a deep breath, gathering all his scattered thoughts back into his head. "I changed my mind," he says. "I don't want to separate." He inhales hopefully, eyes on me.

I reach forward. I brush his messy hair back. "I know."

Then I smile.

V

—

INTIMACY, PART 1

33

Jonathan

I AM THE LAST ROMANTIC IN FRANCE.

What am I doing? I am not thinking with my head. At least not the one on the top of my neck.

I got caught up in the moment. I said things I did not mean—not that I want to take them back.

But what am I doing? What am I going to do? We have to separate eventually—that much is clear—but I can fit a lot into the spaces between the letters of that word: e-v-e-n-t-u-a-l-l-y.

And I am competitive. I cannot just let her win like that, like she was cheating at a game before we started playing.

On the way back to the room, I ask her, "You didn't come, did you?"

And she says serenely, "No." Pure evil.

She waits outside the door. I have the key. My hands are slightly shaking—still—like they are the only ones admitting how much trouble I am in.

I let her into the room. I lock the door. I feel crazy, confused, inconvenienced in the best way.

"Do you want to go to Barcelona?" I ask. I do not have any reason to be in Barcelona, although I can probably pick up a job once we separate. Eventually.

I want to go somewhere—*anywhere*—because I need to get her away from Paris. My heart is in Paris, and if she gets too close, she will find it. Besides, I like Barcelona.

Go to Barcelona. Beat her at the sex. Clear my mind, and everything will be fine.

I do not remind myself that the sex we just had was supposed to fix everything, unglue her from my consciousness. I do not remind myself that it did not work.

"Why?" she asks.

I consider. "Have you ever been to La Sagrada Família?"

She shakes her head.

"Well, you need to go." It is that important.

"Barcelona," she repeats, tasting the word. "Sure."

A beat. "Now?"

She looks around us, at the florgasm hotel room. "Okay."

34

I DO NOT WANT A DRIVER FOR THIS; OMAR IS ALREADY TOO IN-volved. I do take my suitcase—I always travel with an entou-rage of weapons, even on romantic excursions—but I need my own car. The hotel can help us.

"What kind of car are you looking for?" the concierge asks.

I look at Eva.

She smiles. "You want one of those fancy fucking things, don't you?"

I turn to the concierge. "What she said."

The concierge suggests a Bugatti. It takes her an hour to track one down, but she does. It is amazing what you can do with money, how much the world can stretch to accommodate you. I myself have a tendency to overspend, which is why I have to work so much, to keep up with the amateur theatrics of being alive.

But easily enough, Eva and I are steaming down the dark high-ways of France toward the Pyrenees.

There is nothing like driving through Europe at night. There are castles everywhere—great big swarms of them—and pictur-esque villages and enough churches to reform almost any sinner.

Europe is better at night because you can see the past so violently. The way it must have been when soldiers made campaigns like ours, fighting for something more substantial than good sex, but probably not as worthwhile. I am a soldier in love's war. I am the walking wounded.

I turn to Eva. The distant lights peel through the car and slide up her body and across her face. Desire winds like a crown around my head, opening up my mind with an illicit light, like revelation.

She is watching me. She is watching me so often that I am starting to feel apprehensive.

"You drive like I thought you would," she says.

I laugh and shift gears. "Do you want to drive?"

"No." She leans back in her seat. "I'm good." She has her arm cocked casually against the door. I wish she were touching me.

"I just want to be clear," I say, firmly facing forward. "I'm not exactly sure what this is."

"Wow, that is *so* clear."

I smirk. "Well, what do you think it is?" I ask. She lets her shoulders shrug. "I got the impression on the train that you weren't exactly enamored with relationships."

"How did you get that impression?" she says.

"You said, *There is nothing worse than two people in a relationship.*"

"Oh, that."

"Yes, that," I say. She gazes out the window, stuck on a sigh. "Do you really think that?"

Her eyes pinch when she frowns. "I'm not sure." She angles her body toward me. "Have you ever been in a relationship?"

"Actually, no." This is a truth that does not interfere with the lie.

"Why not?"

"Because . . ." I swallow. "Because there are people who want to kill me, and anyone I love."

This is technically true. I have to be very careful, not just with myself but with Mas. Not even my handler knows about him. Thomas does not know my history either. Or my real name. I changed my identity when I moved to Europe. I was afraid that Thomas might not want to work with me if he knew the whole truth about my past. As hard as it may be to believe, people want their contract killers to be dead sane. Obedient. Efficient. Soulless is a bonus.

"So I can't love anyone." I shift gears again. "Is this turning you off?"

"Do you really think I'm in danger?"

"Not yet," I say, but I do not really know. I do not know how much danger *I* am in. I have killed a lot of people, and I have to think that one day I will pay for it—and not just through the punishments I give myself.

Sometimes, late at night, when I am not sleeping, I consider that every person I have killed had a life. They had friends and family. They were more alive than *I* am. I took that away, a cipher turning the living into the dead like me.

I know there are people out there who want me dead. Sometimes I wish they would try me. I should not get away with all the things I do. It should not be this easy, but the network protects me. Sometimes I consider that one day even they might turn on me. If the network has enough power to keep me from being punished for my sins, God knows they could annihilate me.

"Have you ever been in love?" I ask her. The question sticks in my throat. I truly am the most merciless romantic. You would think no one had ever looked at me before.

"I've been engaged."

My nerves tighten. "Where is he now?"

"He died." *Oh.*

"I'm sorry."

"It's okay." She stretches, uncomfortable with the conversation. "Shit happens." She tries to keep it light, always.

"Was it recent?" In other words, are you over him? Although I did not miss the way she dodged my question. She said she has been engaged, not that she has been in love.

"Um, it was over two years ago. Actually, it's kinda funny. That's why I was in Florence, for the anniversary. We were both living there when he died."

"Oh." I have a funny feeling. How ironic. She was there to put flowers on someone's grave and I was there to kill someone. Three people actually. What are the odds? "Can I ask how he died?"

"He was killed." A shadow crosses her face, the first true sign of darkness. I want to take it away, to turn her into stardust again. She sinks in her seat. "I guess it wasn't *love* love, but he was my best friend. He taught me so much. He changed my life. His name was Andrew. Cartwright."

Holy shit.

The car veers. There is no one else around.

"Sorry," I say. "I thought I saw a rabbit."

I try to look normal, but I have no experience. If I thought our reasons for being in Florence were a coincidence, then I do not know what to call this.

I do not need to worry about killing her fiancé. I already did.

I thought she looked familiar on the train. I told myself that it was fate, but it was not fate. It was a photograph. It was Thomas on the phone:

He has a fiancée, but they're a little estranged.

You might think I would have remembered her, but I try not to think about the people I have killed. And I have killed so many people. I cannot really keep track of them all, let alone their friends and family. She looked different in the photo. Her hair was darker and her makeup was thicker and her anger was palpable. She was robbed of her essential life force.

"God, I'm so sorry," I say. "That is just truly terrible."

My jaw is tight. My heart is electric. I feel more sick than usual. I have always known I am a villain, but sometimes it still catches me off guard.

It seems so beautifully apt that I would fall for a woman who I have destroyed. I always assumed that I would destroy her *after* we got together, but finding out I had destroyed her before has an element of surprise that I appreciate.

I knew my attraction to Eva was hopeless. I should have guessed that I was the reason it was hopeless. Somehow, I always am.

We are driving fast now, steaming through the mountains. The sky is a dark, lonely blue. The exact color of my death, and we are headed right for it.

35

Eva

WE DON'T MAKE IT TO BARCELONA. I FALL ASLEEP, AND when I wake up, Jonathan is parking the car on a narrow street in a picturesque village.

"Where are we?" I ask, blinking sleepily at the white cottages with red accents and overflowing flower boxes. It's like the setting of a European Hallmark movie.

"Burguete," he says. "It's a Basque village near the border." He unfastens his seat belt.

"Why have we stopped?" I ask.

"So you can sleep. There's a hotel here. Hemingway played the piano downstairs."

"Oh God, you like Hemingway?" I shake my head. "That is such a red flag."

"You're not wrong." He says things like that all the time—wry, under his breath, like they're a joke. I don't think they're a joke. I'm sweating him out. He's releasing little weaknesses all the time. I just need him to release something I can use.

He gets out of the car and hurries to open my door. He helps me, like I've never gotten out of a car before.

"Thank you," I say.

Jonathan threads his warm fingers through mine as we walk down a sidewalk lined with sparkling aqueducts. This village was designed for romance. It was designed for fantasists and fly-by-nighters and assassins pretending to be in love.

I'm not gonna lie; part of me really wants to run right now. This whole thing is starting to feel too much like the dreams I never let myself have. Dreams that I would meet a guy who wanted me and only me. That he would whisk me away—not just on vacation but away from my actual life, like reality was a thing I could discard if I just found the right man. Like if we got together, I would become someone else. I wouldn't be a killer. I wouldn't be afraid. I would be a girl who was loved. I would be a girl who *could* love.

It's all a little overwhelming.

There's love bombing and then there's whatever this is. People like Jonathan and I keep ourselves separate from the rest of the world. That's probably what drew us to each other in the first place. That's probably what keeps us drawn to each other.

Normally we exist in our own little bubbles. When we do try to be like everyone else, we do it wrong. We run too fast. We dance too hard. We want too much. We crash. We burn. And we retreat to our little bubbles again, to stay longer, to hide more, until we die, always alone, because we couldn't love the world just a little. We had to love it too fucking much.

Jonathan leads me to a hotel with a steep roof and green shutters. There's a night manager watching *Lupin* on his laptop.

Jonathan knocks on the hotel windowpane. The night manager notices us but doesn't seem interested until Jonathan presses a few large bills against the glass.

The night manager lets us in. He leads us to the front desk.

"Do you want your own room?" Jonathan asks me. His eyes go bright, then dark again.

"No," I say. "Why bother? We're here for a limited time only."

I honestly wouldn't be surprised if Jonathan was gone in the morning. If he went out to get milk and never came back. That's the thing about people like us. We love hard, but we fear harder. We scare easy. What scares us the most is intimacy, which is what is making finding Jonathan's weaknesses hard.

So far I've established that he has a guilty conscience, but I'm pretty sure the agency already knew that. It's probably part of the reason I'm here, because of the bad things he's done.

I also know he doesn't like himself, but who fucking does? And that probably ties in to whatever bad thing made him a mark in the first place.

Physically, he's in impressive condition. He's smart. He's sharp. He's very handsome. He puts up a fairly competent front. To find weaknesses I can use I'm going to need to go deeper. I'm going to need to find out what's behind his front.

I need to create *real* intimacy, not just the sexual kind. I know how to do it. There's only one way. People create intimacy by telling the truth. I'm a liar, so I know. The truth just tastes different. You can't fake it.

But if I want Jonathan to tell me his truth, I have to create intimacy. I have to tell him my truth first.

36

W E'RE GIVEN A ROOM AT THE TIPPY TOP OF THE HOTEL.
The ceiling is arched, so we know we can't get any
higher.

As soon as we walk through the door our eyes go to the bed.

"Is that mattress stuffed with hay?" I ask.

"To think we gave up Versailles for this," he says, but he chose
this place.

His eyes stay on the bed. He doesn't step any farther into the
room, as if realizing what he's done. We're going to sleep in that
bed together. Sleep, which is so much more intimate than having sex.

I cross to the bed.

"I sleep in my underwear," I say casually.

"Fuck."

"Yeah."

I strip, not lingering. I don't want sexy; I want the other kind
of intimacy.

Jonathan watches me. I have a reasonably nice body. At least
I think I do. It doesn't look like the bodies in movies but it does

all the same things. Once I'm down to my underwear, I pull back the covers and climb onto the bed. Jonathan hasn't moved.

"Are you just gonna stand there?" I ask.

"I don't really sleep."

"You said," I say. "Not ever?"

"I mean, of course I do *sleep*, but only for a couple hours. Maybe. If I'm lucky." He takes a step toward me.

"We could just lie here," I say. "You don't have to sleep."

He takes off his jacket—slowly, cautiously. He takes off his shirt. I involuntarily hiss. He's armed under his undershirt. He sets his gun on the bedside table, then removes a knife from his ankle.

"For protection," he says.

"Sure."

"I never use them." He strokes the blade absently. "It's just nice to know they're there."

"You're fun," I say. "Anything else?"

He smirks, playful, dangerous. "Nothing you need to worry about." It's another one of his joking-but-not-joking lines. He probably has razor blades sewn into his coat lining. He definitely has lethal drugs somewhere on his person.

He told me he confiscates weapons, but his body is an arsenal. His suitcase was an armory. Sherri was right: He's definitely lying to me about who he is. I need to stop trying to make excuses for him. I need to stop thinking any part of what is happening between us is real. I need to stop thinking he's hot. I need to switch off my pussy and treat this like the mindfuck of a hit that it is. I need to be a professional.

Most of all, I need to stop smiling.

I loosen the covers, make a space for him on the bed. "Come on." I pat the bed, invite him into my web of intimacy.

He climbs into bed. He's so fucking dense that the mattress

sinks, pulling me in his direction. We're uncomfortably close together. I doubt either of us is going to sleep tonight.

I put my hand on his shoulder. I delicately finger his scar.

"Do you know who shot you?" I ask.

"Yes."

"Are they still out there?" Translation: *Did you kill them?*

He inhales lightly. "I don't want to talk about all that . . ."

I pull my hand away. I plan to award emotional intimacy with physical intimacy. I'm hoping he'll pick up on it subconsciously and tell me everything.

"You know," I say, "I kinda miss the old you."

"The old me? We've hardly spent twenty-four hours together." His hand slides along the bed toward mine. I prop my head up with my hand like I don't notice. No truth, no reward.

"I mean the guy I met on the train. Your false identity. From upstate New York."

"That wasn't a *false identity.*"

"You seem different now."

"Well, I'm not high. And I don't have a bullet in my chest."

"Your defenses are up," I point out. "Your armor."

I take a deep breath. I know what I have to do. To get him to share his secrets, I have to share mine.

I sidle toward him. "You know, when you disappeared, I was kind of worried it was because . . ." My tongue sticks. I can't even say it.

"Because of your nightmare." He reaches out and brushes my hair behind my ear. His fingers linger, trace my neck, then my shoulder. I kind of forgot he could touch me, too. I could ask him to stop. I don't want to.

"I have nightmares all the time," I say. "I'll probably have one tonight."

He draws his finger along my jaw. "It's okay," he says. He

doesn't ask me why I have nightmares, because he doesn't want to create intimacy.

Conversation is just a form of combat. I have to be brave. I have to shoot first.

"When I was a kid, something really terrible happened to me." We lock eyes. I'm about to tell him my truth. I have to remind myself that my secrets are safe with him. He's going to be dead soon. I'm going to kill him. "My family was murdered, right in front of me. My mom. My dad." I can see his body contract. "It was a burglary gone wrong. It was just . . . *chaos*," I say, remembering.

Part of me wants to walk him through the whole story. I once had this compulsion to try to make people understand. Right after it happened, I would tell all the dirty details to anyone who would listen. I couldn't stop myself. I thought someone could help me. But after years and years, I realized no one could. No one could ever understand. Then I stopped telling people everything. And eventually, I stopped telling people anything.

Right now, I skip ahead. Past how the burglars got in. Past when I hid in my closet and when I came out. Past the screaming. Past my finding the burglars in my parents' bedroom while my mom and dad lay dying on the bed, crying and bleeding and clinging to each other. Past one thief going through my mom's purse and the other taking off her ring. Right up to when I found the gun on the floor.

"At one point, one of the men put his gun down," I say. "I picked it up. Another man saw me. He reached for it . . . and I shot him. I shot them both. Another one came in from the bathroom and I shot him, too." I shiver with the memory. "It was like something out of a movie. Even after it was over, it was like my whole life was something out of a movie. Like it was never real again."

"God," he says, and then something truly terrible happens. He looks me dead in the eyes and says, "I know exactly what you mean."

He doesn't flinch. He doesn't recoil like other people do. I don't feel his wall going up. Instead, he looks warm. He looks almost peaceful. Like I haven't unsettled his waters. He gets it. He gets *me*.

He pulls me toward him, into his chest, and it's so strong and cozy. I try to remind myself that this is just work, but the truth hurts. It hurts to share it, and it feels so fucking good just to be held.

"I'm so sorry," he says. His fingers run through my hair.

I told myself I was doing this for him, but I suspect I was doing it for me, too. I wanted to tell him. I wanted to tell him the truth. I wanted to tell Jonathan because I knew he was dark enough to take it. And as he holds me to his chest I think: *Fuck*.

This isn't just a job anymore. I made it something real.

37

Jonathan

I NEED TO LEAVE.

I killed her fucking fiancé. I triggered her childhood trauma. I ruined her life, and she has no idea, and all I can say is "I'm so sorry."

This is no longer an escape. This is something to escape from. I should run, and yet I feel the magnetic pull of her sadness, like I have been engaged, assigned: Fix this.

"You can leave, if you want to," she says suddenly, reading my mind.

"I don't want to leave." I cradle her chin. I can feel the blood pumping in her neck, the puff of her breath on my cheek. "I am so sorry."

She forces a smile. "It's not your fault." *Well.* She moves in closer, burrows her head into my shoulder. She sighs into my chest. "What about you? What was your childhood like?" she asks, as if this is a trade, as if my secrets might cure hers. I have a feeling that is not the case.

"Nothing like that," I say. Although it was similar; people did die.

"You can trust me." She burrows deeper into my chest. I roll onto my back, and then she rests her head on top of me. It rises and falls with my breath. "After all, we're only here for a limited time."

If I tell her, that limited time will end now.

SHE FALLS ASLEEP FIRST. OF COURSE SHE DOES. I NEVER SLEEP. When you do wrong, the saying goes, *How can you sleep at night?* I never do, out of respect for whoever coined the phrase.

I watch her sleep. At around three o'clock, she has her nightmare. The one I contributed to. She jerks on the bed. She cries without tears. I hold her in my arms, like I can slow her beating heart.

I wish I were someone else, someone who could protect her from me. I need to leave her. It might hurt her in the short term, but it will save her in the long term.

It is the right thing to do.

But when have I ever done that?

VI

ATTEMPTED MURDER,
PART 1

38

Eva

WHEN I WAKE UP IN THE MORNING, JONATHAN'S ASLEEP beside me: arm thrown back, chin tipped to the sky. He doesn't even stir when I get up. So much for never sleeping.

I almost want to yell *Gotcha!* But I have better things to do, just marginally. I need to check in with Sherri. I should've checked in last night, but I was half asleep when we got here.

I left my phone hidden under the front seat of the Bugatti. I get dressed quickly and grab the car key. The lobby is empty. Hemingway's piano is tucked silently into a corner, being pretentious.

I unlock the car and pass my hand under my seat. The space is empty. The phone is gone. Jonathan must have taken it. *He knows.*

I plunge my hand farther and my fingers brush against plastic. *Thank fuck.*

I yank the phone out from under the seat.

Sherri is calling me. She's called me seventeen times. *Fuck.*

I scan the sleepy little village. It's deserted at this early hour but I still head out toward the pasturelands, just to be extra careful.

"What's going on?" I say when I'm far enough away to feel safe.

"Did you sleep with him?" Sherri asks. *Double fuck.*

"No. I mean, we slept in the same bed, but we barely even—"

"At Versailles."

"Oh, *that.*"

"Yes, that." Sherri is pissed.

"How do you even know that?" I ask. I spoke to one guard. He said he would turn off the cameras.

"The agency has access everywhere."

I feel my chest contract but I remind myself that I told Sherri where we were going. She even helped me break into the Hall of Mirrors. It's creepy to think that someone was watching, but it was probably for my protection.

Besides, I didn't do anything wrong. She never said I couldn't sleep with him. Again. "Yeah, I slept with him. I'm trying to find out his weaknesses—remember?"

"Not in bed," Sherri points out.

"James Bond does it all the time." It's true. It's part of the fun of being an assassin. Sex and death just go together.

"They asked me if we should take you off the job."

"Wait—what?"

"They think you may have been compromised."

"That seems a little puritanical. Besides, you knew I slept with him before, on the train."

"They think you might fall for him."

"How misogynistic. I'm a professional. Even if I did fall for him, I could still kill him. I'm trying to create *intimacy.*"

"All right, have you got any new intel?"

". . . Not exactly. Not yet." Sherri's concern is a little justified. Not only do I not have new intel, but I've also shared my secrets with Jonathan. I'm the only one revealing their weaknesses.

This is starting to get messy. Maybe Sherri is right to be concerned. Maybe I should just let the agency take me off the job. I don't want a Fail to Kill on my record, but maybe I'll fail no matter what. Maybe I can't do this.

"Are you sure you *want* to stay on?" she asks, reading my mind. "I'm starting to feel a bit guilty. Maybe I shouldn't have asked you to do this." She switches from boss to friend so fast, it makes my heart lurch. "I know how lonely you've been, especially since Andrew. Maybe you're too vulnerable. Maybe this isn't a risk worth taking."

It's funny how she's asked me to risk my life time and time again but she wants to draw the line at me risking my heart. Still, she does know me, better than anyone else in the world. Maybe she's right. Maybe a heart is not something to risk.

I think through what will happen if I stop now. I'll leave. I'll never see Jonathan again. Someone else will kill him. No matter what, he's going to die.

Meanwhile, I'll lose all the goodwill I've built up at the agency over the years. I'll be back to smaller jobs and smaller paydays—I might not even be assigned new jobs. Things have always been stacked against me. I'm a woman. The powers that be are always looking for excuses. *She's too moody! She's too sensitive! What if she gets her period?*

If I Fail to Kill after fucking my mark, the agency will one hundred percent believe that it's because I fell for him. They'll think, *Never should've hired a woman to do a man's job!* Which will only make it harder for all future aspiring female assassins to get work. If I don't kill Jonathan, it'll discredit my entire gender.

And what if the agency really does stop giving me jobs? What'll happen to me then? It's not something I've ever thought about—although I really should have thought about it. Will they just let me go back to my normal life when I know so many of their secrets? How will I explain the gap in my résumé?

There's a very real chance that if I don't kill Jonathan, my life as I know it will be over.

I shake all the icky thoughts from my head. I realize I'm standing in a cow field.

"Of course I want the job," I snap, like I can't believe she's asking.

"Are you sure?"

"Of course I'm sure."

"Because it's a green light."

"What?" I say, startled, but I know what a green light is. Red means stop. Yellow means reconnaissance. Green means go.

"It's a green light," she repeats.

"Great!" I say, too fast. "It's probably better that way. Just get it over and done with. In and out."

"Eva," Sherri says.

"It's fine. He'll be dead in an hour."

"You don't have to do this."

I pull myself together. I stand tall. "You believe in me, don't you?"

"Of course I do," she says.

"Consider it done." I need to kill Jonathan. I need to kill him now. Before I change my mind. Before I fall too hard. Before I'm in too deep.

I've killed thirty-six people; what's one more?

———

I START PLANNING AS I HEAD BACK TOWARD THE HOTEL. NOT THE kill but the escape, which is the most important part. Killing is usually easier than getting away with it.

Sherri told me that I don't need to worry about the body.

"Just leave it in the room. Checkout is at eleven. We have plenty of time to get a cleanup crew in there, if you do it as soon as possible."

This makes me curious about how close the other agents are,

how closely I am being watched. Sherri knew about Versailles, which means someone was watching me there. I remind myself that I don't need to know who or how. It's not my job. My job is simple: Kill.

"Just worry about getting yourself out of there," Sherri cautioned me.

Our room is at the top of the hotel, which gives me privacy but not escape. The hotel is an old one, and there are only two exit doors: one in the lobby and one in the café. I went out through the lobby this morning, so I enter through the café.

I pass by a storage room where there are backpacks and dirty sneakers—dozens of them. I'm not sure why so many hikers would be passing through a tiny village until I realize: the Santiago Trail. It's a five-hundred-mile religious pilgrimage across Spain, and the French route starts near here, in Saint-Jean-Pied-de-Port.

It's the perfect escape. I can just walk away.

I scan the hallways. There are no security cameras, no other guests in sight. I scoop up a backpack—I'm sure the hiker gods will bless the previous owner for their generosity. I slip the straps over my shoulders and head toward the lobby restroom.

Unfortunately for me, the backpack belongs to a man who sweats a lot. I hold my nose and change my clothes. I even find a hat to hide my hair. I stuff my old clothes inside the backpack, stick on a pair of cheap sunglasses and start up the stairs.

Jonathan left a gun and a knife on the table. Hopefully he's still asleep. The gun is the obvious kill weapon but I need to grab them both. Fingers crossed that he doesn't have access to any other weapons if he wakes up before he's dead.

I will use my pillow to muffle the gunshot and I will shoot him in the head. It's practically mercy. It's the gentlest way to go, to die in your sleep. To die before you know you're dying. He'll probably be dreaming. He might even be dreaming of me.

I can do this. I can wash my hands and walk away. I'm not attached to this stranger. Even if he seemed to understand me. Even if he wasn't afraid when I told him my truth. Even if he's hot and adventurous and seems to genuinely like me. So what? I'm sure I'll find someone else. It took me thirty years to find him, so if I live to be sixty, I should come across somebody just as compatible. Everyone knows that dating is just a numbers game.

I might have loved him in another life, but in this one I'm going to kill him. I'm going to walk away from whatever this thing is and go back to my life as an assassin. The exact life I want. Where nothing matters and nothing feels real.

Perfect.

I push back against the door as I open it, to keep it from making a sound. I crane my head into the room. His body is as I left it—arm thrown back, shut eyes facing the sky, chest rising and falling with the slow regularity of sleep.

It's now or never.

I deposit the backpack in the hallway, to pick up on the way out. I slip off my shoes to quiet my footfalls. I leave the door slightly ajar, preparing my escape.

I let the rhythm of murder fall over me like a veil. I notice things I never saw with my nonkiller eyes: the grade of the floor, the thickness of the pillow, the make of his gun, the length of his knife relative to the depth of his heart, at an angle between his second and third ribs. Everything speaks to me; everything encourages me; everything in this room is a pathway to a murder.

I follow that path to the bed.

And just like that, I'm standing over him, looking down on his now-familiar face and telling myself:

Here is your villain.

39

Jonathan

I WAKE WITH A START TO SEE EVA STANDING OVER ME. I FEEL THIS warmth ooze through me, as if I can be fully in love with her only when I am half asleep. Reality has not quite settled in to breathe the truth that will separate us.

I start to smile. She goes for the gun. It happens so fast. Her pillow passes over my face. I do not understand why until I feel the muzzle of the gun pressed to my temple, then hear that sound—not a *bang* but a *click.*

I am off the bed so fast. I ram her back against the wall, then feel bad about how hard we both hit, until she stabs me between my second and third ribs.

Holy shit.

It is the strangest thing that has ever happened to me in a very strange life. I grab her hands around the knife before it goes too deep, and I force it out.

"What are you doing?" I say, as if all this could be an accident. People say stupid things when they are in shock.

She has dropped the gun in the heat of the stabbing, probably assuming the gun was not loaded. She assumed wrong.

I launch her off the wall. She staggers to catch her balance. I scoop up the gun. I point it at her head.

"I always leave the first chamber empty," I tell her calmly. "For situations like this." It is an old trick, in case someone happens upon your abandoned gun. I should not be telling her this. I should kill her, but I do not want to. I do not understand why she wants to kill me. "Why are you trying to . . ." And then it hits me. "Oh." She did not appear in the Hall of Mirrors by accident. She did not appear on the train by accident either. There was a reason she gave me a fake name. She has been after me all this time. I was looking for her, and she was looking for me for a very different reason. "This is about Andrew."

Somehow she found out I killed him, and she followed me. That is why she arranged for the hotel room at Versailles, why she sucked my cock in the Hall of Mirrors. She does not want me. She wants me dead. And yet I take a step toward her, feel my hands reaching for her, as if I want to comfort her for failing to murder me.

She blinks in surprise. As if she cannot believe my reaction.

"I have to go," she says abruptly, charging for the door.

I want to go after her. I want to convince her not to kill me. I want to beg her to forgive me. I want to persuade her to love me. It is this last urge that stops me, more than the fear of my own death.

Dying would be easy, so much easier than loving someone. So much easier than being loved.

VII

LOSS, PART 2

40

Eva

AS SOON AS I HIT THE HALLWAY, I SLIP ON MY SHOES AND I shoulder the backpack. Not to escape a murder, but to escape a murderer.

I need to be alone. I need to think. But most of all, I need to get very far away from Jonathan. I just tried to kill him. He knows I just tried to kill him. There's a good chance he'll try to kill me back.

Jonathan doesn't seem to be coming after me. In fact, he seemed downright warmed by my murder attempt, but people act crazy when they're in shock.

I'm a little shocked myself. Not only did I completely botch my kill, but my head is spinning with his words: *Oh. This is about Andrew.*

What the fuck does that mean?

I follow the preplanned path I set for myself: down the stairs, through the café.

I step out the door and into the adorable village in Spain. I walk along the aqueduct-lined sidewalks. The village is not deserted anymore. Pilgrims walk past me carrying enormous backpacks.

They're all going in the same direction. I fall into step with them. It strikes me that Jonathan probably won't try to kill me if I am surrounded by religious pilgrims. I mean, probably.

People walk this trail looking for answers, and I'm no different. Does Jonathan think that my relationship with Andrew fucked me up so badly that I'm willing to kill to avoid love? Because that would be totally believable.

But that's not it. I'm lying to myself again because I like Jonathan. I don't want him to be the villain that I know he is. Sherri told me that he's a henchman for bad people, that he's killed many times.

When Andrew was murdered, I was told it was a job gone wrong, that the bad guys got him. Jonathan is the bad guy. Jonathan killed Andrew.

I need to talk to Sherri.

I reach a wooded area and veer off the trail. I walk deep into the woods, until I can't hear the hikers' footfalls or their early-morning chatter. I come to a stop in a dense patch of trees. I call Sherri.

"Is everything all right?" She sounds worried. I did promise her Jonathan would be dead in an hour.

"Did he kill Andrew?" I ask.

"I beg your pardon?"

"Jonathan." I drop against a tree. My nerves are still sparking under my skin. "This guy I'm supposed to be getting secrets from? I got secrets."

"He told you he killed Andrew?"

"More or less."

"I'm sorry. I didn't know that." What else does she not know?

"How could you not know that?" It's a rebellious question, but I'm feeling a little rebellious, and more than a little disappointed.

"I don't know everything, Eva." She sounds a little deflated.

"But you said the agency does. You said they have access everywhere." She is silent. "Do you think *they* knew?"

"Does it change things?" she asks. "If anything, it just proves what I've been telling you all along. He's killed innocent people."

She has a point. I shouldn't be angry at Sherri. I *should* be angry at Jonathan.

My nerves are starting to settle, leaving behind a familiar feeling of emptiness. The draining of adrenaline that follows every job. Even this one, my first Fail to Kill.

"Where are you now?" she asks. "Where is he?"

I fill her in, even though I'm a little frustrated with myself. I shouldn't have assumed his gun wasn't loaded. I should've just kept shooting. If I had, Jonathan would be dead, and all this would be over.

When I finish catching Sherri up, she tells me: "If you want off the job, just say the word." It isn't exactly a vote of confidence.

I sag against the tree. I feel disappointed. I feel pathetic for feeling disappointed. But the thing is, all the reasons I had for killing Jonathan this morning still stand. If I don't do it, someone else will. I need the work. I need to stand up for women's rights, or something.

If anything, I have *more* reason to kill Jonathan now. He killed my fiancé. I owe it to Andrew to avenge his death.

I should hate Jonathan for what he did, but the truth is more complicated. Because I have killed people, too. People I didn't know, with families and loved ones and lives. And I doubt it mattered to them if their loved one was a hero or a villain.

I keep waiting for anger to come. I keep waiting to hate Jonathan, but I don't. And it just makes me mad at myself.

"I don't want off the job," I insist to Sherri. "I want it more than ever now."

Killing Jonathan is the simplest way to relieve all these complicated, conflicted feelings. It's the way I solve every problem in my life. If something makes me uncomfortable, I end it.

"Do you have a plan?" Sherri asks.

Back in the day—even *days* ago—Sherri and I would plan the hit together. I trusted her with my life, but now I'm not sure. I'm starting to think maybe Sherri doesn't always know best. She doesn't know Jonathan, but I think I do.

"Yes," I say, pushing myself up off the tree and starting back toward the trail. I walk fast. The air is bright. The sun is rising over the trees. "I think we've been going about this all wrong. I don't need to find his weakness; I need to *become* his weakness."

IN ESPINAL I CALL A CAB TO A TRAIN STATION, THEN CATCH A TRAIN to Barcelona. Jonathan's driving a fucking Bugatti, so no doubt he will beat me there, but at least I have some time to think. Some time away from him, when I can think clearly.

The train is almost empty. I've been on many trains since that sleeper train, and on all those trains I thought about Jonathan. Or who I thought he was.

He killed Andrew.

I can hardly get my head around it. It's wild that a complete stranger—someone I was so strangely attracted to—changed my life in such a major way.

I think back to that last night with Andrew. I had convinced myself that his death was inevitable, but really, it took me by surprise.

We had been fighting a lot. Andrew thought I was working too much, getting lost in the job. I had—a little bit arrogantly, I can admit now—thought that he was jealous. I was better at killing than he was. I had better aim. I was faster. More efficient.

I remember the night I surpassed his kill number. I came back to his apartment expecting congratulations. He was the closest thing I had to family. I wanted him to be proud of me. But instead, he said, "Don't you think maybe you're taking this too far?" And later, "It just seems like you're a bit obsessed." When he was the one who got me into the job in the first place.

It was like the better I got, the more the job became a bad thing. I couldn't help thinking that it was about me.

The night before Andrew died, we had a big blowup. He wanted me to leave the agency.

"I don't think it's good for you," he said. "I think it's trapping you in your childhood trauma." I honestly thought that was a low blow.

"This has nothing to do with my past," I said back. "It has nothing to do with me. This is about *you*. You want to control me. You want to tell me what to do."

That made him laugh. "When have I ever had the least control over you?"

That annoyed me, too. "You got me into this. You trained me. You *made* me. And now I'm better than you, and you don't like it."

"You were always better than me," he insisted, trying to pull the nice card, trying to make me the bad guy.

I stormed out. I wandered the city for hours, walked across Ponte Vecchio, to the Palazzo Pitti, all the way to Piazzale Michelangelo.

The thing is, I knew Andrew was kind of right. My childhood trauma had propelled me into this job. I couldn't go back and change my past. I tried not to even think about it. I rarely ever talked about it. But it was the reason for almost every major life choice I made. Every time I killed a bad guy, I felt a surge of power. I felt like a hero. I felt like I had saved the world from becoming me.

But it wasn't just that. I created new chaotic memories to burn over the old ones. Like I thought I could drown my past trauma in violence and adrenaline.

The morning after our big fight, Sherri called me and told me Andrew had been killed. She said that he had been taken out while on a job. I was a little confused, because Andrew hadn't mentioned a job the night before, but then I just figured he might not want to share his hypocrisy.

I didn't know what to do. We were engaged, but I had no legal claim to him. I hoped his estranged family would take over the funeral arrangements. I left Florence. I asked Sherri for another job, as soon as possible, so I could bury the trauma of that loss, too.

Andrew became just another thing not to think about. Another piece of my past to erase. And now here he was, at the worst possible time, in the worst possible place, mind-fucking me during the hardest job I've ever had to do.

Sherri had told me Andrew was killed on a job. What if the job was Jonathan? The implications of that were a little scary. It would mean that the agency was sending me to kill the guy Andrew—a pretty competent assassin—had failed to kill. But worst of all, that would mean the agency has been trying to kill Jonathan for years.

That can't be true. The agency might believe in me, but there's no way they believe in me *that* much. This is starting to sound like a suicide mission.

You would think all this would make me want to quit. You would think it would make me want to turn around. Give up. You would think. But Andrew was right. I use violence and adrenaline and the challenge of a kill to bury my past, and this thing with Jonathan is the *most* adrenaline and the *most* challenge and it's about to be the *most* violence. I don't want to stop.

I'm gunning for Barcelona on a rickety train. I'm tracking Jonathan down to kill him. That's one way to put all these complicated emotions to bed.

That's one thing that has always dragged me from my darkest thoughts: a plan to kill.

Jonathan thinks I wanted to kill him to get revenge for Andrew. He doesn't know I'm an assassin. I have to make sure that he doesn't even suspect it. I have to get close to him again. A seemingly impossible task now that he knows I tried to kill him. He might not want to hang out after that. Unless he's like me.

Unless he's a little addicted to the thrill of the game.

41

Jonathan

I CALL THOMAS ON THE WAY INTO BARCELONA. HE IS NOT HAPPY to hear from me. He is never happy to hear from me anymore.

"I thought we agreed you needed to slow down," he says. "Work–life balance, all that shite."

"I'm not calling about work," I say, although that is not totally true. "I'm just letting you know that someone tried to kill me."

He laughs. What a guy. "You're joking."

"A girl I was seeing—thought I was seeing. Turns out I killed her fiancé. I thought we had something, but it was just revenge."

"Where is she now? Did you kill her?"

"Of course not. I'm not a monster; I only kill for money." I change lanes, four times in a row. "I think I like her more now. Is that weird?"

"Everything about you is weird."

"She made a pretty competent attempt at my life." It is true. She knew to muffle the gun. She was very handy with the knife. Most people do not know the exact placement for a knife to connect with a heart. I stopped the blade before it did major damage. I did not even have to stitch up the wound. I want it to leave a scar, a tattoo over my heart. "So competent, I'm wondering if she's a professional. Is there some kind of database or something? Could you look her up?"

"What's her name?"

"Eva."

"Just Eva?"

"I mean, if she is an assassin, it's probably not even that."

"All right, female assassin. I'll look into it."

"One more thing," I say carefully. I am supposed to be slowing down. And sometimes I think that I am, for all of ten, twenty-four hours. I think I have turned a corner. Then I call Thomas at two in the morning and demand another job.

Thomas has warned me at least a dozen times over the past six months: "You're being reckless. You're making yourself too conspicuous. If you're not careful, something bad is going to happen."

He was right; someone just tried to kill me. But instead of slowing me down, it makes me want to move faster, like I am finally getting somewhere.

I thought Eva and I had something, but of course we did not. I am a killer. I am not made for love. I am made for murder.

"I need something to take my mind off of all this."

"Talk to a therapist."

"I'm talking to you."

"Jonathan."

"Please," I say tersely.

"This is getting out of control," he says, like it was ever under control.

"Don't act like you haven't benefited," I say. "Don't act like you're above it. You hired me. You're the reason I'm here."

"Oh, fuck off."

I pull myself together. Threats will not convince him. "I'm headed to Barcelona. Just find me something nearby."

"Jonathan, I'm warning you—"

"Just do it. Or I'll find another handler."

I do not know how I would do that, but right now I do not care. Maybe Thomas and I are not a good fit. He treats me like a human being. He has never understood.

I am something so much worse.

42

Eva

BARCELONA IS LIKE A CITY THAT GOT DRUNK ON THE BEACH: loose, sprawling and bleached by the sun. It smells of sangria. The air buzzes like a Spanish guitar.

I hop into a cab and head straight to La Sagrada Família.

As I'm driven through the rowdy streets, I question whether Jonathan would have continued to Barcelona without me. The city definitely doesn't seem his style, but it's the only lead I have.

La Sagrada Família is what would happen if a church went to a rave. If there is a God, I hope he's like this. This God is fun, all Day-Glo colors and stars and stilts. The stained glass windows turn the sunlight into rainbows.

The church is almost closing when I arrive. If I don't find Jonathan soon, I'll have to come back tomorrow. I'll have to stake out the church. I'll have to live here, and I'm not totally averse to that.

I pass through the crowds of tourists and worshippers and people who look lost. I try to keep my eyes from drifting up to the epic ceilings.

Somehow, I know he's here. Call it the killer instinct. I can feel it in my bones. I just need to find the most pretentious place. I just need to look for the most well-dressed person here.

I smile when I see him, because he's exactly where I thought he would be.

He's kneeling on a bench in front of an altar of candles. They flicker in front of him like fireflies. My throat catches. I recognize the backs of his ears, his neck, the frames of his glasses.

The dizzying church spins as I walk toward him. I pass under an arch and into the quieter place where he's waiting.

We've been drawn to each other from the beginning. Both of us felt it. Both of us still feel it. Both of us are broken people. That's the truth, and the truth just *feels* different.

He senses me coming. I'm not even kidding.

He gets to his feet. Now that I know he killed Andrew, he transforms in my eyes, like a predator has slipped under his skin. I can see how attuned he is to everything around him, to me.

Hundreds of candles glint behind him as he turns toward me. What if he lit them all? A candle for every person he's killed.

The candles scatter light across his cheeks as he smiles hopefully at me.

"That one." He points at a candle. "I lit that one for you." I'm flickering on a table surrounded by prayers. "It worked." His smile grows limp, uneasy. "You're here."

"Praise God," I say.

His eyes flick down. "Why are you here?"

"You mean, do I still want to kill you?"

I drop some coins into a wooden box, then light my own candle. He watches me set it on the altar, next to his candle for me.

I turn back to him. "It's kind of fun not knowing, isn't it?"

He laughs in surprise. It echoes through the chapel.

43

Jonathan

I NEVER EXPECTED EVA TO COME TO BARCELONA. NOT IN A MIL-lion years.

I asked Thomas to check if she is a contract killer but I do not think she could be. A professional would never run a job like this. She showed up unarmed. She had sex with me, twice. She tried to kill me and failed, and instead of doing what any sane person would do, instead of running as fast as she could, she is standing here now like all of this is just entertainment.

Now, I know I am pretty sick, but her coming back? That is sick as fuck. That is another level of sick.

She is crazy, and it is so fucking hot. I want to get down on my knees and worship her, the only God in this whole chapel.

Instead, I wait, uncertain. "What now?"

She tilts her head. The candlelight flickers in her eyes. "Are you hungry?"

I am surprised. "You want dinner?"

"Well, whatever happens next, both of us have to eat."

"I suppose." I trail her to the exit.

She threads her fingers into mine as we walk out of the

cathedral. It is purely insane. And yet I feel my heart expanding in my chest, taking up all the space.

I am fairly certain she still wants me dead, but I still want to be with her. I am not sure what that says about me, but it is not exactly surprising.

I would die for her, I think. I might even let her kill me.

44

Eva

AS WE WALK OUT OF THE CHAPEL TOGETHER, I CAN TELL HE'S scared of me—and I don't mean scared that I'll kill him. He's doing that thing with his fingers, his nervous tic, and I wonder if it's because he feels safer when he's holding a weapon.

It might seem deranged that I can break bread with the murderer who I'm about to murder, but the truth is, I do stuff like this all the time. Deranged feels normal to me.

Plus, it's a good way to initiate my plan. It's called mirroring. He took me out to eat; therefore, I take him out to eat. He wants the girlfriend experience, so that's what I'll give him. We'll eat and we'll contemplate all the ways that we can kill each other, just like a normal couple.

"There's this really great tapas restaurant in Barrio Chino," he says. "They have private rooms—for eating, obviously." Private means no cameras. We don't need a repeat of Versailles.

"Perfect." I smile. "No witnesses."

He laughs, a little uncertain.

He thinks I'm crazy. He's not wrong. But who is he to judge?

WE GET A PRIVATE ROOM AT THE TAPAS PLACE. JONATHAN ORDERS A selection of tapas, consulting respectfully with the waitress.

She nods and backs out of the room. "The tapas, we are going to spread them out," she says. "So you will get all different things at all different times. Traditionally, you take your time. You sit, you eat, you talk, you drink your wine. It's all very nice." It's a good thing we came equipped with conversation.

The waitress leaves, but the threat of reentry, of *all different things at all different times*, hangs over us.

Jonathan looks to me for guidance. I'm in a bit of an awkward situation. I need to work my plan, but I also need to make sure he doesn't realize I have a plan. And to do that, I need to address the murderous elephant in the room.

I take the first shot. "Why did you kill Andrew?"

He shifts in his seat. He'd better get comfortable being uncomfortable, because I'm just getting started.

"If I tell you, it could put you in danger." He recognizes my disappointment. For the record, I wasn't hiding it. "Do you believe that?"

I cross my arms. "I don't care. Do you believe that?"

"I kill people for a living," he says, so abruptly that it catches me off guard. I thought I was ready for anything, but I didn't expect the truth.

ROUND ONE: *Melon and Serrano Ham, King Prawns*

We both jump when the door opens. The waitress enters with the wine and a tray of small plates. She arranges them on the table.

She places wineglasses in front of each of us. She pours my wine first.

190

"Please tell me when to stop," she says. I completely blank. She reaches the top of the glass and stops pouring before it spills over.

"Thank you so much," I say, remembering myself.

"This looks exquisite," he tells her in Spanish.

We both watch her exit, beaming like lunatics. She makes a face. The door closes.

I chug the wine. Jonathan neatly dissects a prawn, then pops it into his mouth and chews contemplatively. He swallows.

"Your fiancé did, too," he says.

"What?" I try to sound shocked, but my voice hits an odd note. I hope he doesn't notice.

"I know it sounds outrageous, but it's the truth. He was an assassin. He leaked privileged information to the Italian police. He was identified as a threat by powerful people."

"Wait—what?" That I did *not* know. Andrew went to the cops? It takes me a moment to realize that Jonathan might be lying, but admitting he was a killer was pretty damn honest.

What Jonathan is claiming makes a little sense. Andrew seemed so preoccupied, and yet I know he was taking fewer jobs with the agency. He was also pushing me to quit.

A few days before he died, Andrew showed up at my apartment with some pretty serious bruises. It didn't ring any alarm bells with me back then because it was pretty normal for us. Both of us were getting banged up all the time. But what if it was because of something else? Something he kept from me?

Andrew had seemed disillusioned with the agency. Maybe he was leaking secrets, but wouldn't the Italian police be on the agency's side? We were supposed to be the good guys. We were taking care of the bad guys for them.

"Who do you work for?" I ask. But what I really want to know is: Who do I work for?

Jonathan shrugs, snaps the tail off a prawn. "Whoever pays

me the most," he says, trying to be blithe, but I can tell he is nervous about what I'll think. Sherri told me he was a henchman, that he worked for a very bad man, but that doesn't seem to be what he's saying. "I'm an assassin." He spells it out. "I have a handler who finds me jobs. I pick and choose what I want."

Fuck. That sounds a lot like what I do.

Sherri warned me not to believe anything Jonathan said. She told me he was deranged, but he's being a perfect gentleman, even after I tried to kill him. He could probably take me now, in this private room with no cameras. He's definitely still armed. But I know he won't, and that means that part of me does trust him.

What if he's not a bad guy? What if he's *me*, at some other agency?

As much as I want answers, I need to be careful. I can't risk blowing my cover.

"Maybe we should talk about something else," I say.

"Oh, *thank God*," Jonathan says.

ROUND TWO: *Squid in Marinara, Goat Cheese and Grilled Pepper*

The waitress enters and exits again. This time things are altogether calmer. We smile pleasantly at her. We thank her only a little too profusely.

The wine is working through my system, making me feel good about things I should feel terrible about, as wine does.

"So," I say, "why did you come to Barcelona? Killing someone?"

He flinches. He's really sensitive about his job. "I thought we were going to talk about something else," he says hopefully.

"I meant not Andrew specifically, but we could go back to that."

"No," he says. "I'm not here to kill anyone. Although I did put in a pickup, in case something convenient comes up," he admits. He's being very honest with me. I'm a little shocked. I'm a little charmed.

I wish we *could* talk shop. There was something about him

192

from the very beginning, a feeling I got that we were connected. I wonder if this is where it came from. "Did you know who I was that night on the train?"

He considers. "I thought you looked familiar, but I wasn't sure why. I had seen your picture, but, uh, that was a very busy year for me . . ."

"Of course," I joke.

"You know"—he pauses to taste his wine—"I have to say, you're handling this a lot better than I thought you would."

"The world is full of all kinds of people," I say. The wine is making me philosophical.

He leans forward. "You knew . . . ," he says. I go cold all over. I feel a sure and violent chill that he knows everything. That he brought me here, to a private room—alone—to kill me. The waitress is probably in on it. It's possible she poisoned the wine I've just polished off. I'm dead. It's over. ". . . what Andrew did for a living."

I swallow the biggest sigh. "Maybe," I say, because I haven't had time to think this line of thought all the way through. The wine is slowing me down. I never drink on jobs. I need to remember this is a job.

"You're not an assassin, are you?" he asks. "I mean, you did make a fairly competent attempt on my life."

"Fairly competent?" I repeat. I could tell him the truth. I could tell him everything. I could trust him all the way. "Andrew taught me. Self-defense."

His eyes are tracing me, downloading my aura. I try to hold tight to my cool, my casual, my devil-may-care. "Fair enough," he says. "You don't seem like an assassin."

See, now, that annoys me. "Why not?"

He sips his wine, then says, "You're not fucked-up enough."

"*Excuse me?* Do we need to go over my childhood again? Because I remember it being pretty fucked-up."

"What happened to you was fucked-up," he says gently. "But you're not."

"I tried to kill you this morning and I'm having dinner with you right now."

"I think that's optimistic," he says. "You know, I didn't mean it as an insult." He's watching me closely. I wonder if he's trying to spark a confession. Maybe he knows. Maybe he's trying to goad me into admitting the truth.

Or maybe he really thinks he's more fucked-up than I am. And I can't let that go. "You know, women are just better at hiding how fucked-up they are," I point out. "We have to be. Men can act unhinged and people think they're troubled and romantic. Meanwhile, a messy woman is always—always—ostracized by society."

"You're right. I apologize." I wish more men knew what a turn-on apologizing is.

I shift in my seat. "Anyway, if I were an assassin, you'd be dead by now." If I were a good assassin, he would be. I should be killing him now, in this private room with a lock on the door and with no witnesses. That's the truth. Instead, I'm questioning my handler and my job and my life.

"Probably."

"Do you think I'm crazy?"

"No . . ." His eyes find mine and lock on. "I think you're so fucking hot."

Oh.

ROUND THREE: *Some Kind of Sausage, Tiny Potatoes, Olives, Something That Looks Like a Meatball*

"How is everything?" the waitress says.

"Excellent," Jonathan says.

"*So* good," I agree.

We beam at her. It's pretty clear that she's starting to get a little freaked out. She shuts the door quickly. It rattles in the frame.

I try a tiny potato. "What is it with you and stranding us in eternal meals?" I ask.

"It's not me; we're in Europe." He is still watching the door.

"What is it?" I ask.

"Nothing." He eats an olive, then notes, "There's a lock on the door."

I try the meatball thing. "I noticed." I do not add that I noticed when I was contemplating killing him.

He shifts uncomfortably.

"What?"

"It's just . . ." He drifts off. "I owe you an orgasm."

My eyes shoot toward the door, like we've given the waitress a cue.

When she doesn't enter, I lean forward. I grin at Jonathan. I lock the door.

45

Jonathan

I HAVE NEVER TOLD ANYONE OTHER THAN MAS WHAT I DO FOR A living. Up until now. I told Eva. She did not give a fuck. She was fine with it. It was hardly a speed bump. She is so much more twisted than I ever dreamed possible. It is starting to scare me, and it is *really* turning me on.

She smiles at me. She reaches for the door and she locks it.

"What should we do?" she asks.

"Get on the table," I say. She did ask.

"But there's—" There is food on the table, all different food in all different places.

"Get on the table," I repeat.

She cocks her head. For a moment, I think she will not take direction—she has been calling most of the shots so far—but then she makes up her mind.

She smirks. She moves. Her sneaker slips slightly on the leather seat as she stands. She places her knee in the gap between the bread and where it's buttered. She puts her hands out, sliding the little plates aside to make a place big enough for her.

"On your back," I say.

She gets down and rolls over. The plates orbit her. She is the perennial sun.

I climb over her. I am not careful to move the plates first. They crack beneath my knees. I grab the waistband of her trousers and I yank their bright plastic button off as I strip her. It is messy work, but somebody has to do it.

I put on a condom. She grunts as I enter her. I start to move inside her. She tries to hold her place on the table. I thrust into her and her body jerks, trying to hold the impact inside that magnetic belly, trying to keep still, to keep the plates from falling.

"Oh! Oh! Oh God!" I am really moving now, thrusting inside her. I want her to remember this tomorrow. I want her to remember this forever.

She claps her hand over her mouth as the first plate drops. It cracks against the floor: a whole, perfect sound. The others are all going to go the same way.

The prawn shells. The olives. The little sausages wrapped in bacon. I am sorry it had to end this way. We are going to have to let you go.

"Fuck!"

The plates fall in droves.

Crack! Crack! Crack!

It is a natural disaster, a force of nature. The table is textured: Parts of it are swamped in oil; others are mountains of bread and broken porcelain. My palm slips on marinara sauce and finds purchase in the ropes of her dark hair.

"Fuck!"

Everything must go. If I am not careful, she will go, too.

This will take some fancy footwork, but luckily I am well studied in the gymnastics of physical extremes.

"Put your knees up." She does and I lift her with me, backward off the table and *thwack!* onto the leather seat. I get an orgasm for my efforts. Girls love surprises.

"Oh . . . *Fuck.*"

I release myself inside her, too exhausted to carry on. My breath is pumping inside my chest. Hers does the same.

I lift her and place her beside me, somewhat overexerted by our efforts.

She tries to catch her breath, peering at me from between the fronds of her marinara-coated hair. She starts to laugh, deep in her belly. In a moment she is hysterical, doubled over, laughing infectiously.

"That was so, so naughty!" she exclaims.

"We should probably clean this up," I say. The wreckage is spectacular. Her ass is printed in oil on the table. The broken plates on the floor have created an apocalyptic skyline that looks surprisingly like Barcelona.

"And leave a big tip," she says.

"I've wanted to do that since the day I met you," I confess. "No, from the moment I first saw you, on the sleeper train to Paris."

"It's probably a good thing you waited," she says, zipping up her now-buttonless pants. "I don't know if our seatmates would have appreciated it."

"We'll go back there someday, won't we? And we'll get our old compartment? The same train?" I have half a mind to drag her back there now.

"Someday," she repeats, like she finds the phrase suspicious. She bites her lip and her brow crosses. "What exactly do you want from me?"

"I want you," I say. "Just you."

I AM A LITTLE TIPSY ON THE WALK HOME. I DO NOT NORMALLY DRINK, because I tend to go dark. Well, darker.

But I got caught up in the moment, in being with her. I started to think—in small moments, here and there—that I could be like everybody else. That I could drink for fun. Eat for fun. Live for fun.

Eva and I walk to the hotel along La Rambla, the main artery of Barcelona. I have walked this street dozens of times before, but I have a sense that this is *the* time, as if all those other times were in preparation for this moment. The lights, the trees and the cobblestones are all lit. My life before her was a dress rehearsal; this is the main event.

I am maybe more than tipsy.

She is holding my hand. Her fingers are tangled in mine. I can still taste her pussy on my lips from when I kissed it goodbye.

I am cataloging all of Eva's parts—her skin, her moles, her lips—so I do not see him coming until it is too late.

Suddenly there is a man beside me with a knife at my ribs, demanding, in English:

"Give me *everything.*"

I admire his lack of specificity. Why ask for anything when you can have everything?

I am used to thinking on my feet, but I am not entirely sure how to handle this situation. You might think, *You're a contract killer! Kill him!* But I do not like killing honest criminals. And it is not safe. When I kill people for work, I have a cleanup crew. I have killed people outside of work before, and I ended up imprisoned for my efforts.

I also do not want to offend Eva by knocking him out. I decide to calmly unsheathe my wallet. There is no reason we cannot all walk away happy.

Except the thief misreads my reaching into my coat—in fairness, I do have a gun in there. He stabs me—just lightly. It is practically foreplay.

That is when Eva takes him out.

It is objectively impressive. She hits him in just the right spot—her palm, the bar of his columella. The luckiest strike.

Crack!

"Oh," I say.

Blood gushes down his shirt, then through his fingers, which are now stapled to his nose to stop the bleeding.

"You fucking bitch!" he says, then staggers away.

I start after him, but she stops me.

"He can't talk to you like that," I say, feeling a little heated.

She starts laughing, still holding me back. "Oh my God!" Her hand brushes my wound. "You're actually bleeding."

She spreads my coat and I am bleeding. Blood has never really bothered me. It does not seem to bother her either. She ties up my shirt to quell the wound.

"Thank you," I say, catching her eyes.

She smiles at me. "No problem."

We are both far too serene for people who have just been mugged.

"I'm glad you're not an assassin," I say. I slip my fingers through hers. I can feel her heartbeat through her palm. Feel her fast breath slowing as we start toward the hotel again. "I wouldn't stand a chance."

"You really wouldn't," she confirms.

La Rambla seems even more beautiful now, as if it has become an integral part of our story. The night she saved me.

"I can't believe you're real," I muse. "It's like you were made for me."

"Excuse me—maybe *you* were made for *me*."

"Okay," I agree. "I like that better." I do. I would much rather have been made for her than for what I originally thought I was made for: chaos.

Her existence is such a trip. It is rearranging my entire world—not to be dramatic.

Before this moment I thought I was wicked. I thought I was placed on this earth for my torture—and maybe a little for everyone else's. But she is making me think, making me believe, that there is another, more playful reason.

That I am a little here for love.

46

Eva

JONATHAN TAKES ME UP TO HIS HOTEL ROOM. IT'S ALL WOODEN floors and dark walls. High ceilings, a private patio, an epic shower.

I need to call Sherri, but I don't want to. I don't have the energy right now to find someplace secret to grill her. I'm also afraid of what she might tell me.

Once inside the room, Jonathan takes off his clothes to examine the stab wound. He has a neat cut between his sixth and seventh ribs, to add to his scar collection. The scar I added myself this morning is still an angry red.

He sits on the bed and starts to clean the cut using items from his very extensive first aid kit. I recognize a lot of them.

"Here." I sit beside him. "Let me." I dress his wound. He watches me with reverent eyes. I'm doing exactly what I told Sherri I would do: I'm becoming his weakness. I'm not sure how I feel about it.

"You've done this before," he says. I don't have to make up an explanation for my skill. He thinks I did this for Andrew, and I did. What Jonathan doesn't know is that Andrew did it for me, too.

"So," I say, focusing on the wound so he won't see my wheels turning, "how did you get into assassin work? Job fair? College major? Bet gone wrong?"

"No," he says. "Nothing like that . . ." He hesitates, as if debating how much to tell me. How much I can take, maybe. How much to trust me with, definitely. He catches my eyes. His eyes seem deeper than other peoples', but I wonder if they're deeper for me, like I can dive further into them than anybody else. "I don't want to scare you," he says.

"Do I seem scared?" I ask. I know I don't.

He takes a deep breath, preparing himself, preparing me. "I realized that I could kill people. I realized that it was a kind of talent, not something everyone could do."

I have to hold back a smile, because I've sometimes thought the same thing. How great and how terrible it is that I can do this thing that other people can't do. "Who was your first kill?" This is just pure curiosity.

"My father," he says.

My hands freeze for a second. He notices. I force myself to focus, to finish bandaging him up. "I'm assuming he deserved it?" The agency warned me that Jonathan was dangerous, the most dangerous, but this still surprises me. Maybe because I want to believe he's safe.

"I shouldn't have done it," he says. "He was abusive, but I didn't have to kill him. We had found someone to help us. We were leaving the next day. I knew that." His eyes grow distant, sinking into the memory. "I didn't think it was enough. And I was afraid he might find a way to take us back. I couldn't let that happen. So I killed him. The next morning, we left. The next day, I was arrested. I was charged with murder. I did murder him. I was so fucking stupid, I thought . . . I didn't even try to cover it up. I was just a dumb kid, who was fairly ambivalent about murder."

His story is intense, but I'm not even thinking about it. Not thinking about what he did or why. All I can think about is one thing. He said "we."

I know Jonathan's weakness.

"You don't have to stay," he says, startling me from my thoughts. I realize he's expecting me to be horrified. He's expecting me to be afraid of him. But I'm not. I've killed dozens of people. Killing a parent so negligent that Jonathan and his sibling had to find a way to escape seems fairly tame in comparison.

"Why would I leave?" I ask.

"I'm not a good person." He sounds almost frustrated with me. Frustrated that I'm staying. That I'm not afraid of him. "It should be obvious. I shouldn't have to explain it."

I shrug. "It's not obvious to me." I'm saying what he wants to hear, but as I say it, I realize I mean it.

All my life, I have never felt that anyone could ever understand me, because of what I did, because of who I was.

I would meet people, anywhere, anytime, have ordinary conversations until it would hit me—and it always did—*If they knew what happened to you, if they knew what you did, they wouldn't want to be around you.* The wall would go up. The real me lived in a separate world. No one could ever reach me.

Sometimes I thought I was exceptional. Sometimes I thought I was cursed. But I never thought that I would find someone like me. As exceptional and as cursed. I think I could forgive Jonathan anything, and I know just how dangerous that is.

I reach out. I brush his jaw with my fingers. Then I lean in and kiss him. It's like kissing my own broken heart.

He pulls away from me and pushes himself off the bed. "You shouldn't be okay with this," he says. He starts pacing in front of me. He runs his fingers over his palms again and again.

I watch him calmly, quietly. I don't even know who's the real predator here. I guess only time will tell.

"Do you want me to leave?" I ask.

"No . . . I don't know."

"You keep asking me if I'm scared, but it seems like you're the one who's scared. I don't mean scared of me. I mean scared of yourself." I cross my legs, feeling very Zen.

"I'm scared that you're not scared."

"And you've lived your whole life this way? Hating yourself? Blaming yourself?" Just like me.

"Eva, I'm a bad person. I've killed a lot of people."

"How many?" I have to know. I told you I was competitive.

"I haven't kept count. Over a hundred." Damn, that's way more than me.

I shrug. "If it bothers you, don't do it anymore."

He laughs in surprise.

"I'm serious," I say. "Just stop."

He shakes his head, climbs back onto the bed. He takes my hand, squeezes it tight.

He kisses me. It's like no kiss we've had before. It's better, even, than our first kiss.

I've never had that happen before.

47

Jonathan

I AM SICK, BUT THIS TIME SHE IS THE SICKNESS. SHE HAS CRAWLED into my brain and into my veins and into all the locked-up, fucked-up parts of me.

I wake before her the next morning. I have a missed call from Thomas. I force myself out to return it, but I am so fucking pussy whipped that I write Eva a note first. I leave it right in front of her nose so she will not think even for a moment that I have left her again without saying goodbye.

The city of Barcelona is part nightmare. Never has another civilization succeeded so well in making the dreamscape a physical reality. Who else would ever intentionally make a cathedral appear to be melting?

I walk along La Rambla, the street Eva and I walked together last night. Only now it is drenched in the nostalgia of a few hours ago. Last night was the pinnacle. We have left the before. We are living in the after.

It is very unclear where things will go from here, but I almost do not need to know.

I still have a little money left from the last job. We could crisscross through Europe, or go farther—maybe that would be safer. South America. Antarctica. The moon.

I find a quiet corner off the beaten path to call Thomas. The sun is shining. The world is right.

"Something's come up," Thomas says.

"I don't want a job," I say. "You were right. I think I'm going to take a break. A real one." I want to give Eva my full attention.

"Oh . . . Wow. I never thought I'd see the day you'd say no to a job."

I am not proud to say this rankles me, like part of me needs to be the most fucked-up. "Yep," I say.

I think of what Eva said last night: *If it bothers you, don't do it anymore. Just stop.* I would not go that far, but she is right. I do not *have* to do it. I can stop, for now. Do something else. Mostly her.

"I think this is a really positive step forward for you," Thomas says. "However, I'm not calling you about a job."

Shit.

"Why are you calling me?" I say, even though I know why.

"Because the woman who tried to kill you is, in fact, an assassin. She's not out for revenge; she's on assignment."

"Of course she is." I am not an idiot. I am something worse. I am a romantic. I do not even know if I cared whether she was lying to me or not. I wanted to be with her so badly, I was willing to believe anything. We are all liars in love's war, but it still hurts to hear the truth.

"I warned you to slow down," Thomas scolds, like this is my fault. "I told you that you were making yourself too conspicuous, that you were getting sloppy."

"Who took out a hit on me?"

"I'm not entirely sure."

"Shit." In all my years in this job, I have never had someone take out a hit on me. In all honesty, I thought that being a hit man granted me a certain level of protection—never kid a kidder; never kill a killer. I thought my reputation preceded me. I thought they would know better. "What do I do now?" I know what to do when I am the hit man, but I have no idea what to do when I am the hit.

"I'll try to figure out who wants you dead. In the meantime, I suggest you not get killed."

"Sure." My mind is moving a thousand miles a minute, but my body is still ahead of it. I start toward the hotel.

"Jonathan? I would advise you not to confront her."

"You do your job," I say, "and I'll do mine."

VIII

ATTEMPTED MURDER,
PART 2

48

Eva

JONATHAN IS GONE FOR A SUPER LONG TIME. SO LONG THAT I take a shower, blow-dry my hair, order breakfast and eat it. So long that I start to get nervous. Force of habit. I'm used to things going very, very wrong. Fast.

Maybe he took a job. Maybe he's hurt, trapped, dead. Maybe he's not coming back.

Sherri's called me half a dozen times. I should call her back. I should quiz her about all my doubts: about Andrew and the agency and everything Jonathan said. With all these doubts, I'm not even sure if I *can* move forward with this job. Maybe I'm making excuses to save Jonathan, or maybe I'm making excuses to save myself.

Last night I told Jonathan he should quit. "Just stop," I said. Projecting much?

Maybe I'm the one who wants to quit. Even if all my doubts are unfounded. Even if I really am saving the world, maybe I don't want to do it anymore. Maybe I want to have my own world that's worth saving.

Maybe Jonathan and I could both quit, together. I don't know exactly where we would go, but I have a feeling we could go anywhere. I don't know what any of that would look like, but I know that it's fucking hard to meet someone. I know that it's worth taking a chance. I know that if I don't, I might regret it for the rest of my life.

So I wait. Even when Jonathan is gone for way too long.

Then I hear his key card in the lock.

The door opens. He walks into the room. I can immediately sense that something has changed. Call it an instinct. I don't want to overreact. I don't want to jump to any conclusions.

"Sorry I took so long," he says. His voice is light. "I got lost." I don't believe him.

I watch him walk toward me. His walk is a little stiffer than usual, a little slower. What's different? What's changed?

I look down at his hands and see that they're not moving. They're perfectly still. And I realize: He's not nervous anymore. The whole time I've known Jonathan, from day one on the train, he's been nervous, anxious, a kid with a crush.

Now he's totally calm.

This job favors those who act before they think.

I dart for his ankle. I pull the knife from his sock and throw him off-balance, so he stumbles backward. I charge him. I force him back against the wall. I press the knife against his throat.

He hardly even seems bothered. His breath is a little heavier. His eyes a little duller. With incredible nonchalance, he draws an antique rapier from a sheath behind his back and points it into the soft underside of my jaw.

"I got this at the flea market you told me about," he says. "I wanted to show you." He's talking like all of this is totally normal. It's a tactic, I think. A part of his gift. His ability to do things other people can't do. He observes his knife in my hand. "I can't believe whoever sent you sent you unarmed."

"They said it would be worse if I came armed," I say. "Were they right?"

"I don't think it could be worse." He traces the rapier along my jaw until he reaches the sweet spot, the exact angle from which he could kebab my brain.

I press the knife against his neck until I gently cut him. His blood runs down my fingers. He even bleeds politely.

We are at an impasse.

The most valuable skill an assassin can have is—no surprise—the ability to actually kill someone. Jonathan wasn't wrong when he said it was a special, twisted gift. Not everyone can do it. In fact, most people can't. They think they can, but when the time comes, they hesitate. With people like me, with people like Jonathan, if you hesitate, you're too late.

"I really like this sword," he says. "I'll always remember you when I look at it."

"You'll be too dead to remember anything."

"If you slit my throat, I won't die instantly. You know that—you *must* know that. I will live long enough to make your life a living hell." He adjusts the angle of the blade, demonstrating all the ways he could end me. "What type of brain trauma do you prefer? Cerebellum? We could take out your hypothalamus. You wouldn't be able to run and you wouldn't be able to fuck." I have to give it to him; he's a little chilling. I should have known he would make murder overdramatic.

"I'm going to kill you," I say, straight to the point.

"I can't wait." He's hesitating. We both are.

With a practiced move, I shove the rapier off. The blade barely knicks my throat, but my knife does a little more damage. Blood drips down into his shirt.

213

"You're kind of a bleeder," I point out.

He wipes the blood from his neck. "You're not wrong. I've had seven blood transfusions."

He pulls his sword on me. I pull the knife. Honestly, his is a lot bigger. It's a little unfair, but we fence anyway. Forward and backward across the hotel room. Both of us are just biding our time. Maybe we're looking for an opportunity. Maybe we're looking for an escape.

Most of my kills are made using an element of surprise. Yes, it's a little cheating, but murder isn't about playing fair.

But right now, I don't even know if I want to kill Jonathan. I'm also not sure why he's suddenly turned on me. That's the tricky part. I don't really know how he feels about me. Right now, he doesn't look like he feels anything.

"Can I ask what inspired this sudden change in attitude?" I say as we dash across the room.

"It was brought to my attention that you, in fact, *are* an assassin," he says.

"Oh, that."

"Yes, that," he says. "You lied to me."

"And you've been totally honest."

"Someone hired you, which means someone wants me dead. Don't you think I might want to know that?"

"No offense, but I would guess that a lot of people want you dead."

He allows me to thrust him into a corner, where we cross weapons more intensely. He strikes so forcefully that I have to back away. "Who trained you?" he asks.

"Andrew," I say.

"You're much better than he was."

"Thank you." I beam, genuinely pleased. "But you know, I feel like you're not really trying."

He stabs me, deep enough for me to bleed. "Do you feel better now?" he says.

"Fuck you. Seriously." He knows it's not fair. He has the better weapon. I'm fencing with a knife.

We continue to fence back and forth but it's clear both of us are losing steam, looking for an out.

"How do you do it?" he says.

"Do what?" I ask.

"How do you kill people?"

"As if you don't know."

"I don't mean physically."

I hesitate. I'm not sure if I don't know the answer or if I'm afraid to admit it. I've always told myself I was the hero. That I was saving the world. But I know that Jonathan won't buy that, and not just because he's a cynic. He won't buy it because he understands me. He might be the only person in the world who does. "How do *you* do it?"

He boxes me against the wall. Our breaths are both pumping—mine slightly more, which annoys me. "I think the world is a terrible place," he says. "I feel like I'm doing these people a favor."

His glasses are crooked on his nose. I reach up with my free hand and adjust them.

It's bait; I'm setting him up. If he tries to stop me, I will slit his wrist, but he doesn't. He lets me fix them, then blinks in polite discomfort.

"You want to know how I do it?" I ask. "The same way you do, and I mean the *real* reason. Not all this crap about the world being a terrible place. Killing people is just one of the self-destructive things I do because of the trauma I experienced as a child." I'm not just hurting other people; I'm hurting myself. I'm staying stuck in trauma instead of moving on, instead of growing up, instead of *living*. "It's not about killing other people. It's about killing myself."

He jumps back, like my words have hit.

I hesitate, and he unleashes the real moves. He pitches the sword across the room. It buries itself in the wall like an arrow. I realize it's a distraction.

He shoves me back while tripping me from behind. I land on my back on the floor, staring up at the ceiling. But not for long, because he throws the duvet over my face, bundles me up like a burrito and stuffs me under the bed—I'm not kidding.

As ridiculous as it sounds, it's well planned. By the time I have fought my way out of the duvet—which still smells like him—he's gone.

I just have to decide if I'm going to follow him, and for what.

49

Jonathan

I DRIVE OUT OF BARCELONA, AS FAST AS I CAN. AS I AM BROACH-
ing the edge of the city, I find myself turning back. Before I
know it, I am circling the city like a hawk, round and round
like I cannot escape.

It's not about killing other people. It's about killing myself.

I have never been read so accurately, and she was not even
talking about me. She was talking about herself. She was talking
about us.

I want to run but I feel like I am bound in a web stronger than
fear and stronger than fate. Even if I drove as fast and as far as I
could, she would be there, sticky in my mind.

I am searching for a way out when Thomas calls again. That
was fast.

"Please tell me you know who hired the hit, because I am
about to go nuclear," I say.

"I'm actually calling you about something else," he says.

"Full of surprises today," I say. Hopefully this surprise does not
hurt as much as the last one.

"A job just came in over the network."

"You really think I have time for another job right now?" I switch lanes three times, even though I do not have a destination.

"*She* is the job," he says. I inhale sharply. "I thought it might be a sort of two-birds, one-stone thing. Earn a little pocket money. Send a message to whoever wants you dead."

"Who wants *her* dead?"

"Does it matter? She's trying to kill you."

"I suppose not." I exhale, but I do not have time to think. "I want the job. I don't want anyone else to take it."

I end the call. I keep circling Barcelona. I try to come up with a plan. Do I want to hide? Or do I want to be found? I have never had a mark who was chasing *me*.

I do not want Eva dead, but part of me does want to kill her. It is what I have been doing all along. It is self-destruction in its purest form. I am sorry for making her collateral damage. I am sorry it had to be her, but this is the culmination of a lifetime of murdering myself.

Soon I am driving almost aimlessly, changing lanes at random, traveling in a loop. I cannot think straight. I cannot get a grip on this. Any plan runs like sand through my hands.

I am not sure if I can do this.

I remind myself that she is trying to kill me. I do not have a choice. I am a cold-blooded killer. I am not a romantic. I am not a nice guy. I can murder the person who is trying to murder me.

But there is something about her assignment that bothers me—and not just that someone wants me dead. Something in this scenario does not quite add up. They sent Eva to kill me. They sent her unarmed. That does not sound like a plan; it sounds like suicide.

Maybe they knew there was an attraction? Maybe they thought I would fall in love, get dumb and get fucked. Or maybe . . .

They did not send her to kill me. She had so many opportunities that she did not take.

They sent her on recon. They sent her to talk to me. They sent her to get me to spill and I did. I told her things I have never told anyone else. I think through all these things. Search my words for things she could use, things they could use, to get to me.

The tires squeal as I spin the car around. I shift gears four times and I steam north, toward Paris.

I told her about my first murder. I remember the way her eyes lit up, not with the tragedy but with the words I used so carelessly:

We *had found someone to help us.* We *were leaving the next day.*

50

Eva

I LEAVE HIS SWORD IN THE WALL. IT'S NOT MY JOB TO CLEAN UP after him. He ran, like they all do eventually, but for a different reason.

I walk out of the hotel, moving without thinking, the way I sometimes do. The sun is high in Barcelona. The city moves with the music of itself. I hail a cab and tell the driver where to take me. I know where I'm going. There was never really any question of that.

Jonathan told me he'd been staying in Paris. He took an overnight train to see a doctor there, as if there were not doctors between Florence and France. It doesn't make sense. Unless the doctor is someone he trusts. Unless the doctor is someone he knows. Unless the doctor is family.

I head to the train station. I book the high-speed train to Paris. I'll be there in six hours. Assuming Jonathan is driving, I'll probably beat him there. Probably. He is driving a Bugatti.

I know that Jonathan likes me, but I also know that part of him doesn't like liking me. I remember his expression when I told him why we kill, his terror at being seen, at being understood.

Jonathan likes his darkness. He likes his weapons and his tragedy and his unhappiness. He likes being a killer. I know because I'm like him. I'm married to my trauma, and one day I will be buried by it.

I take a seat next to a window. I watch the city flatten into fields that then undulate into hills. I have six hours to decide what to do—not just with Jonathan but with the rest of my life.

SHERRI'S BEEN CALLING FOR HOURS. SHE'S LEFT ME DOZENS OF messages coded "SOS." I'm not sure if she lied to me. I'm not sure of anything just now, but I can't keep avoiding her.

When I'm halfway to Paris, I lock myself in a bathroom and call her back.

"We need to ta—," I start, but I can't finish, because Sherri interrupts.

"Thank fuck! Oh my God! Thank fuck!" She's in a panic.

"Are you okay?" I say, forgetting my anger and confusion. I've never heard her sound so distressed.

"Do you not understand the meaning of 'SOS'? Where the hell have you been? I was sure you'd been killed!" I honestly feel a little warmed by her fear. Maybe I can trust her. Maybe she can explain everything.

"Sorry," I say. "It wasn't safe to talk."

"Is he there? Please tell me you're not anywhere near him." This feels like a major turnaround considering I'm supposed to be killing him.

"No, he's not here." I take a deep breath. "To be honest, Sherri, I'm not sure if I want this job anymore . . ." This is a pretty big admission. I'm testing the waters. I don't tell her that I'm not sure if I want *any* jobs. That's a problem for future me.

"I'm so sorry. This is all my fault." She starts to cry. I'm shocked.

Sherri and I have been through a lot together: murders and missions and midnight chats. She has kept her cool through some extremely hairy situations. I didn't even know she *could* cry. She must really not want me to quit.

"Hey! No. Don't cry. Look: It's a good thing. I think maybe I should just take some time off, try something else for a while." She cries harder, so I try harder to comfort her. "It's okay. We'll still see each other. We can go for drinks anytime."

"I lied to you."

"You—" Fuck. "What?"

"I've lied to you about everything. The agency—it's not some benevolent organization. It's not even an organization. I made it up."

My heart goes cold. "I don't understand."

"It's a forum on the dark web where people order hits. It's called Hire-a-Hitman."

"Please tell me you're joking."

"I wish I were," she says.

"I don't believe it," I say. I am so far from believing that I don't even know where to begin. My brain is trying to convince me that she's lying now. That my life as I knew it *was* real. That this isn't happening. Sherri was my "M." She was smart and brave and *moral*—even when she was instructing me to commit murder. "Why would you ever be on a website called Hire-a-Hitman?" I don't mean to focus on an unimportant detail, but the name is distracting.

"My husband—remember I told you I found out about the agency through him? That was partly true. Roughly seven years ago, he suddenly started making bundles of money. He said it was bonuses at his job, and then investments, but as the years went by, I started to get suspicious. I had a look at his computer when he was at the pub and I found out what he was up to."

"I was going to confront him, but then I thought—I quite like the money. And I'm just as good on a computer as he is, so why not have a go?"

"But . . . what about Andrew?" Andrew was the one who sold me the agency story. He wouldn't have lied to me.

"I knew Andrew from school. He'd been in and out of prison for assault, all sorts. He used to be very troubled. I invited him to meet me, said I had a job he might be interested in. I was going to tell him the truth, but I panicked. I didn't think he'd want to work for a housewife pulling jobs off some dodgy forum. So I made up a whole story, told him I was part of a branch of MI6. I don't even *really* know what MI6 does. I've just seen them on telly. Luckily, Andrew didn't really know either. I never thought I'd convince him until I told him about the money. I even borrowed from my husband and paid him in advance."

"Why?" I ask. "I don't understand why you would want to do this."

"But you *do* understand. That's what I liked about you from the very beginning. From that night we met at that club in Chelsea. You understand what it's like to want something more. Before I met my husband, back when I was a dominatrix, my life was chaotic and exciting. Then I got married and it was like I buried that part of myself. I think I wanted to go back. To feel that powerful, yes, but maybe even to feel imperiled. This job made me feel like I was more than just a wife. Like I was something dangerous."

I feel so fucking stupid. Hearing Sherri spell it out makes me realize how naive I was to ever believe it was real. A benevolent organization that takes out bad guys? I can't even fault Sherri for getting her MI6 information from TV, because I'm pretty sure I bought into this whole assassin thing because I'd watched movies

223

play out this way: with heroes and villains and omnipotent assassins.

"You told me we were killing the bad guys," I say weakly. I trusted her. That was my biggest mistake. To ever trust her or anyone.

"I did independent research to make sure we were only taking the villain hits, but . . . ," she says. "I'm so sorry, Eva. I'm a terrible person. I convinced myself that if it wasn't us, it would be someone else taking the jobs. And you were so good at it, just as good as the men. I think I felt like we were winning somehow."

"You were my only friend," I say before I can stop myself. I'm embarrassed by it.

"I'm so sorry."

The train rattles and I brace myself against the sink. The world steaming by out the window is the same world as before, but it feels different. My stomach is sinking, and it's not just because of what Sherri's told me. It's because of what she hasn't told me. "Why are you telling me this now?"

"Because it's your only chance."

I grip the counter. "My only chance at what?"

"You've been identified as a defector. They think you're an enemy of the organization."

I laugh in surprise. "How can I be an enemy of an organization I didn't even know existed?"

"Because you've failed to kill Jonathan. They think you've been compromised." I want to argue, but she's not wrong. I don't want to kill Jonathan. I want to quit. I kind of *am* a defector, even if I didn't know what I was a part of in the first place.

"What happens to defectors?" I remember what Jonathan told me about Andrew.

"They're terminated," she says.

224

"Fuck." I sit down on the toilet. I don't even put one of those paper things down. "Fucking fuck." What am I going to do?

"Where are you right now?" Sherri asks.

"I'm in a bathroom on the fast train from Barcelona to Paris."

"Why Paris?"

"Because that's where Jonathan is going. *Fuck.*" I have no idea what happens now. A global forum of contract killers wants me dead. I'm going to die. It's so weird.

You would think that, being surrounded by death all the time, I would've contemplated my own mortality, but I'll be real: I've hardly thought about it. When I have, it's been in passing, thinking about how no one would come to my funeral, or how I shouldn't adopt a cat because I'd have no one to leave it to. The important stuff.

The truth is, when you're faced with your impending death, you think about death in a whole new way. I don't want to die, it turns out. I really, really don't.

"Where are you?" I ask Sherri. "Are you okay?"

Her breath hitches in surprise. "Please don't worry about me. I'm the one who got you into this mess."

I am angry at Sherri, but I'm worried about her, too. I am a woman of many contradictions. "I *am* worried about you. You're still my friend. You were also my handler, and it just happens to turn out that you were really fucking bad at that."

She chokes down a chuckle. "Please don't make me laugh."

"We're going to get out of this," I promise, like I have promised before. "You and me. And then we'll meet up for drinks to celebrate. On you."

"Of course," she says. I can tell she feels unworthy. I can tell because I've often felt that way myself. "Don't go to Paris, Eva. You need to run."

"Run where?" I say, and when she doesn't answer, I repeat it. "Run *where*, Sherri?" The agency is a forum on the dark web. The internet is everywhere. I'm fucked. I am totally, wholly fucked. But I can't give up. "What do you know about this forum?"

"Not much. I know that it's existed in some form since the dawn of the internet. It was a place where people could order hits, and it used to be completely unregulated. People paid deposits to criminals, and there was no incentive for them to follow through with the job. It was the Wild West.

"Until the administrator took over. They make sure that the payment is held until the job is completed, for a fee. They make sure everything runs smoothly. There's a cleanup crew and a reconnaissance team and a department for dealing with local and international governments. And there is a strict policy of terminating anyone who doesn't follow the rules."

"Who's the administrator?" If I could track this person down, maybe I could convince them to let me go.

"I don't know. It's the internet; everyone is invisible. Whoever they are, even you wouldn't stand a chance against them. They command dozens of skilled assassins all over Europe." She has a point. Even if I could identify this person, it wouldn't be as if I could just talk sense to them—with or without my Glock. They run a murder-for-hire empire.

I find my face in the cloudy bathroom mirror. It looks deader than normal: pale, haunted. The train rattles around me, hurtling toward my destiny. Always forward, no matter what happens. Never look back.

I take a deep breath. I remind myself that I have been fucked before. I have been in situations with no way out. I got out. I can do things other people can't do. I can do *this*.

I need a plan—that's all I need. I'm used to making plans on the fly. The secret is to play to your strengths, and I know mine: I'm really, really good at killing people.

I set my jaw. "What if I don't run?"

"You have to run."

"What if I face Jonathan? What if I kill him? Won't that prove I was never compromised?"

"I'm not sure . . ."

The train seems to be moving faster, steaming toward the inevitable conclusion. It's a day like any other, so someone has to die.

"I don't really have a choice, do I? I have to face him. I have to kill him."

51

Jonathan

I AM FLYING PAST BOURGES WHEN A COP APPEARS IN MY REAR-view mirror. He is driving fast. I am also driving fast. Shit.

I slow down. He slows down. And turns on his sirens. Shit.

Perhaps surprisingly, police are something I rarely deal with in my line of work. I am not a fan of cops. A detention center will do that to a person.

I pull over to the side of the road in the scenic French countryside. I keep my hands where the cop can see them, on the wheel. I stare straight ahead. I have a gun strapped to my torso and a knife on my belt but nothing exotic.

The cop takes his time getting out of his car, then takes his time walking over. He is a cop; cops can do whatever the fuck they want. They make contract killers look tame.

I roll down my window. "Good afternoon," I say in French. "Sir."

"Good afternoon," he says in English. They always know when you are American. It is a gift God gave the Europeans. "Do you know how fast you were going?"

"Yes." The question is, does he?

"Three hundred and fifty kilometers per hour." He does.

"How much?" I motion for my jacket pocket, where my wallet is. I am not trying to bribe him. In France, you pay speeding fines on the spot.

"No." He wiggles his finger. "I need your *license*."

French cops are also able to confiscate your license on the spot. Your vehicle is towed at your expense. Shit.

If this were a movie, I would kill him, then drive off in his car and never hear from him again. But there is one class of people I do not fuck with. When you play with cops, you lose every time.

"Of course." I grit my teeth and hand him one of my licenses. He steps back and allows me to get out of the driver's seat. Looks like I am taking another train.

But first, we have to wait for a tow truck. Everything takes so long. This is Europe, a place where it is easy to fall into the cracks between things, to wait for so long that you forget what you are waiting for.

I sit in the passenger seat of my rental car and worry my hands until they ache.

In my life, I never stop. Like a shark, I keep moving. I never think about what drives me.

But right now, on the side of the road outside a picturesque French village, I realize I am terrified. I have been killing people for almost seven years, ever since I got out of prison, and I have never revealed Mas's identity to anyone.

I do not have friends. I do not have relationships. I find that I am mostly afraid of people, perhaps ironically. I am afraid of what they might do to me.

Eva said I kill people as a way of killing myself, and she is partly right. It keeps me separate. It keeps me locked in my trauma, but there is more to it than that.

I do not trust anyone. I think everyone is out to get me. I

think that way all the time. I was a child of abuse and then I was a child in prison, and as much as I might try to look normal, to look *good*, even—rich and flash and in control—on the inside I am fucking terrified.

Not just for myself but for Mas. Always for Mas.

I did not lie to Eva about everything that first night on the train. I did grow up in upstate New York, on a different planet—it sometimes seems—than the one we are on now.

We had locks on our bedroom doors—not on the inside but on the outside, to keep us in. That was one of my first memories, of not being able to get out, for hours and hours and hours. That was how it started.

My father would leave us locked in our bedrooms, and then, seemingly at random, we would be let out into the rest of the house. It was like an amusement park by comparison. With a TV and a recliner chair and a refrigerator. Mas and I would go crazy.

Sometimes we would be allowed in the yard, or in the woods. We would swim in the lake for hours, screaming, delirious with freedom. But we just looked dirty and wild and badly behaved.

I think at first Mas and I were just an inconvenience. I assume our mother, at least, had wanted children pretty badly. She had adopted Mas; she had gotten pregnant and kept the baby. But then she had died, and my father did not want us.

I do not know when exactly it changed—if it was upon her death or after or before. I do not know how it changed. I do not know why he kept us at all. He used to act like we were the problem, like he was heroic for taking care of us.

"You're lucky you have me," he would say all the time, with the edge of a threat.

He would lock us in our rooms. He would starve us and then be annoyed at how thin we were, how unhealthy we looked, how naughty we were.

He locked the fridge because we kept eating food.

He stopped letting us out because the neighbors were talking.

He would scream at us, all the time, "Why are you doing this? Why are you like this?" When we did perfectly normal child things, he acted like we were monsters.

Then he started hitting us. He slapped Mas across the face for crying and then he demanded, "Why did you make me do that?" Over and over, pleading, distressed, wild with it. Like it was Mas's fault.

He did it again and again and again. So much that I started to suspect some perverse part of him enjoyed it. The hurt, the guilt, the blame. He would jump up and down when we were too loud, or too sick, or too whiny. "Do you want me to get the belt?" He would practically beg us. "I want you to count. I want to hear you say it out loud."

When I got older, I started to fight back, to protect myself, to protect Mas. That was when it got messy, because I started to lose sight of who the real bad guy was. Was I bad because he was punishing me, or was he punishing me because I was bad?

It was always presented as being my fault. As something he *had* to do. And I believed it. I still believe it, for myself. But not for Mas. Never for Mas. I might have deserved it, but he never did.

School complicated things for our father, but not as much as you would hope. It was easy for people to just say that we were wild kids. "They live out in the middle of nowhere," our teachers would say to one another. "You just have to put up with them."

I would get into fights—perhaps unsurprisingly—all the time. I honestly loved fighting. The only time I felt good or in control was when I was completely out of control. The consequences of these fights seemed so tame compared to the consequences at home. *You have detention. You have Saturday school. You have to think about what you did.*

Saturday school was my favorite activity, especially when Mas was there with me, because then I knew he was safe, too.

Saturday school was also where Mas befriended the teacher who got us out. It took months to arrange. There were moments when it seemed like it would not happen—when our dad got suspicious and threatened to move, when he stopped letting us go to Saturday school—but the teacher did not give up.

And then it was the night before we were supposed to escape. We would take the bus to school the next morning and we would go home with the state. Our dad did not know. We just had to make it through one more night.

All day I was petrified. I was so scared to leave. So scared that I was the problem and that wherever I went, wherever someone took me, I would turn those people against me, too.

But Mas comforted me; he explained to me that it was not my fault. That our dad was an evil person, that every bad thing I thought about myself came from him.

"Once he's gone, we'll be okay," he said. "Once he's gone, we'll be like everyone else."

But he would not really be gone.

"What if he won't let us go?" I asked. "What if he comes and gets us?"

"He won't," Mas said, but I knew he was as worried as I was. The teacher who was helping us had told us that nothing was guaranteed.

"He might try to get you back," she had warned us. "But we'll keep fighting."

I could not let that happen, not to Mas. That was how I justified it.

That last night, I kept waiting for something bad to happen. I kept waiting for my dad to do something horrible so that I could retaliate. But he never did. We watched TV together like a normal family, and then we went to bed. He even forgot to lock us in our bedrooms. His mistake.

At around two in the morning, I left my room. I got my dad's belt. I used it to strangle him to death.

I did it for Mas. It drove me crazy that my father hurt Mas—beyond crazy. It drove me as far as I could go, which it turned out was pretty far. Further than anyone else I knew.

I went to school the next morning sincerely believing that there would be no consequences. My dad was a bad person. I took care of him. I saved my brother.

Of course, the body was found. I did not even try to hide it. I just assumed no one would ever look for it. I was not a professional back then. I left DNA and other evidence. I was naive enough to think that if I acted like a god, then I was one.

I was not.

I pled guilty to a lesser charge. Mas and I were separated. I was put in a detention center. Mas was placed with a good family. He became a doctor. I became an assassin. I kill people. He brings them back to life.

And now I have put him in danger again.

I have to get to Paris as fast as I can. I try to focus on the present—on the beautiful landscape and my nice clothes and my will to kill—but instead I find myself sinking into my past while I am waiting for the tow truck, while I am waiting for the cab, while I am trying to appear normal, while I am trying to appear nice. I am trapped, and the only way out is to fight.

The only way out is to kill.

52

Eva

AS SOON AS I GET TO PARIS, I GET A CAB TO LES PUCES. I'M
sure Jonathan will go to his sibling first. Once he sees that
they're untouched, he'll know to come here, to the place
where he searched for me. We've had a date here since day one.

I could probably track down Jonathan's sibling pretty easily.
They're an American in Paris. More specifically, an American
doctor. They probably live somewhere trendy. They probably
know how to dress. I could find them. I could try to use them as
leverage, but it's not what I want. I want a fair fight. Me and Jonathan and the market.

I stake out locations. I search for the perfect place to murder
him. I'll know it when I see it.

Then I see it: an antique-weaponry shop tucked behind a
wrought iron spiral staircase inside a two-story market hall.

There are a few shops and stalls that sell antique weaponry,
but this one has the best selection. It also has a broken window.
The pane has been replaced with fairly new reinforced metal.
Jonathan said he got that rapier in Les Puces. He wouldn't want
to leave a paper trail.

I hang around the shop for a while, pretending I'm interested in a sword, a cannonball. I actually *am* interested, but not in buying them. I'm interested in using them tonight.

I don't want to hang around too long, in case I look suspicious, so I break for lunch and then wander around other parts of the market. You can get amazing vintage pieces here. I find this gorgeous Dior bag, but of course it's the right bag at the wrong time. I'll come back tomorrow, if I'm still alive.

No lie: I'm pretty nervous. Jonathan has a way higher kill number than I do. He's physically stronger and definitely darker and possibly even more fucked-up. I don't want to kill him, but I also really don't want to die.

I pass by a psychic. I wasn't lying when I told Jonathan that I had my palm read all the time, even though my readings were always wrong. I mean, who wants an accurate psychic? There's something safe about being misunderstood.

I step into the psychic's office. It's fairly sparse, but there are limp nods to other realms: evil eyes, crystals, tarot cards.

The psychic is dressed in scrubs, ready to operate.

"Hello," I say in French. "Do you have time to read my fortune?"

"Yes," she says back in English. "Sit down."

She gestures to a repurposed card table. I sit on a squeaky chair. My heart is racing. It's been racing all day. I'm nervous—and slightly giddy at the prospect of seeing Jonathan again, even under these objectively terrible circumstances. It's all very confusing, to be honest. I don't expect the psychic to help, but I do feel better just having something silly to distract me.

The psychic takes the chair across from me. She pulls a stack of tarot cards from her front pocket.

"I want to know if—," I start.

She holds up a hand. "I know." I smile. Oh, she's *good*.

She shuffles her cards, then arranges them in a pattern facing down. She pulls the first card: death.

I gasp.

She looks concerned. "It doesn't always mean physical death," she notes. "It might mean spiritual. Or ego death."

"With me, it's probably physical."

She turns over cards. She doesn't explain them right away. "We have to see how they fit together."

Once she has pulled them all, she stares at them. She moves her eyes from one card to the next, trying to divine conclusions. I feel like I've stumped her.

"It's okay if it's too hard," I say. "Maybe I have no future."

I try to keep my voice light, but I'm definitely feeling like this was a bad idea. I thought it might be funny to listen to some psychic tell me a windfall is coming my way. Ridiculous shit like that. It kind of stopped being fun when she pulled the death card.

She startles at nothing, then meets my eyes. "You are in a very dangerous position," she says. Accurate.

I wriggle in my seat.

"You will have to make a choice that has deadly consequences." Also true.

"What should I do?" I ask.

She narrows her eyes at me, like she blames me for something. "Stop guarding your heart." Ugh. I hate that for me.

"Really?"

She starts to put her cards away. I think she seriously doesn't like me. She's taking my fortune back instead of giving it out. "If you want to win at this game, you need to open your heart."

I mean, God.

Way to fuck with my head before a kill.

53

Jonathan

I STRAIGHTEN MY JACKET AS I WAIT IN THE HALL. THE SLEEVES are dusty from the rural train station. I smell lightly of sweat and other people.

Giselle answers the door. She is very pregnant and very unhappy to see me. I am so relieved that she is alive that I almost hug her.

I stop myself, but she still puts up a hand. "What are you doing?"

"I'm just so pleased to see you," I say.

She rolls her eyes, then yells, "*Mas!*" down the hall. She glares at me. "You better not upset him," she says.

"I—" I am about to say I will not, but what planet am I living on? Instead, I say, "I'm glad he has you," which registers concern on her face.

Mas comes out of the living room and hurries toward us.

Giselle seems relieved to escape. "He's scaring me already." She waves in my direction as she passes down the hall and disappears into the living room.

"Ethan." My brother's lips form a hard line. He steps into the doorway, clearly to keep me out. "What are you doing here?"

I am honestly surprised there is no sign of Eva, or of anyone else. She is smart. I am sure she could have tracked him down. I wonder if I am being set up. I worry that this is a trap. That she is waiting to destroy everything I love.

"What are you looking for?" Mas asks as I scan the hallway. "And again, why are you here?"

"I fucked up," I say.

Mas checks that Giselle is out of earshot. He leans forward and lowers his voice. "More than normal?"

"Remember that girl I told you about, from the train?" I ask. I see him tighten everywhere. "She's been assigned to kill me."

"Oh. Okay . . . Weird."

"We've been getting close—obviously part of her plan." I feel stupid now that I know the truth. But I also wish that I did not know the truth. "And I've been, you know, telling her my deepest, darkest secrets. Like people in relationships do, right?"

"I'm not sure that's exactly what people in relationships do, but okay." He leans into the doorframe.

"I didn't tell her everything, but I told her enough to figure out there was a you. And maybe even where you are."

He sighs his big sigh. "What does that mean, Ethan?"

"It means I need to stay here and protect you until the threat is gone." I do not tell him that it might never be gone. "I can get an apartment in the building. You won't even notice me."

He backs away a little. "No. Absolutely not."

"I'm sorry. But I have to."

"No. You don't *have* to, Ethan. That is something you never really got. You don't have to protect me. You don't have to do anything *for* me."

He is still pissed that I killed our dad. To be fair, it was a huge mistake. We were supposed to get out together. We were supposed to stay together, change our lives together. To overcome our past *together*.

I fucked it up.

"That's a real no, Ethan," he continues. "I don't want you waiting in the wings. We don't want a personal Batman."

"I need to protect you."

"I'm not an excuse for your behavior." He gently directs me backward, into the hall. "I don't care if we're in danger. If I am on *fire*, I do not need you to piss on me or kill the arsonist."

He starts to close the door.

"You know, Mas, I—"

He pauses.

"I love you."

Mas shakes his head. "I know. But your love keeps blowing up my life."

54

I CANNOT BELIEVE EVA DID NOT FIND MAS. MAYBE SHE REALLY does want to play fair, with everything except my heart.

I have considered the alternatives to killing her, and I mean *all* of them.

I have considered that we could be together. Team up against the people trying to take us down. But even if I want to, even if I *can* get over all my fucked-up modes of thinking, I will never know if she truly wants me. I will never know what she is thinking. I have been wrong about her all this time, from the beginning.

She could slit my throat on our honeymoon. Relationships are hard enough without having to worry about whether your partner is trying to kill you.

The truth is, I cannot imagine a world where I am not a killer. No one retires from this job. You end up in jail or in a body bag.

I do not know all the details of who I work for, but I know there is a reason I have never been caught, and it is not just that I am fast and clean. Nobody is that good all the time. These people have power. These people own me and a hell of a lot of other people.

I cannot imagine they would let me go. I cannot imagine they would let her go.

The world is too small for us to ever live in it.

I have no choice. She has no choice.

I walk to Les Puces. I know she will be there. It is like we had this meeting arranged from the very beginning. I just went too soon, and now I am late.

The market creeps up on me with the darkness of nightfall. The street vendors have left. The market stalls are shut, locked and lightless.

The whole city echoes with regret.

I wind through the wreckage.

I know exactly where to find her. The cage is pulled down when I arrive, so I can see her in pieces: one eye, dark hair, white sneaker.

This is it.

The less I think about it, the better. I need to block everything out. Think only of these three things:

Her heart.

Her breath.

Her arteries.

IX

MURDER

55

Eva

EVEN THOUGH I KNOW HE'S COMING, I JUMP BACK WHEN HE walks through the door. Like a phantom. Like a vampire. Like Death has been chasing me across Europe.

People believe love is fated, but what if death is fated, too? What if he's my soul mate and my death mate?

I took all the best weapons. Unfortunately, the antique guns didn't come equipped with antique bullets. If they did, I could blow him out the door right now.

I've disabled every camera. Not just in this shop but in the entire market hall, except for a tricky one above the twisted staircase on the south side. He's lucky I think of these things.

He observes my weapons: a sword and a shield, and a backup blade around my waist. He considers his own choices, mounted on the wall, hanging over our heads.

"You didn't bring the rapier I gave you," he says. "I wanted you to have it."

"In the hypothalamus," I joke.

It might seem like an odd time to make jokes. After all, within the hour one of us is going to be dead. But I'll let you in on a little secret: Laughter is a weapon. Whether you're fighting off sadness or anger or a deadly assassin.

Jonathan pulls a machete from a wall, tests its weight. It looks pretty rusty.

"I'm not sure if my tetanus is up to date," I point out.

"If you die of tetanus, it still counts. A kill is a kill," he says, but he puts the machete back on the wall.

"Anyway, that rapier was so not my style," I say. "It was *your* style."

"What does that mean?" He tries a sword with jeweled inlays. Seriously.

"It was a little pretentious," I say. "In fact, all of this is a little pretentious." I gesture to the walls around us. "Antique weaponry? Give me a Glock any day of the week."

"Well, when you do this job for as long as I have—"

"Oh, here we go."

He cocks his head. "What?"

"How old are you? You've got to be early thirties tops. And you were in prison until you were at least eighteen—"

"Twenty-five," he corrects. Damn. How exactly did he kill his father?

"I've been an assassin for over three years," I say. "You haven't been doing this that much longer than me."

He finally settles on a sword. It matches his shirt. I'm not even kidding. Style will be the death of him. Tonight.

"I'm sorry my pretentiousness so offends you."

"You don't need to apologize for anything. I'm going to murder you. Problem solved."

He smirks. "Don't make me laugh, or I won't want to kill you."

My throat catches. "Do you want to kill me?"

He looks me dead in the eyes, like he did on the train, like he did in bed, like he did the last time we fought. "No. But I'm going to. Do you believe me?"

"Yes."

"Good."

We cross swords. We fence. Right away it feels different from the fight in the hotel room. Jonathan is not fucking around. Not only is he planning to kill me, but he plans on doing it fast.

I start with the upper hand. I spent time on recon. I learned the space. I chose the best spot, with higher ground and room to move. Jonathan immediately tries to get me out of this spot, to drive me into a corner. I suspected he would do this, and I used those suspicions to my advantage.

I set up a trap. An antique cannon on a high shelf. When he drives me into the corner, all I have to do is hit the wall and the cannonball will fall, shattering his shoulder.

I just have to be careful not to make the setup too obvious. I have to fight back, to resist just enough to make him feel comfortable, to make him feel safe, and then . . .

He thrusts me into the corner, not realizing I allowed him to thrust me into the corner.

I hesitate. I feel my reluctance, a split second of regret. The problem is, I like his shoulder. I've buried my head there before, and it would be a little gruesome to see it shattered by a cannonball.

The cannonball drops. It does hit him, but not squarely enough to do major damage.

He gives me a look. "That was a trap," he says.

"Or an act of God."

He drives me into another corner. He lunges. I parry. Then he surprises me: He throws his sword at the display wall. Weapons rain down over our heads. I go for cover, ducking under a shelf. He runs out of the shop.

I wait until the dust has settled, and then I follow him.

He is waiting for me with another sword in the aisle of the market.

"It was getting hot in there." He is lightly sweating.

He draws his sword. I draw mine. We fence, now with a lot more room to maneuver.

"You know," I say, "fencing is really not my thing."

"Are you seriously trying to suggest that I have the upper hand?" he asks. "You chose the weapons and the location. You could've had your Glock. You could've blown me to pieces." He's right and he's not right. I could've tried to shoot him when he walked through the door. He has his gun, too. This could've been a gunfight. But I didn't want it to be. I didn't want it to end that fast. "You could have used my brother," he says, and his breath hitches, his eyes lock on mine and I can see how grateful he is that I didn't.

"I want to play fair," I say.

"We can't play fair," he says. "Fair is: Everyone gets out alive. The longer we delay this, the harder it gets."

"I know."

"Someone has to pull the trigger, metaphorically speaking."

"I know."

He flies into a driving attack, forcing me back through the market hall until we almost reach the twisted staircase.

"Stay away from that staircase," I say.

He pauses his attack. I take the opportunity to riposte. "Why?"

"I didn't disable that camera," I say. "I couldn't reach it."

He gives me a look, then holds up a finger. There is a shop selling Venetian masks just beside him, and he walks over to it. He neatly cracks the window with the pommel of his sword and extracts a mask. He removes his glasses and tucks them into his pocket. He puts the mask over his face and jogs casually up the stairs until he is just beneath the camera. Then he jumps up and smashes it.

He lifts the mask off his face and casually travels back down.

"God, you're such a show-off," I say.

"You could have said thank you." His breath is pounding. He is standing at the bottom of the stairs with the mask now on top of his head and he looks so beautiful, like some kind of angel of death. I can't stop looking, and he can't stop looking back, and it's like something turns over inside us both.

"Eva?" he says.

"What?" My head feels oddly light.

"I'm sorry, but I'm going to kill you now."

"I'd like to see"—he stabs me beneath the shoulder, with frightening precision—"you . . ." I stagger back. Blood is pumping, pretty quickly, down my side. Pumping is not good. "You *asshole*."

His face is pale, but his voice is perfectly, chillingly calm. "You probably know this, but that is your brachial artery. If you keep fighting, you'll bleed out faster." Pumping means artery.

"Fuck." What did I think was going to happen? He told me he was going to kill me, several times. I acted like it was foreplay.

"If you don't get immediate medical attention," he continues, "you'll bleed out slowly. I would estimate that you have approximately twenty minutes to live."

"You fucking asshole." I feel lightheaded, and I'm pretty sure it's not because I love him.

He reaches into his jacket and pulls out a loaded syringe. "I brought this. I don't want you to suffer."

"You're so thoughtful." My voice sounds weird. The whole world is pumping with my blood.

"It's how I would want to die." His eyes are filled with genuine concern. He is genuinely insane. "You won't feel any pain."

"I can't believe you killed me." I feel my knees start to give out, not from loss of blood—not yet—but from shock. Maybe I could save myself if I called an ambulance, but he could stop me. He's standing right in front of me now, perfectly intact.

"Try to focus," he says. The audacity. "Do you want me to administer it?"

"Killing me once wasn't enough?"

He flinches, like he's the one hurt. Like he's the one dying.

I try to tear my sleeve to make a tourniquet.

"You shouldn't do that," he says. "You'll just prolong your suffering." And his. He looks miserable. I actually feel bad for him. Not that bad.

"Give it to me," I say.

"What?"

I put out my hand. "The needle. I know how to inject myself."

He seems to understand that this is the honorable way to go. He won't even have to feel bad for killing me; I'll have killed myself. He moves to hand me the syringe, then hesitates, like he doesn't trust *me*.

"Killing me is one thing, but I draw the line at torture," I say. Still he hesitates. "Do you know how many times I could have murdered you but didn't? You really think I'll bother now? I have better things to do with the last nineteen minutes of my life."

He sighs, then tosses me the syringe.

I catch it in the air. I lunge. I swing my sword wildly to distract him, then jam the needle into his jugular vein. It's extremely dangerous to inject a needle into the neck, but if he dies, he dies.

"Shit!" He jumps back, grabbing his neck. He looks at me in shock.

"I would apologize"—I grit my teeth—"but I'm not sorry. You killed me first." I didn't inject everything. I don't want him dead.

I just want *me* alive. But it's hard to guess how much to administer when I don't even know what's in the needle.

"I don't . . ." His eyelids start to flutter. His chin drops.

I slap him. *"Try to focus,"* I tease. "Now, where is your brother?"

"He's close . . ." His voice is faint, far away. I may have given him too much.

I search his pockets until I find his phone. I force it into his hands. "Call him. Tell him to come *now*."

He dials, squinting at his phone. "Mas, I need you to come *now*." He repeats my words, slightly slurring. His brother seems to protest. "It's not for me. It's for my girlfriend." He just called me his girlfriend. What in the headfuck? He tells Mas where we are and what we'll need, then ends the call. "He's coming."

"Can he fix this?"

"He was an army surgeon. Yeah, he can fix this." He seems relieved, even though he's the one who finally pulled the trigger.

"Good." We need to get to the street. I need to keep Jonathan awake. If I lose him, I don't think his brother will save me. "How far away is he?"

"Seven minutes, but Mas drives fast."

"I guess it runs in the family."

Jonathan starts toward the street, fighting the drugs. He seems to realize that if he passes out, I can kill him before he wakes up. I have him, and he has me. We need to stay alive for seven minutes.

He leads me to a street corner. "It's probably better if we don't move," he says, and then he collapses onto the curb, barely catching himself on a streetlamp. So dramatic. I mean, I'm the one bleeding to death. He's just high.

He fishes sloppily through his pockets as I sit down beside him.

My wound seems to be bleeding faster now. I can feel it with every pump of my heart, my blood leaving, my life leaving. I thought dying would hurt more. All in all, this isn't a bad way to go. At least I'm not alone. If I could choose anyone to die with, ironically, it would be him. The guy who killed me.

Jonathan finds what he's looking for, then leans over me and examines my wound.

"May I?" he says.

"You think I trust you after this?" I ask. I try to move away but his eyes stay locked on mine, keep me trapped in place.

"I know you do," he says. He opens up his hand and reveals a pair of forceps.

"Oh, you have got to be kidding me," I say.

"It's not what you think," he says. "I'm really good at making tourniquets. I've done this before. Many times."

"Is that another brag?"

He tears a strip of fabric from his shirt. "Please?" he says.

I sigh. "Fine."

I watch as he loops the fabric around my arm and the forceps. Once he has tightened the knot, he twists the forceps, pulling the tourniquet tighter and tighter, until the bleeding seems to stop. He clips the forceps to the fabric to secure it.

"Neat trick," I say.

I can tell he wants to brag again, but he says nothing. I appreciate that even more than the tourniquet.

"I still can't believe you killed me," I say. "For someone who claims to be so miserable, you sure seem to want to live. *Hey!*" He lists sideways and I grab him, shake him back awake. "Don't fall asleep." I need to keep him awake, and this could be the last time we ever talk. So I might as well tell him the truth. "You know, I really like you."

"Hmm," he says, either doubtful or on the verge of passing out.

"Do you like me?"

"I love you," he corrects, and then he lets his head drop onto my good shoulder. He nuzzles his nose into my neck. His breath is warm against my skin. "That's why I had to kill you." His voice sounds far away, and I'm not sure if it's because I'm dying or because he is.

"I get it," I say. I do. I understand. There's a thin line between love and murder.

I stare out into the hazy, graying streets. The buildings seem to throb with my blood, like the whole world is bleeding out, losing all its chaos and color and meaning. The only thing that stays, the only thing that lasts, is my ever-pumping heart.

"It's scary," I say. "It's not even that you're afraid of getting hurt. You're afraid of hurting someone else. And you know that you will. That you're dangerous. A killer. And the ones you love are the ones you hurt the most."

His body sags against mine. His breath is so shallow, I'm not even sure he's breathing anymore.

Only then, in the quiet between the fights, between the passion and the arguments, in those moments when we are holding our breath, do I realize how much I could lose if I lose him. I didn't think that I would ever find someone like him. Someone I didn't have to make myself smaller for, or sweeter for, or more normal for.

I have been apologizing for myself all my life, and I finally found the one person I don't have to apologize to and I was willing to kill him—for what? Survival? What the fuck is the point of surviving if I'm not even living?

I've been alone for so long that I thought that was the only option. I was sure there was no one in the world who could really love me, who I could love. I've been living without hope for so long that I couldn't even recognize it in him.

"Wake up, buddy." I nudge him, softly and then harder. "Come on. Jonathan." He falls onto my lap. My blood seeps into his hair. "I love you, too," I tell him.

I don't know if he hears it, but I hear it.

I don't remember anything after that, except Paris. The old gray buildings and the misty yellow lights and the cobblestone streets. I remember them.

56

Jonathan

MAS IS NOT HAPPY WITH ME.

I am in the waiting room. Mas shot me up with Narcan as soon as he picked us up, so I am out of the woods now. Eva is in surgery.

She said she loved me. I said I loved her. We tried to kill each other, but that seems less important.

I never thought I would meet someone. In fact, I would say I actively worked against it. I am so fucked-up that I never thought I could hope to find someone who understood me, but she does. I understand her, too, and that is worth something.

I jump the moment Mas comes in. "Is she okay?" I ask.

He shakes his head at me. "Not yet, but she will be."

I hug him. He is taken aback.

"What the hell happened?" he says.

"I told you—she's a trained assassin; she was assigned to kill me." She is still assigned to kill me, but I have not dealt with that yet. All the minor details will have to work themselves out. "But I don't want to hurt her. Again."

"Right. Well. You two need to have some kind of talk or

something. Maybe several different ones." He pinches the bridge of his nose. "In fact, we need to have a talk." He gestures me toward a chair.

I sit. I keep my mouth shut. Mas and I have needed to have a talk for years, but one of us was always avoiding it.

He takes the seat across from me and fixes his eyes above my head. "Do you know why I joined the army?"

"Because you're a saint." I am not joking.

"Yes. But also because I didn't know what to do with myself. I didn't know how to exist in the world. How to be like everyone else. A little like you, I imagine?"

I nod, not wanting to interrupt.

"But that's not the only reason. I wanted to understand you better. You were still in jail; we weren't talking."

"I was talking," I have to clarify. I sent him letters all the time. I had no one else to send letters to.

"The less said about those letters, the better," he says. I will admit, those letters were a little disturbing. I was a minor in prison for murder, pleaded down to voluntary manslaughter. I had grandiose delusions that I did it all for Mas. I had to kill our father so he could never hurt Mas again. It was maybe a little less than charming after a while.

He takes a deep breath. "I thought joining the army would help me understand why you were different. But you know what I learned? You're not different. Everyone is exactly like you. Everyone can do what you do. I don't mean just soldiers. I mean civilians. Children.

"Our father put you in survival mode and you never left it. You never turned it off. You're trapped there, always thinking something terrible is around the corner." He sighs. "You need therapy. *Intensive* therapy. With the right therapist this time."

I know he is right, but I have never admitted to him what I am

256

about to admit: "I don't want to be fixed." I swallow hard. "I might need it." That is the problem, the principal issue. I do not want to be cured. I might need my darkness. I might need my fear. I might need my trauma to protect my life.

And the truth of the matter is, right now, I *do* need it. I am up to my eyes in a network that kills. I am in danger all the time. Better to be sick than to be dead.

"I know," Mas says.

His understanding makes me feel so much better. For years I wanted Mas to believe I did not have a choice in the matter, that my urge to kill was beyond my control, because the truth was so much worse: I chose it. I chose not to repair myself. I chose not to get fixed. When given the choice between a future and a murder, I chose murder every time.

"But you can't have a life like that," Mas says, laying it out exactly right. "Do you think she's gonna put up with it?" He nudges his thumb toward the exam room, toward Eva.

"We're the same."

He thinks it over. "That sounds dangerous."

57

Eva

WHEN JONATHAN COMES IN, I'M ON THE HOSPITAL BED, attached to a morphine drip that works at the press of a button. I haven't pressed it once. At this point I know better than to take my hands off the wheel.

"How are you feeling?" he asks.

"Alive. You?"

"Slightly less than that," he says. I'm actually a little pissed that he's relatively unscathed. He probably has a nice buzz. I have stitches.

"Thanks for not taking out a nerve," I say.

"Right back at you." He rubs his bruising neck.

I sigh, scanning the trendy hospital room. "No offense to your brother, but I have to get out of here."

I hate hospitals. I mean, *everyone* does, but a hospital is the first place I landed after my parents died. I had medical treatment while the police waited outside to interview me. After that, my life was never the same.

"I have a room at the Ritz," he says carefully. "I can book another. I'm sure you don't want to share a room after what I did."

"It's fine," I say. I can practically see his heart catch in his throat. "I might need you. I might pop a stitch or something."

"I have a fully stocked first aid kit."

"Of course you do. Your brother said no sex." He didn't, but it's funny.

"We'll have to get a second opinion."

I laugh. I shake my head, and then suddenly I'm overwhelmed with sadness. It's like the sadness that has been chasing me my whole life catches up with me all at once. Dying will do that to a person. Because I did actually die.

Mas was there when I woke up. He walked me through everything.

"I didn't tell Ethan this—God knows he's dramatic enough—but you flatlined," Mas said. "You were dead. I brought you back."

"Did you have to?" I joked.

He made a face. "Oh my God. You're perfect for each other."

It was bravado; I'm sure Mas knew that. I didn't have a near-death experience. I didn't see the light. Not that I should be surprised. Odds are, Heaven is not where I'll land. But all this time—through every reckless, silly, stupid thing I've done—I've never really believed I could die. Death is scary. Even scarier than living, it turns out.

Jonathan gets down on his knees beside the bed. He clasps my hand. "I want you to know that I meant what I said. I love you. I promise I will never hurt you again." Even if he's not still trying to kill me, that seems pretty unlikely.

I'm so sad that I can't even laugh. I can't even force a smile. "This is never going to work, is it?"

"I think both of us just need to stop," he says. "Stop jumping to conclusions. Stop thinking three steps ahead."

"Easier said than done."

"I know." He kisses my knuckle. Then my palm. "But I trust you."

"You better. Mas told me your real name."

"What's yours?"

"Annika."

He kisses my pinkie knuckle. "It's so pretty."

"I know. Never say it again."

"Right back at you," he says to me.

58

Jonathan

PARIS WAS MADE FOR THE NIGHT. DURING THE DAY IT IS washed out, almost shy, embarrassed by its own gaudiness. But at night it is confident, full of shadows and secrets, piss-soaked cobblestones, uneven footing and spilled red wine, and someone, somewhere, is always playing the saddest song you have ever heard.

Eva and I are walking to our hotel. Mas gave her scrubs to wear. He offered to drive us to the hotel, but we both wanted the walk. We wanted to be in the world again.

She catches me up on everything that happened with her and her handler and the network. They want her dead because she did not kill me. I cannot blame her for wanting to kill me to live.

I can tell she is shaken. I am, too. I tried to kill her. If it were not for her quick thinking, she would be dead.

"I truly am sorry," I say again.

"Will you please stop apologizing?" she says.

"I just want you to know that—"

"Please." She puts a hand up. "It's irritating. You tried to kill me. I tried to kill you—"

"To save yourself."

She cocks her head. "I'm not talking about tonight. I tried to shoot you in the head. And stab you in the heart. Two days ago." She makes a face. "It's kind of concerning that it's so easy for you to forget."

She is right. She did try to kill me. I feel better.

I lace my fingers in her good hand. Her skin is a few degrees colder than before. It will take days for her body to warm up again. Bleeding out will do that to a person.

She smells like blood. Not just hers but someone else's. Significant blood transfusions, like the one she just had, change the way a person smells. Forever.

It scares me how close she was to death. How close I brought her to it. She was right. I am not afraid of getting hurt. I am afraid of hurting her.

I feel this need to protect her from me. I do not know how to be the killer and the lover, but I am going to try. I am going to try for her.

We turn down a dark alley. Neither of us is prepared. Neither of us sees them coming. That is the dangerous thing about falling in love.

59

Eva

THEY'RE ARMED WITH GLOCKS, WHICH I APPRECIATE. NO CHEESY antique weapons here. There are three of them. We don't have the time to ask who sent them.

It doesn't really matter, I guess. They didn't come to talk.

One shoots Jonathan in the arm. Another aims at me but Jonathan charges him, so quickly and so ferociously that the man falls back—I'm guessing he's heard of Jonathan. A reputation can be a weapon.

Jonathan pulls his gun and blows the man's brains out right there in the street. That kind of decisive action tends to end a party quickly.

Most of the time in this job, hesitation is what kills you. If you're the kind of person who can stick to their guns—metaphorically speaking—you've won half the battle.

Jonathan tosses me the man's Glock as the other two men try to find cover.

I shoot one in the back. The third man runs.

"You let him go!" I say to Jonathan. I meant it as a joke, but I should have known better. Jonathan takes off after him.

They disappear down another alleyway. I hear the crack of a gunshot.

It's kind of funny, actually, how quickly we end this assassination attempt. These poor guys probably planned this; they probably took time strategizing and encouraging each other, and now they are all dying in the street.

I meet Jonathan in the alley next to the third body.

"Do you want his gun instead?" he asks. "I don't think he ever took a shot."

"Sure," I say, making the trade.

"We should probably leave Paris, just to be safe," Jonathan says. "We don't have a cleanup crew on this one." He's right. We need to run. We need to hide. At least until we're feeling better. Until we have some kind of plan. We can't just keep thwarting public assassination attempts.

Jonathan is examining his arm. I forgot they shot him. I watch in fascination and horror as he removes a bullet fragment from his deltoid.

"Ouch," I say. "Wait—they shot you."

"I am aware," he says, gritting his teeth as he removes another fragment.

"I mean, you and not me. I'm the defector."

He looks up. "You're right."

"If they think we've joined up, they're gonna bring out the big guns, aren't they?"

"Probably." He doesn't look impressed by their first attempt.

I scan the alleyway, expecting more assassins, but Paris is quiet. "Why don't they just let us go?" I ask. I know it's kind of a naive question, but it seems wasteful to go after us. "I mean, wouldn't it be easier for everyone to just part ways amicably?"

"They're afraid of us," Jonathan says. "Because they can't control us."

"What do we do now?" I can barely think straight. So much has happened in the past twenty-four hours. I told Jonathan I loved him. I died. I killed someone. It's been kind of a lot.

I want to go back to the hotel and take a bath, like I do after any other job. Only this isn't a job anymore. This is my life now.

Jonathan takes my hand and starts toward a busy street, probably thinking we're safer with an audience. "Have you ever been to the Cotswolds? Charming piece of English countryside: woodlands, stone walls, thatched-roof cottages."

"Sounds lovely."

"My handler lives out there. We need to find out everything we can about the network." As Jonathan speaks, he bunches the sleeves of his shirt and jacket, hiding the bloodstains with a practiced hand.

"Sherri said there was an administrator. We should focus our efforts on finding them."

"What kind of person would start a murder-for-hire business?" he muses.

"Someone who likes money more than morals."

"I'm not sure if that narrows it down."

We reach the main road. It's sometime between morning and night, but the city isn't completely asleep, not ever. This is the crossroads hour. Revelers are returning from the Great Last Night while early commuters charge past, scowling at the limp boys at bus stops, the girls sharing the last cigarette.

We disappear seamlessly into the crowd. We're experts at it. We've been doing it our whole lives.

"Why do you want to see your handler in person?" I ask. "Can't we just call him?"

"I don't trust him . . . I mean, I don't trust him without a gun to his head."

I think of Sherri, who's lied to me all along. Do I still trust her?

I remember how panicked she sounded on the phone when she told me I was the mark this time. She warned me. She didn't have to. She could've just cut and run. "My handler lives in London. We can see her, too."

"Perfect." Jonathan checks his watch. "The first Eurostar leaves in two hours. We need to be on that train."

"Fuck." I can't catch my breath. Anymore. Ever.

Jonathan stops in his tracks. He turns to face me. He looks deeply into my eyes, like he did on the train all those months ago. I want to wish I had never met him, but I don't. I don't wish that.

"What do you want to do?" he says. "Tell me, and we'll do it. Whatever you want."

Decisive action. He'll do whatever I say. He would stay here. He would go down in blazes. He would die. He might even enjoy it. But I don't want that for either of us. I want us to make it out of this alive.

"Remember you said one day we'd go back on that train?" I ask. "The sleeper train from Florence to Paris. Same car. Just the two of us?"

"Yes."

I swallow. "Let's go to England. Let's find out who's trying to kill us, and let's murder the fuck out of them."

He kisses me.

X

INTIMACY, PART 2

60

Eva

WE BOOK OUR OWN PRIVATE CABIN ON THE EUROSTAR. MY artery aches, which is something I didn't know could happen.

Jonathan is very careful with me. Too careful. He sits across from me in the compartment. It reminds me of the day we met, except this time we're both injured.

He's crammed in his seat with his smudged glasses. He's wearing a sweatshirt that says *I Left My Heart in Paris.* I bought it for him at the station because he couldn't exactly go around with bullet holes in his clothes. If I ever questioned whether he really loved me, now I know he does. I know because he is wearing that sweatshirt.

"You can sit over here," I tell him.

He's trying to read the newspaper. He looks so normal, it kind of breaks my heart. "I don't want to hurt you," he says.

"It's too late for that."

He shifts, uncomfortable, then scans me up and down before he stands and crosses to my side of the compartment. He drops carefully down beside me. "Do you feel okay? How are your stitches?"

We had to make some adjustments after the gunfight. Jonathan and I went into an empty restroom at the train station. We secured the door behind us, and then Jonathan repaired my stitches with his expert fingers.

I place those fingers on me now.

He looks up at me. "I thought Mas said we couldn't have sex?"

"That was a joke." I smile.

"Not funny," he says seriously.

There are an infinite number of ways to have sex. There are ways I never imagined. This is one of them:

On a train, trying not to move too much because I don't want to strain my injury, as he scatters delicate kisses down my body, searches me for any and all exposed flesh. Checking in with me all the time.

"Are you okay?"

"Are you sure?"

"I love you."

It smells earthy outside the window, the swelling landscape of flesh. The train is thrumming, vibrating through my thighs, drumming in my teeth.

Something about the rush of the train makes it all feel so urgent, yet every movement seems impossibly slow, as if it is happening in the stars first and we are down here interpreting it, in controlled movements and human sounds.

He sticks one finger inside me. His finger curves naturally with me as I take him in. My clitoris is its own tiny universe, a territory even I haven't completely explored. He stakes his claim there and everywhere.

I cry out, trying to let go and grab on at the same time, trying to get a grip on sensation.

So much of the sex I've had was bravado. It was a game of one-upmanship. A chance to prove my value: how strong I was, how flexible, how sexy and desirable and even, sometimes, how crazy and how wild.

This sex is nothing like that.

It's so much more dangerous.

61

A T THE STATION, WE PICK UP A CAR TO DRIVE OUT TO THE Cotswolds. Sorry—we pick up a McLaren to drive to the Cotswolds.

"You know," I say, climbing into the front seat, "you're basically unemployed. You might want to consider budgeting a little."

"I was right. You *are* optimistic." He reaches over and helps me fasten my seat belt. "There's no way we're making it out of this thing alive."

He steps on the gas.

On our way out of London, we stop at an abandoned flat near Latimer Road station. Jonathan goes inside and comes out with a suitcase.

"Is that your getaway bag?" I joke.

"Something like that," he says, stowing it neatly between the seats. I'm sure it's filled with his signature pretentious weapons. I'm a little worried that he thinks we need them to meet his handler, but I guess it's better to be prepared. We left our guns in Paris. We couldn't get them past the metal detectors at the Eurostar station. Jonathan wiped our prints and tossed the guns in a trash can at the Gare du Nord.

The Cotswolds are ridiculously pastoral. Fields of green; quaint villages. England is featured in so many classic children's books that it kind of feels like a storybook land.

I settle into the drive. I've tried to get ahold of Sherri but I haven't heard from her yet. I'm not worried, though. It's still early.

"So," I say, "how do you know where your handler lives? Has he invited you over for tea?" I've never been to Sherri's place.

"No," Jonathan says, switching gears. "I tracked him down. He doesn't know that I know."

"Creepy," I note as he switches gears again. "You might want to slow down. Unless you want to burn another identity." He told me that he had a license confiscated on the way to Paris.

"Shit, sorry." He downshifts, twice. "I'm a little nervous." I can see that. He's practically vibrating. His fingers rub his palm whenever they're not busy doing something else.

"Why?"

He frowns. "I don't know . . . I guess I've never had so much to lose before."

His fingers start to worry again. I reach across the console and take his hand.

WE ARE IN THE COTSWOLDS IN JUST OVER AN HOUR. JONATHAN'S handler lives in a historic thatched-roof cottage at the top of a rolling hill. It's delightful.

We park just out of view, behind a row of manicured hedges. Jonathan studies the cottage, strategizing.

He unfastens his seat belt. "I think maybe you should stay in the car."

"What? Why?"

"You were gravely injured twelve hours ago," he says. "It's not safe."

"It was safe enough to have sex with me," I point out. "Who's your handler? Do you actually think he'll get violent?" I can't imagine Sherri getting violent. In my experience, handlers are much more the IT types. They're the brains of the operation. If they weren't, they'd be the ones doing the killing. Jonathan wriggles in his seat, and it dawns on me: "Oh. You think *you'll* get violent."

"I might have to be convincing."

"You might choose violence, but literally."

"Exactly," he says. He opens the suitcase. It's not filled with antique weapons. It's filled with some very modern, very gnarly guns.

"Not your usual style," I note.

"Not my guns," he says. "That was a safe house."

"Seems pretty dangerous for a safe house."

"There are armories scattered all over Europe," he says. "You can find coordinates on the dark web. Thomas—or Alfie—told me about that one."

I had no idea. "Why are they there? Who are they for?"

He picks up a gun and a multitool. "Whoever needs them. That's what I love about the internet. It's so egalitarian."

I pick up a Glock. He looks at me. "You know I'm not the kind of person who waits in the car," I say.

He nods. "All right," he says. "Cover me." He means for me to stay behind him, which is fair enough, I guess. I do have to be careful of my stitches.

We follow an angled path toward the house, avoiding the view from the windows.

We reach a side door. Jonathan uses the multitool to cut out the door lock. It falls and I catch it in my hand. He smiles.

"Teamwork makes the dream work," I say. I'm a little jazzed. It's kind of fun to have a buddy, and to be on a job where no one has to die. Just a friendly in-and-out to ask some questions, get some answers. Easy peasy.

Jonathan pushes the door open. It seems I spoke too soon.

He takes a step back, protective. "Is that . . . ?" he starts.

"Blood," I finish for him. A lot of it. In a trail down a far hallway ahead of us.

"Shit," he says.

"Super shit," I confirm.

It's not just the blood. The house around us is silent. So quiet, you almost wouldn't recognize the sound, but I do, and I know Jonathan does: This house is echoing with death.

"Someone might still be alive." I break rank to hurry toward the hallway, toward the blood. I can't help myself. This is massively triggering. The blood, the house, the silence.

After my parents died, I didn't even call the police right away. I was in shock. I had just shot three people, and I wasn't sure how the cops would respond to that. One of the burglars took forever to die, thumping the floor with his fist and gurgling obscenities. I was in a stupor for hours. Another thing I felt guilty for: I might have been able to save the burglars—the people who killed my parents—if I had called the police right away.

Right now, I streak down the hall, careful not to step in the blood or touch anything. I skid to a halt when I see the body. For a second my mind snaps apart. I think I'm hallucinating; I think I'm imagining things.

It's not a stranger on the floor. It's not Jonathan's handler. It's mine.

62

Jonathan

I CAN SEE EVA START TO SCREAM, SO I GENTLY PUT A HAND OVER her mouth. She bites my fingers. God, I love her.

"Ouch," I say, taking my hand away.

"I wasn't going to scream," she says defensively. Her voice is hushed. Her eyes are locked on the woman's body on the floor. "That's my handler," Eva explains. "That's Sherri."

"That's Alfie's wife. Laura." Another coincidence. I am starting to think the network is smaller than we thought.

Eva staggers back. "The last conversation I had with her, she told me everything. She warned me. She went against them. Do you think that's why . . . ?"

"I'm sorry." I do not know what else to say because yes, I do think that is why.

"Fuck!" She punches the air, not wanting to touch anything.

"We need to get out of here," I say. Whoever killed Laura did not bother to clean up, which means they probably wanted us to find her. It could be a warning. It could be a trap. "But first we need to find out if Alfie's here." I cock my gun. "I'm going to sweep the house, okay?"

She takes a deep breath. "I can help. We need to work fast."

"You take the upper floors," I say, because the murder happened on the ground floor.

I sweep the rooms as fast as I can. I consider calling Alfie, but I have to consider carefully. Alfie might know that Laura warned Eva. He might know she was killed for it. He might even have been involved; he has always seemed a little spineless.

I am just finishing the living areas when I see a line of blood leaking from underneath a closet door. I find Alfie inside it.

Eva is coming down the stairs, and I stop her with a gesture.

"They got him, too." I suddenly remember the phone call Alfie and I had six months ago, right after Eva and I first met, when he told me, *You are putting dozens of people behind the scenes—with families, and loved ones—at risk. And no amount of kills is going to make that worthwhile to the people who want to live.*

Even if Alfie was not all good, he was also not all bad.

I feel terrible, and then he gasps.

63

Eva

I RUSH TOWARD JONATHAN'S HANDLER.

"Are you okay?" I check his vitals. I search his body for injury. "He's fine. I don't even think he's been hurt."

Jonathan helps him up by his shirt collar. "Your wife is dead in the hallway," Jonathan says, straight to the point. "And you're fine?"

"I wouldn't say I'm fine," Alfie says. His face is drawn. His shoulders are lightly shaking. I know shock when I see it. I have a feeling Sherri's death hasn't hit him yet. He's still in the moment, soaked in adrenaline. In the next few days, or the next few weeks, his old life will quietly die. His whole world will change. But for now, he's at the beginning of the end.

"Whose blood is this?" Jonathan asks. Is he suggesting that Alfie had something to do with what happened to Sherri? Alfie starts crying. Jonathan is not dissuaded. "Answer the question."

"She put us both at risk." Alfie hiccups. "They didn't give me a choice. I know you—of all people—understand." Jonathan's grip around Alfie's collar tightens, like he is preparing to strike. "You told me to track her handler down!"

"I didn't tell you to kill her," he says.

"They made me do it! They said I had to prove my loyalty. What was I supposed to do?" Alfie gazes down the hall, where death hovers in a cloud we can all see. He seems to pull himself together for a moment, riding the waves of his grief. "They asked me to give you a message."

"What's the message?" I ask.

"They're going to kill you both." His voice is chillingly calm. "There is no way out, and you are absolutely fucked."

Jonathan takes a deep, cleansing breath and then releases him. "He's all yours."

I step forward. "We need to know who's running the network. Who's the administrator?"

"I haven't the least idea."

Jonathan gives me a look. I sigh, then lift my gun to Alfie's temple. He cowers, starts to snivel again. "You must know something," I encourage.

"It never seemed important who it was," he says. I cock my gun. "Blowing a hole in my head won't give you any answers."

"This is my fault," Jonathan says. It's not a question.

Alfie scowls at him. "I wish I could blame you, for everything. But I did this to myself."

"What do we do?" I ask.

It's practically a rhetorical question at this point, but Alfie still answers. "I suggest you run and hide, and hope that eventually they decide you're not worth the effort."

I laugh once in surprise, then realize he's not joking. That really is our only hope, that they'll just decide to stop. Decide we're a waste of resources. Whatever happens, we'll spend the rest of our lives looking over our shoulders. They're after us, just like they were after Andrew. They eat their own.

"Let's get out of here," I say, lowering my gun.

"You're not going to kill me?" Alfie asks. "God knows I deserve it."

"No," Jonathan says, stowing his weapon. "I'm getting tired of killing people." This is a pretty staggering admission from Jonathan.

He follows me out, although neither of us has any idea where to go.

Life is so twisted. I finally find the right guy, and an invisible network of murderers wants both of us dead.

64

J ONATHAN AND I GO FOR DINNER AT A PUB SOMEWHERE BE-
tween Albion and nowhere.

One of the best things about England is the sprawling countryside pubs that fill up only on the weekends or during football matches. The one we select—the Butcher's Arms—is totally empty. Just a lonely barmaid and a series of empty rooms. We sit in the smoking garden, armed to the teeth. The sky is dark and portentous, the way the last night sky of your life ought to be.

Jonathan—who's a bit of a downer at the best of times—now seems sincerely depressed. He's staring out into the dark blue sky, gripping his untouched ale.

"We need to come up with a plan," I say.

Sherri's death hasn't really hit me yet, or maybe death can't hit me anymore. Maybe I fucked myself up by surrounding myself with it, and I can't feel loss anymore. Maybe that was always my intention. Maybe that's why I took this job in the first place, to solve death with more death.

I have to force myself to think about her. I'm going to force myself to mourn her, because I know that I need to. I'm not an emotional undertaker; I can't just keep burying my tragedies. Sherri was my best friend, even if she was also my handler. She died saving me. She put her life on the line to protect me.

She also lied to me. She made it seem like we worked for a benevolent organization, when really it was just a free-for-all on the internet.

I remember the first night Sherri and I met at that nightclub, how gleeful we were talking about the job. *Wasn't it crazy? Wasn't it wild? To kill for a living. Wasn't it free?* We used to laugh so loudly to cover up the lies. It wasn't crazy or wild and it *definitely* wasn't free. Both of us were trapped in a dark machine. A machine that kills. The same machine that killed my fiancé.

"Wait." Something occurs to me. I sit up. "You said Andrew leaked privileged information to the Italian police. What information?"

"I don't know." Jonathan seems to have really given up hope. I think it's mostly an act. I'm just not sure if he knows where his acting begins and ends.

"When I was in Florence," I say, "the night we met, I passed by Andrew's old apartment. No one had cleared it out. There might be something there, some clue about the network." I don't know what I'm expecting to find, but I'm not one for giving up. Not on Sherri, not on us and definitely not on myself.

"That seems like a long shot," he says. He's right, but we don't have any other leads. We can't stay here. I, for one, am not waiting around to die. "Somebody will have swept it. They had to have known where he lived." I give him a look. "But if you want to. Of course. Whatever you want."

"Good boyfriend."

65

T HE NEXT DAY, WE TAKE THE TRAIN TO FLORENCE. IT'S NOT THE
fastest method but it's the one both of us prefer, for the
same reasons. You can jump out of trains. You can reroute.
You have some semblance of control.

Plus, trains are just aesthetically superior. Europe is fucking
gorgeous, and it's a shame not to spend every moment of your life
looking at it.

The last time we rode these tracks, we pretended to be a couple. Now we really are one, and I like to think we are just as insuf-
ferable. We put up our armrest. We cuddle. We kiss. We check
each other's vitals. We buy each other coffee and Fanta and Skittles.

Knowing we might be killed actually makes being together
easier, because we don't have any angst about the future.

"If we do die," I tell Jonathan, snuggling into the new suit he
bought en route, "I hope we die at the exact same time."

Our fellow passengers look a little disturbed.

Jonathan absently strokes my hair. "We'll certainly die eventually."

"Will you kill me if you're sure you're about to die?" I joke.

"Of course," he jokes. I think.

"Perfect. You're the best."

Outside the window, the landscape is turning Italian. We're going back in time, to the place where we first met, to the place where I lost my fiancé, to the place where Jonathan killed him. What could go wrong?

66

Jonathan

I SHOT ANDREW UNDER THE ARCHES OF THE PONTE VECCHIO. HE fell into the Arno. I had been reading a lot about harmonic principles at the time, so it was one of my most pretentious hits.

Of course, Alfie fought me on it. It was too public, he said. Too attention getting. But what he did not realize was that there are two ways to hide a death: in the dark and in the open. People die at national monuments all the time. In fact, statistically, they die at memorable locations more than anywhere else. Famous cliffs. Notorious hotels. Suicide bridges.

Alfie was also not happy because it was hard to confirm the kill. The body did not turn up right away. There was a dispute about my payment, and then, luckily, Andrew was found.

It drives me crazy now. Not that I killed him, but that Eva was out there then, hurting. Eva was out there all this time when she could have been with me. Now that we have found each other, there are people who want us dead. Life is the only thing more unfair than death.

We stop at Eva's old apartment in Florence to get the keys to Andrew's place. She searches cupboards and drawers.

"I haven't taken them out in years," she says, "but I know they're in here somewhere."

"Is this your home base?" I ask. It is a collegiate-style artist's loft above the Arno. It is actually disconcertingly near the Ponte Vecchio.

"It's supposed to be." Eva sighs and puts her hands on her hips. "But to be honest, I'm never here anymore. I should probably just let it go."

The walls are halfheartedly decorated with unframed prints from various museums: Renoir and Monet and van Gogh. It could be Eva's personality; it could be someone else's. That is the life we lead, never wanting to give anything away.

"Can I sit on your bed?" I ask.

"'Course you can." She is searching the kitchen drawers.

I sit on her bed, run my fingers along the musty covers. It smells of her and it smells of dust.

"I wish I had known you were here," I say. "I wish I had known you were anywhere."

"Maybe it would have been too soon," she says. "Maybe the timing was off."

"I don't believe that."

"We can't go back. I think both of us need to realize that."

"You're right," I say, lying back on her bed, gazing up at her ceiling, imagining all the nights she lay like this alone when she could have been with me.

"Found them!" She jumps up, wiggling the keys with her fingers. They are held together with a red ribbon.

"Come here," I say. "I want to congratulate you."

She climbs over me and slaps me playfully. "We need to focus—remember?"

I do not want to focus. I am nervous about going to Andrew's apartment. Afraid of seeing her love for him on her face. Afraid of knowing I turned her love into grief. I keep waiting for her to wake up and realize how dark I really am. She says she knows, but I do not think she does. I am not sure she can.

She sits back, observing me. "What is it?" she says, like she can read my thoughts.

"I'm sorry," I say, even though I know it will annoy her.

"You don't have to be sorry. You killed people. I killed people. We have to let it go. We have to move forward." She slides off me. "It's the only way we're ever getting out of this."

But she is wrong. She knows she is. Because to get out of this, we are going to have to kill a lot more people.

67

Eva

JONATHAN'S SO NERVOUS THAT I DON'T THINK HE REALIZES HOW nervous *I* am. I haven't been back to Andrew's place since he died. I sort of stuffed his entire existence into the past, with the rest of my baggage. It's awkward enough going to your ex's place with your current partner without having to factor in that your ex is dead and your new partner killed him.

I understand why Jonathan keeps apologizing, but as usual I'm trying to suppress my emotions, so it doesn't help that he keeps bringing it up. Because of course I don't blame Jonathan and of course I do. It's complicated. And it's getting more complicated all the time.

When we reach Andrew's apartment, Jonathan asks me if I want him to wait outside. He can sense that I'm upset and he's looking at me with care and worry.

"Of course not," I say, charging up the stairs. When I reach the familiar front door, I change my mind. "Maybe just wait here a sec?" I say, like I didn't just laugh off the suggestion one staircase ago.

Jonathan stands in the hall. I walk alone into my past.

Andrew's apartment is so familiar that it's a little crushing. The uneven shades he never fixed. The scorched teakettle his grandma gave him. The same ten books he never read on his shelf. The bed is made the way he always made it—with sloppy hospital corners.

Being there makes me think of Sherri. Of our life back then, when I first became a killer. I've lost her, too. Like I lost Andrew. Like I lost my parents. Sometimes my life feels like a series of closing doors. Of rooms I can't get into anymore.

This room is exactly how I remembered it. Exactly.

The mini fridge is still humming. The electricity still works— I would've thought someone would have turned it off. The books are gathering dust but the rest of the studio is fairly clean.

I approach the fridge, already grimacing. I'm expecting to find all of Andrew's old favorites: milk two years past its sell-by date, English mustard, rotten thick-cut bacon. When I open the fridge door I find all these things, only none of them are out-of-date.

"Fuck." I jump into readiness, almost expecting Andrew to leap out from behind the curtains.

Jonathan hears me and comes in. "Is everything all right? Do you still want me outside?"

I shake my head; then I say, quietly, "Close the door." He does. I keep my voice down. Andrew could come back at any second. Maybe we should leave. Maybe we should stay. Maybe a lot of things. "Are you sure you killed Andrew?"

"Yes."

"How did you kill him?"

He seems hesitant to say. "I shot him. Off the Ponte Vecchio. He fell into the Arno."

"Did you confirm the kill?" I ask.

"Not personally. His body turned up a few weeks later, around Empoli. You know rivers."

"I don't think so," I say. "I don't think he died that night. I don't think he's dead now." I reopen the fridge. "This milk goes bad in a week. That's English mustard. Andrew is still alive. And he's still living here."

Jonathan actually smiles. "Really? Because that would be a huge weight off of my mind."

"You're missing the most important part."

"I still got paid?"

"He got out. He defected and he's still alive."

Jonathan seems unsure. "Something's not adding up here. Why would the network let him go? And why would they pay me if he wasn't dead?"

We both hear the sound of the building door opening downstairs.

"Maybe we should leave," Jonathan says.

We stay frozen as we hear footsteps coming up the stairs, but then they become fainter. They're moving away.

My head is spinning. "Why would Andrew let me believe he was dead? Unless— Oh my God, what if he faked his death to break up with me?"

"If he did, I'll kill him. Again. More completely this time." Jonathan jokes, but I'm not in the mood.

Losing Andrew was so painful, and all that pain, all that feeling, was for nothing. It was fake. He let me suffer for no reason. "Men are such *fucking* assholes."

"As much as I understand that you must be pretty pissed off right now, I don't think this is about you. If it was Andrew's plan, it wouldn't have involved me."

It dawns on me. "*I'm* going to kill him."

"We should talk to him first," Jonathan says. "Then I'll let you decide."

We both startle. The footsteps that seemed to disappear down the hall are now right outside the door. We were being so loud that I didn't notice them coming back.

Two things happen at once: Someone puts a key into the lock and Jonathan draws on the door. And then the door opens and my current boyfriend is pointing a gun at my ex.

Andrew seems to recognize Jonathan immediately—I guess their last run-in would have been pretty memorable.

Andrew draws on Jonathan.

Then I draw on them both, which is kind of painful, considering my mortal wound is still pretty fresh.

Jonathan gives me a look. "You're pointing a gun at me?"

"Sorry," I say, but I don't lower my gun. I need Andrew to feel safe.

Andrew's eyes expand when he sees me. I almost wouldn't recognize him, which is probably what he was going for. He has facial hair, dyed dark. He's no longer chiseled. He's dressed in dodgy-looking tweeds. I actually think he looks hotter. Good for him.

"Eva?" he says. "What the hell are you doing here?"

"What the hell are *you* doing here? On earth."

Andrew's eyes go back to Jonathan and don't leave him. "You're here to kill me."

"Don't be ridiculous," I say, although I can very much see how he would arrive at that conclusion.

"How did you find me?" he asks.

"This is your apartment," I point out. "Let's focus on the important things. You let me believe you were dead. For years."

Andrew slides carefully along the wall, not taking his eyes off

Jonathan. As if *I* couldn't kill him. This is exactly what was wrong with our relationship; he never believed in me. I almost want to kill him just to prove myself.

"I'm sorry," he says, apparently to Jonathan, because he still doesn't look at me. "I did it to protect you."

Jonathan speaks. "Why don't we all put our guns down and have a chat? Have a cup of tea or something. English shit."

"I'm not putting my gun down around you," Andrew says. "You shot me."

"He's not going to shoot you now," I say. "He already got paid."

Andrew finally looks at me again. "Then what are you doing here?"

"They want us dead, too," I say. "We came here because we're trying to find out who we were working for. We had no idea you were still alive. And apparently hiding in your own apartment."

"Hiding in plain sight," Jonathan says. "It's a strategy many people don't appreciate."

"Exactly," Andrew says. "I was in the Pantanal for a year. But you'd be surprised how conspicuous you can become in the middle of nowhere."

I look from Andrew to Jonathan, taking the temperature of the room. "How are we feeling about putting the guns down? You can give them to me."

They both laugh. Rude.

Andrew considers. "I suppose you wouldn't kill me here," he says to Jonathan. "You like to make a spectacle."

"I wouldn't call it a spectacle," Jonathan says.

Andrew lowers his gun. I give Jonathan a look and he does the same. I lower my guns, too.

Andrew carefully closes the front door. Then, somewhat haltingly, he makes us tea. "So, what are you two doing together?"

"Well, it's . . . ," I start. "It's kind of a funny story."

"She's my girlfriend," Jonathan says, protectively taking my hand. I roll my eyes, but also, I kind of like it.

"Fucking hell. I really did a number on you, didn't I?" Andrew asks. "Do you still take your tea the same way?"

"Yeah. Three sugars." There are many ways to die.

I take a seat at the kitchen table, my seat. Jonathan takes Andrew's seat, which makes me smile.

"How do you take your tea, mate?" Andrew asks Jonathan.

"Black."

"Could've guessed that," Andrew says.

"You know, you could have told me you were still alive," I tell Andrew.

"It was too risky," Andrew says, filling the kettle.

"You mean you didn't trust me," I say.

He sighs. He glances at Jonathan, then continues. "Things had gotten a bit weird between us. And then the network took out a hit on me. And then I was shot. Off a bridge."

"How did you survive?" Jonathan says. He seems a bit annoyed with himself. "I'm sure I shot you in the heart."

Andrew is pouring out the milk and sugar now. He has this very strong belief that you should pour the milk first. He will fight people on it. "I was wearing a bulletproof vest," he says.

Jonathan scoffs.

"You contract killers are so ridiculous about not doing anything for your own protection," Andrew snips.

"Laura is dead," I have to tell him. I use her real name because he must know it. They went to school together. He doesn't seem surprised, so I guess that's another secret he kept from me. "They killed her because she warned me."

He looks conflicted. "Lucky you." He runs his fingers through his hair. "I'm sorry to hear that she's dead, but she never did me that courtesy."

I can't blame him for being conflicted. I am, too. Everyone I know is so bad and so good. Including me. "So you knew she was lying about the agency?" I have to ask. "And you didn't even tell me?"

"I wanted to protect you," he says. "I started to get suspicious about things. After Laura hired you, to be honest. You were running so many mad jobs. It didn't seem plausible that a government agency would be so reckless. I started asking questions, and instead of answering me, Laura tried to make me feel like the bad guy . . . You did, too. A little."

I remember his questions. I remember feeling like he was jealous. Feeling like I had finally found the solution to my malaise and he was trying to take my new life away. To drag me back to a world where I'd never fit in.

"It was actually one of my marks who finally told me the truth," he says. "Or accused me of it. He said I'd been hired through some dodgy website. I failed to kill him, and then I called Laura and demanded answers. She said if I kept digging, they would have me killed.

"So I went straight to the police," he continues. "I didn't even think about it. There's no way, I thought, that these people could be more powerful than the Italian police."

"What did you tell the police?"

"Oh, you know, that I worked for a top secret internet hit-man request site, but I didn't have any idea how to access it. I couldn't even give them Laura's details, because I wanted to protect her. And you." That doesn't sound like leaking privileged information, but I guess it makes sense that going to the police would be reason enough for the network to eliminate him.

"What did the police say?" I ask.

"Not a lot. It was more of an awkward-silence thing. Especially when I asked them to arrest me because I was afraid to leave. They politely declined. Even I started to think I was a bit mad. Until I ran into an officer on the way out and he busted my face open."

I remember the bruising. "You should've told me." It makes sense now, how adamant he was that I quit. I would have if he had just told me the truth.

At least, I *think* I would have. I was so different back then, so high on the idea that I was destined to be an assassin. I felt like I had a purpose. I felt like all my suffering had been for a reason. I might've not believed him. I might've made excuses. I might've not wanted to walk away.

"I was afraid that if I told you the truth, it would put your life in danger." It would have. I know that now. "Anyway, after this fella shot me off that bridge, I went into hiding for a bit. Then I had an idea. Bodies are found in the Arno all the time. All I had to do was bribe a few officials with the money I kept hidden, and I had a body in Empoli. I made sure it was cremated, but in any case I didn't see the overlords sending someone to check.

"I flew to Brazil, spent a year exploring the Pantanal—nearly died there a few times, mainly from frogs—but I missed Florence. I came back, just on a lark, thinking I'd stay a few days, and before I knew it, I had the exact life I'd always wanted." He pours the tea and distributes it.

"They will find you eventually," Jonathan muses.

"Yes," Andrew says, taking the open seat. "I expect they will, mate."

I grip my too-hot tea. "Were you ever going to tell me you were alive?" I ask him.

Andrew just makes a face, like he doesn't want to admit the truth. Then he drinks his tea too quickly and scalds his tongue. Small victories.

Jonathan sits back, lost in thought. "I don't want to keep

running . . . and I don't want to keep killing." Both Andrew and I look up in surprise. Jonathan squeezes my hand. "I just want us to be together."

I think on it. "What if it wasn't killing other people? What if we killed ourselves?"

68

Jonathan

EVA IS RIGHT. FAKING DEATH WORKED FOR ANDREW. IT COULD work for us. It might be our only chance.

"They'll want to see your bodies," Andrew says.

"They didn't see your body," Eva points out.

"It's different with you," he says to me. "You're a much bigger threat."

"There are two ways to not leave behind a body," I say. "You blow it up or you burn it down."

"I don't think even you could survive that, mate." Andrew keeps calling me "mate," so I know he really does not like me. But I cannot quite dislike him back, because he may have saved our lives. An idea is forming in my mind.

"We could draw fire. Lead them to us and then . . . boom." That last word is an understatement.

"How would we draw them?" Eva asks.

"We can use Alfie. He must have some way of communicating with them."

Eva seems energized by the idea. "Where would we draw them to?"

"I know a place," I say. It might not be the perfect place, but it is convenient. "I know someone who has a house with an insecure foundation in the French countryside, near Bordeaux. They're in the process of tearing it down. We could help."

"I'm telling you, they're going to want to see your bodies," Andrew insists.

"I could leave something behind." I lean back in my chair. "A finger. An arm. A leg. I know someone who can amputate anything." I am honestly a little enchanted with the idea. I have always wanted to lose something I could never get back.

"Maybe something you don't need," Eva teases. "Like a kidney or a piece of your liver."

"I'm serious," I tell her. "It would be worth it if we could leave all this behind."

"I'd rather you keep all ten fingers." She weaves her fingers between mine. "I might need them."

"How do you feel about toes?" I ask.

"I think it's worth trying to keep *all* our body parts," she says. If she wants them, then I have to keep them for her.

"Fine," I say. "But it is an option."

Andrew stands. He has finished his tea. "Well, I hate to be unsociable, but seeing as you're on the lam and I'm meant to be dead, I think perhaps we ought to cut this session short."

I stand and head toward the door. I have no desire to hang out with him either. "Thank you for the tea," I say.

Eva moves to follow me.

"Eva?" Andrew says. "Mind if we have a quick chat?"

Eva looks at me. "Sure." I should have killed Andrew when I had the chance.

I walk into the hall, then make it sound like I keep walking. I know I should not eavesdrop, but I do a lot of things I should not do.

"Are you sure everything is all right?" Andrew asks.

"I'm sure."

"That guy is a pretty notorious murderer."

"So am I, thank you very much. Anyway, he's changed. You heard him. He doesn't even want to kill people anymore."

"He also said he wanted to amputate his leg."

"Nobody's perfect."

"I don't trust him."

"He did shoot you."

". . . And maybe I'm a little jealous. You never looked at me like that."

"You weren't crazy enough for me. I didn't think anyone was."

Andrew laughs. "Good luck to whoever comes after the two of you. They'll need it."

"I'm glad you're not dead."

"Thank you," he says. "And if the two of you ever need anything, please do not come back here."

Eva laughs, then opens the door, catching me in the act.

"Were you eavesdropping?" she says.

"Yes." At least I can be honest.

"You're such a red flag," she says, and then she throws her arms around me.

"I was joking about the leg," I say.

She pats my cheek. "Of course you were. Come on. We have a train to catch."

69

WHEN I PROPOSED TO EVA, DAYS AND LIFETIMES AGO, that we take the sleeper train to Paris again, I never believed it would actually happen.

We have to wait for hours at the station for night to fall. It does not fall. It creeps over us, like a dark assailant, lulling us into a false sense of security, and then—*wham!* It is night.

We do not have sex on the train. Instead, we sleep. She lies on top of me on the tiny single bed surrounded by six of our newest, closest friends.

I always assumed that when a couple stopped having sex, even for twenty-four hours, it was a sign of a failing relationship. Now I know that is not true. Not having sex with Eva feels phenomenal. She is stitched to my body like she belongs there. She was amputated by accident the day I was born and I have been missing her all my life.

I love her so much that I am scaring myself—truly scaring myself. I will do anything for her. I am so wild with this urge that I am almost asking for it, demanding that anything and everything come my way to try to stop me from loving her.

I want to fight for her so badly that I am scared that I will start the fight.

———————

WHEN EVA AND I REACH PARIS, WE DIVIDE AND CONQUER. I ARRANGE to meet Mas at a café in Pigalle. It is easier than it has ever been to convince him to come and see me. You would think that would make me happy, but instead I feel edgy. I do not like things to be too easy. I, maybe, do not like things to be too fixed.

"You look like shit," he says when I sit down. "You must be happy." The accusation stings a little. I have never been happy, and part of me feels I am betraying my true self.

I try to focus on the future, on my impending death. I can worry about my many *issues* later. "I want to ask you a favor."

"What a surprise." He sips his coffee.

"It's a favor to you, too. I want to help you with your house in Bordeaux."

He puts his cup down. "How do you know where the house is?"

"I'm sorry. I had to find it so I didn't go there by accident," I joke. "I am going to get help. I just have to take care of one little thing first." That little thing being my life.

Mas rolls his eyes. "Fine. How are you going to help me?"

I scan our surroundings, then pick up the complimentary matchbox on the table. I light a match. We watch it burn. "Permit problem solved."

"And how does this help you— No, wait. Strike that. I don't even want to know." He sits back in his chair. He looks happy all the time. I think that is what unsettles me the most about him. He is about to be a father, and his world has not ended. He has a normal life. A life I do not want. A life I am terrified of having. "You know," he says, "I would love to hear something from you that's not a variation of 'I'm sorry' or 'I need a favor.'"

I fidget in my chair. I know I am the fuckup, but maybe I do not always want to be. "Would you really?" I ask. He looks annoyed at the challenge. "I'm not saying you're the bad guy. I know I am. But I also feel that the only things I can talk about to you are things I know you'll listen to. I know that's my fault. I know it is. All I can say is that I am trying to change that, finally. So I can be the brother you deserve. The one who doesn't need you so damn badly. The one who you need. The one who leaves you alone."

"Then you need to quit your job," he says, like he cannot help being the older brother.

"I have quit. I'm getting out. Technically, I am out. Right now."

"It's that simple?"

"It will be." I smirk a little. "If you let me torch your house."

"That doesn't sound simple . . ."

I lower my voice. "I have to fake my death. It's the perfect out for both of us. I won't see you again for a while. Maybe forever."

Mas takes a deep breath.

"It's what you want, right?" I cannot help myself, because that's not what I want. I love my brother. I always have, even when I have not loved myself. What I really want is an apartment in Paris. Not too close, but close enough to invite him and Giselle over for Sunday dinners. To see the kids and catch up and have every normal thing I told myself I did not want because I believed I did not deserve it. Maybe I am old or maybe I am dying, because that is what I really want. Even if I can never ever have it.

"I just want you to be okay," Mas says. "If this is what you need . . ." He pulls a house key off his ring and sets it on the table. "Take it."

"One day I will save you back."

"You already have. Look, Ethan . . ." He fumbles with the

buttons of his jacket, the same way I do sometimes. "I hated you for going to jail. I hated you because you were gone and I needed you. I hated you because I loved you. But I never hated you for what you did." He meets my eyes. "Maybe I'm not as good as you think I am, because I never hated you for killing him."

70

Eva

While Jonathan is securing the location, I walk down to the market. You can buy anything in Les Puces. Anything you could possibly need, to live or to die.

You can buy a new identity—or three, just to be safe—in the little room behind the passport photo booth at an internet café.

You can buy ashes, cremated bodies, bones and teeth in the taxidermy shop on the south side of the market. They might not hold up to DNA testing, but I have a feeling that the neckbeards accessing the network don't want to get their hands dirty in the real world.

I buy two jars of cremains and a few bones that remind me of Jonathan. I stick them in a bag and head back to our hotel room.

On the way there, I stop and pick up Jonathan's suitcase. It's so heavy that I have to get a cab. I feel pretty cool carrying a bunch of ashes and antique weapons across Paris. There's nothing quite like executing a plan to kill.

When I get back to his hotel room at the Ritz, I take the most decadent bubble bath. The thing about me is, I appreciate the small things. I could die tomorrow, or in the next five minutes. I try to enjoy every minute.

I hear the key in the lock. Until I hear Jonathan's voice, I am prepared to kill whoever walks through the door.

"He's agreed to it," Jonathan says. "Made me feel like shit about it first, but hey, that's family." He stops in the washroom doorway. His eyes sweep over me. He loosens his collar. "You look very cozy," he says softly.

"That's your urn on the right," I say. I have both of our jars of ashes on the counter, watching me take a bubble bath. "I wanted them to get to know us intimately, so they can play us well."

"You're delightfully odd."

"I have a surprise for you," I say, and duck under my bubbles. "It's in the hallway closet."

He gives me a look and then follows my instructions. I can hear his shriek from the tub.

"My suitcase!" he says. He comes running back in with a sword. "I can't believe you were holding on to these all this time and never told me."

"I forgot . . . slash was trying to kill you," I say.

"Fair enough." He disappears again and I can hear him drag the suitcase to the middle of the room and start unpacking. "My dueling pistols! My flamberge!"

I snort. I climb out of the bathtub and wrap myself in a robe. I walk into the bedroom and perch on the arm of a chair. I watch him tear through his weapons. It warms my heart.

"You're delightfully odd," I say back to him. "Do those grenades actually work?"

"Everything in here works," he says, absently stroking a serrated blade. "You think I lug all this around for fun?"

"Yes, I do." I stand and cross over to him. "I also think we should leave these at the house. To help sell our story. No one would ever believe you would walk away from your collection alive."

His grip tightens on a sword. "You're right. And I guess I won't be needing them where we're going. Wherever that is . . ."

He gazes longingly at all the weapons spread across the floor, probably trying—and failing—to imagine a place where that could possibly be true.

I can't imagine that place either, but we'll deal with that when we get there. Or something.

XI

NUCLEAR FAMILY

71

Jonathan

W̲E TAKE MY PORSCHE TO MAS'S COUNTRY HOUSE. I AM almost broke. I used to love running out of money, because then I had an excuse to take another job—a more dangerous, more lucrative one. Another chance to blow it all again. But right now running out of money feels more like a death sentence than my actual death sentence.

The sky is dark blue and I know what that means. I have a feeling that I am really going to die this time. All my life I have been terrified of almost this exact moment: me and a girl driving alone to a family house in the countryside.

"We're going to be fine," Eva hums, in response to my unaired worries. She is gazing into the blue, too, like she knows it is the color of my death. Like it is the color of her death, too.

THE HOUSE IN BORDEAUX IS ANCIENT. IT IS FALLING APART, UNINHAB-itable, dangerous.

The front steps are high and bound in columns, like the steps of a courthouse. I lead Eva up.

"Nice," she says. The front door is wooden but carved to look soft. I find the key.

The door opens into a chapel of an entryway. Stairs spiral down from either side of the second floor. The ceiling is spun with a heavenly mural just visible in the light of the sliver moon.

"Do you have a flashlight?" Eva asks.

"No." We are going to have to feel our way around this cavern of a house. "Take my hand."

The house is stunning. Mas has always had excellent taste. It is a shame that it is a death trap, but I know a lot about beautiful death traps. I appreciate them more than most people do.

I am going to have sex in this house. I am going to have sex in every room of this house. It could take all night, but I like to aim high.

We walk into a circular ballroom that somehow looks like it is at the bottom of the sea. Half an organ is crumbling in rusted veins along the wall. The fireplace is as big as a bedroom.

Eva is tired, although she will not admit it. It must be almost three in the morning.

I pull the drop cloth off a horsehair sofa, and she nestles into its corner.

"It's cold," she says, hiding her hands under her elbows.

I inspect the fireplace. I turn a key and hear the hiss of gas. I pull a lever to light a flame. It draws a ring along the floor of the fireplace and spins, narrower and narrower, until it makes a spiral of fire.

Eva watches the flames, then gazes up at me. "You know what would warm us up?" she says. I have an idea.

I climb onto the sofa and kiss her cold mouth warm.

Kiss harder. Kiss deeper. Kiss harder.

She slithers off the sofa. Then she stands, a snake framed in flames. "Where do you want me? I'll do whatever you want me to do." It is like she knows this is my last night alive.

I stand up with her. The heat of the flames covers us like a sheet as I kiss her. Kiss her harder.

I glide my fingers up her ribs until they collect around her breasts. I direct her with kisses. I catch her wrists, and I lift them slowly above her head. I kiss her lips, seal them like an envelope.

"Keep your hands up," I instruct her. "Don't move them."

The heat from the fire is almost overwhelming. It does not crackle but it burns. It burns in light along her bare legs as I remove her pants and her underwear.

Her wrists are crossed above her head. She is naked from the waist down.

A line of liquid leaks down her leg, drawing a crack in the arc of her thigh.

She is being very quiet now. She is thinking very deeply. She has nothing to say.

I rub the pressure points at the base of her skull and her head rocks toward me, nuzzles against me.

"I want to fuck you standing," I say.

Flames blush across her cheek.

I push her wrists higher up along the wall. Her body stretches up, past comfort, almost to pain—that is where the body comes alive.

I slip on a condom. I push into her, and as I do I lift her up along the wall, so that when I hit the deepest part of her, her toes are barely touching the floor. It is a cheap shot, an easy way to make her come, but we are not shooting for one. It is double or nothing tonight.

I stretch her up and thrust into her, grunting like a bull.

"Oh fuck!" She cannot believe it is happening so fast. I can feel her try to stop it and I push back, up and into her until her arms go slack and her legs start to jerk. "Fuck!"

One of her hands slips from my grasp, slick from the heat. It escapes. It curls around my collar. I try to grab it but her insides start to rock. She tightens her grip and she rips open my shirt.

I take her and I lead her, stumbling, onto the drop cloth.

"But what about you?"

"I'm not finished with you yet."

Some of the best sex happens after she comes. The second orgasm does not come so easily. The body bows in twisted pleasure, skims along the ceiling, but it does not break. The pressure cannot crack.

"Hold on to the sofa leg." She does as she is told.

I put my hand on the dip beside her hip bone and I enter her again. I hit her at an angle, pushing her legs up so I get the right spot, the spot marked *Sexual Psychosis.*

I mold her; I elongate her insides. I tease lazy circles into the center of her clit. I press my thumb into it. I flick it. I tease it. I massage it, and as I do I move slowly inside her, building up the wall that I will eventually break.

Her eyes are wild. She is focused on a fixed point on the ceiling and it is telling her things, delicious secrets in radial stutters and long, hungry waves that rotate through her sexy body.

Shadows from the primeval flames are licking up her side. For a moment I am the first man on earth. I blame the fire.

I stroke her stomach and I think, absently, that I would like to impregnate her.

Fuck.

It is obviously an instinct, a side effect of too much sex. It burns like a match in my nostrils and it turns me on in a way that games never do.

Fuck.

I am not an animal spreading its seed; I am a Very Sophisticated Fucking Machine.

Prove it.

I pull myself out.

"Get on your knees." She rolls onto her front.

Wouldn't it be nicer if you could feel her, the real her, if you could feel all of her around you? Like a circle in the fire. Like every star in every sky. Like eternity is a ring of endless light.

Vanilla sex is a dangerous thing. It leads to vanilla children. It leads to animal instincts that ruin human lives.

I ignore it. I cannot be blamed. I am in the thick of it.

One can never be held accountable for what one thinks during sex. You have to allow for stray thoughts. You cannot take them seriously.

I bite my lip and I slide back into her tempting insides. *If you don't want to think about impregnating her, you probably shouldn't be fucking her like an animal.*

Breathe.

I am a professional. I am a Very Sophisticated Fucking Machine.

"Please, may I spank you?" I ask.

"Yes," she says.

I take my hand and I draw the ecstasy particles down to her ass and—*smack!*—make them scatter.

She rocks forward. I feel her juices flowing down the base of my balls.

"Do you like that?"

"Yes," she says. She pushes back for more.

I weave my fingers into her hair, close to the base of her neck, and I tug slightly as I thrust into her. She pushes her ass up against me and I *smack* it once for her.

"That feels *so* good," she says.

I take the palm of my hand and I draw it through the shadows of flames that dip along her spine, and I take all the pleasure, I lead all the pleasure particles to the rosy red cheek of her ass and I *smack!* it as I thrust. I scare all the pleasure away so it runs through her bones. Her knees start to give and her thighs start to shake and I realize she is going to come again but I am not; I am not because my brain has instituted a ban on free thinking.

It would be rude, though. It would be rude not to come and it could create a problem. Just think about it. Just think about it a little bit and then stop. It does not count. It does not count in the throes of passion.

It is just pretend. It is just another fantasy.

I slide my hand down below her stomach and I hold her and imagine driving my seed there and I do. I give into her.

My mind peaks and it all comes pumping out.

"God."

I pull out of her. I toss the condom into the fire. The smell of burning rubber bleeds into the air.

She sits up. Her eyes are half-closed, but she sees everything. "Are you okay?"

"I'm fine," I say. I am not in a secure place. I am in a very suggestible frame of mind; I have just made an imaginary baby. "I'm going to get some water. I'll be right back."

I STALK ALONE THROUGH THE ENDLESS HOUSE, LOOKING FOR A place to be alone.

The night is gathering strength, making one last stab at darkness before the sun rises. I sit down on a chair, a throne masked in white cloth.

I cannot do the things that ordinary people do. I know that. This relationship will be a disaster because ultimately, I cannot keep myself together in situations where I do not have complete control. I need nice hotel rooms. I need expensive clothes and purified water. I cannot live in a broken-down castle. I need electricity.

I need to breathe.

Love is like death in a way. It comes and it catches you by surprise, and it hurts and it hurts and you cannot control it.

I tried to design a world where no one could love me and I failed.

I could go back to work. Maybe a new handler will take me if I give them my soul and I will not have to dream and I will never have to be afraid anymore. *As your hand curls around her stomach* . . .

This has got to stop. I need to stop dreaming.

The sky through the windows is catching light by degrees.

You could watch the sunrise. What a horrible, twisted thought.

These dreams are worse than nightmares. At least nightmares do not sting. At least nightmares do not lie.

We will put the dreams to bed, but not yet. Not just yet.

We will wait until sunrise.

72

Eva

I USED TO TELL MYSELF THAT I LIKED TO BE MISUNDERSTOOD. That I didn't mind it. That I was special. But then I met him. And he understood me instantly, like he recognized me on the train. His twin flame, his soul mate, all those cheesy, scary things.

I love him like he's a part of me. The best part. The worst part. And loving him makes me love myself more wholly than I ever have, more than I ever thought I could.

I find him sitting on a drop-clothed chair in an unstable room at the top of the house.

"Hey," I say. "Is everything okay?"

He shudders. "It's fine."

"We were having sex," I remind him, "and you freaked out."

He looks pale now, sick like he did on the train that first night. "What if we went back?"

"Back to where?"

"To the network. To the job. Pledged our allegiance in some way. I'm good at my job. So are you. We could do it together. It would be different."

I shake my head. "I thought I was killing bad guys. Now that I know what I'm really doing . . ."

"We could do independent research, only take the villain hits," he says, repeating Sherri's intention. Fuck. He's serious.

I walk across the faulty floor. He withdraws. "What happened? What scared you?"

He swallows. "I can't do this. I can't be like everyone else." He laughs, but it's a mean sound. "What am I going to do for a job? I'm almost out of money. Where are we going to live?"

I can't believe he's doing this. It's so predictable, but I still didn't expect it. I sigh in frustration. "We can live anywhere. We can do anything."

"No, we can't. We're killers, both of us. You were wrong about the reason we do this. We're not killing ourselves. We're already dead. We kill because we can't do anything else."

"That's not true. I was a pretty good real estate agent," I say lightly, but he doesn't laugh.

He is working his fingers over his palms. His chest is pumping. He is on the verge of a panic attack.

He's wrong. He's dead wrong. Neither of us is dead inside. Life would be so much easier if we were.

"I don't want to live in some shack in the woods with babies," he says.

"Um, neither do I," I say, and then I get it. The reason for the panic. The reason for the freak-out. "You know, we don't have to have kids."

He starts, like he can't believe I've figured him out.

I climb onto his lap while he's thrown off, before he can run. I draw my fingers through his hair, down his cheek. "We can design the exact life we want, just like we designed our hits. We can do anything, just like we always have. We can have sex in luggage compartments, steal swords from antiques markets. We don't have to be saints; we just have to be free."

He gazes up at me. "I'm afraid of being free. All my life I've been in one prison or another."

"Then be my prisoner. And I'll be yours." I draw my finger along his jaw. "We don't have to solve everything tonight. We don't have to see the future. We just have to get through today. And honestly, with the day we have coming, that'll be enough." I shrug. "Who knows? Maybe you'll get lucky and we'll both die."

He lets his head drop onto my chest. "I'm sorry. I panicked."

"It's okay." I stroke his neck. "I don't know what I'm doing either. Nobody does. It's normal. We're normal. We just have to learn to live with it. Killing is a lot easier than living."

"What if I did want kids? What if I wanted everything that everyone else has?"

I lift his chin so I'm looking directly into his eyes. Speaking to him like I'm speaking to myself, my own soul. "Then you can have it. We can have it. Maybe we're not really that different from everyone else. Maybe that was just something we told ourselves because we were scared."

73

THE NEXT MORNING, WE ARRANGE EVERYTHING. THE BOMBS
that will go off in all different sections of the house. The
balcony we will jump from. The net that will catch us. The
steel safe in which we will bury ourselves alive with the laser cut-
ter that we will use to cut our way out.

It's not a completely foolproof plan, but it's hard to come up
with a plan under pressure. I'm sure that tomorrow morning I
will wake up—if I wake up—with a better plan. It's easy to come
up with a perfect plan once it's too late.

It was Jonathan's idea to bury ourselves alive. We've tried to
arrange the explosions to minimize the amount of debris that
will fall over us, but there's a chance we won't be able to escape.

Jonathan seems to think this is a good thing. "We have to get
as close to dying as possible," he says, "to make it believable that
we have." I think he's a little too jazzed by the possibility that we
will actually die.

"Sure," I say, trying not to think about being trapped inside
the steel safe, for however long we decide to wait, not knowing if
we'll be able to get out.

Jonathan calls Alfie at five fifty-three a.m. We're both terrified, but we're also both good at pulling the trigger.

On the third ring, he picks up. Jonathan puts him on speaker. We can hear breathing down the line. The breath crackles.

"Alfie?" Jonathan says.

"Alfie can't come to the phone right now," a tech-warped voice says.

"Where is he?" Jonathan asks like he knows the answer. I know the answer, too.

"We took care of him," the voice says. "We thought you would take care of him for us, but you really don't like to work for free."

"We want out. We just want to quit our jobs. That's all." Jonathan looks at me. It was worth a shot.

"That's not how it works. Blaye," the voice says. Blaye is a commune outside Bordeaux, not far from us.

"We just want to walk away," Jonathan says.

"No, you don't," the voice says. "You want us to come to you. You're setting a trap. At the Château du Cap. Oh. This is interesting." They are clearly typing as they talk, like most techies. "The owner of the château is a doctor in Paris. Masood Ahmed."

Jonathan goes pale as paper. I lose my breath. How did we not see this coming? We thought we were so much smarter than them, but we just seemed smart because we were their pawns. Neither of us says anything, because neither of us knows what to say, and this reveals everything.

"He has a wife," the voice says. "Oh. His wife is pregnant."

"What do you want?" Jonathan says. His voice is hoarse.

"I'm offering you a double hit," the voice says. "I hope you'll take the job. The marks are both of you. The payment is Masood Ahmed's life. You have an hour. Even you can't get to Paris that fast."

"Wait—"

"And just so we're clear: I want bodies. Not bones or ashes or broken pieces. I want you, dead."

The call ends. The clock starts now.

74

Jonathan

I AM WILD WITH RESOLVE. I HAVE TO KILL MYSELF. I HAVE TO DO it now. In my pocket I have an end-of-life concoction that would see me dead in three minutes. I reach for it.

"What are you doing?" Eva grabs my hands to stop them.

"You heard him." I am shaking. "But it doesn't have to be you. It can just be me. Maybe they'll be satisfied."

"I don't think so," she says.

I force her hands away and pull out the pills. They start to melt in my sweaty hands.

"Jonathan, no. We have to stick with the plan. The plan was to die anyway."

"You heard him. He wants bodies. It's not going to work." She knows I am right. "We only have an hour. You know they'll kill him. They'll kill him so fast."

"You can't protect him. They're right—we don't have time."

"I need to call him." I try Mas but he does not pick up. The fucker. I text him, They are sending someone to kill you in an hour, but I have always been so paranoid about him that my credibility on these things is dust.

"It's going to be okay," Eva says. "I mean, as okay as it can be." She squeezes my hand. "We should move forward with the plan. We don't have another option."

I avoid her eyes. I am shaking everywhere. I feel like a mess, like a child. I feel completely out of control.

"I can't." I pull my hand away. "I'm sorry, but I can't. I have to go to Paris." I start toward the door, toward the drive, toward the car, disoriented.

She follows me. "Jonathan, this is a mistake. Your brother is smart. He can take care of himself."

"You don't have to come with me," I say. I would die for my brother. In some ways, that has been the highest aspiration of my life.

I reach the car. I take the keys out of my pocket, but my hands are shaking so badly that I drop them.

Eva picks them up. I cannot read her expression. "Get in the front seat. I'll drive."

"We'll never make it in time," I admit.

"We'll take the TGV. It's faster." It is not fast enough. She sets her jaw. "If they kill him, they lose their bargaining chip." She rests her hand on my shoulder. "We're gonna call their bluff."

She opens the door for me. I get into the car.

XII

LOSS, PART 3

75

Eva

I REALLY HAVE NO IDEA WHETHER THEY'RE BLUFFING. THEY DON'T seem to have any compunctions about murder, just as a rule. We're lucky that when we arrive at the station the fast train to Paris is set to leave in seven minutes. Neither of us talks much at the station, or on the train. Jonathan stares out the window as we speed past vineyards and lazy hills and postcard views.

The hour has almost elapsed when Jonathan says, "I can't do this." It's not immediately clear what he's talking about, but my first thought is that it's us.

I want to take his hand but I'm afraid he'll take it away. We haven't exactly had a normal relationship, but if we had, I would say that our honeymoon period is over. Does he blame me for what's happening? Is he afraid of losing me? Or does he think that loving me has made him too reckless, too careless, too out of control?

I tried to talk him off the ledge last night, but I'm not sure if he ever really came back. I thought we would have time. I thought we could work things out, but the chasm between us is widening. It was easy to be in love when we were only risking ourselves.

He looks at his wrist to check the time, but his watch is gone. We left it with the ashes and the bones, our stand-in decomposed bodies.

He picks up his phone and starts furiously texting, and calling Mas again and again.

I check the clock at the front of the train car.

"One minute," I say. Jonathan goes completely still. We are both silent as the minute changes, and in some theoretical world— maybe even in this one—Mas is killed.

"Where do you think he'll be?" I ask. "Where will we find him?" Dead or alive.

Jonathan rubs his wrist. "The office." Would they really kill him in a doctor's office? "He's always the first one there. He'll be alone, if he's there."

"He'll be there," I say. "He'll be fine." Jonathan won't meet my eyes. He knows I'm the one bluffing. I know it, too.

76

Jonathan

WHEN I WAS A KID, THERE WERE TIMES I THOUGHT MY brain would break. You can push someone only so far. There were scars all over my body, and I could not remember where all of them came from. I stopped being able to see my face when I looked in the mirror. Sometimes I forgot my own name. Forgot everything except pain and fear and vengeance.

Mas brought me back from the brink, again and again. He knew my name. He saw my face. He could tell the story of every scar.

We used to hide out in the woods. We would sit beneath the trees and watch the sun draw time across the sky and Mas would promise me, "When we get older, we'll leave all this behind. We'll be completely different people, with completely different lives."

He was right. And he was wrong.

Paris is over three thousand miles away from the town we grew up in. I do not think that anyone who knew us then would recognize us now: rich and clean and cutthroat. But underneath everything, beneath my bones even, I am still back there, and I always will be.

I cannot be with Eva. I cannot be with anyone, because no matter where I go, no matter what I do, I am still back there, and I always will be.

As we pull into Montparnasse, I realize I have stopped shaking. My tics have vanished. I have gone completely still, like time has stopped inside me. There is nothing more tragic than knowing something terrible has happened before it has been confirmed. Because you cannot scream; you cannot cry.

All you can do is hold your breath.

I wait for a taxi like a prophet. I give the driver the address. Eva looks confused, even awed, by the change in me, by the person I have become: cold and expectant and ancient.

She leans closer. She whispers in my ear, "Should we get weapons somewhere first?" We do not need weapons to find a body.

I know of a safe house in the thirteenth arrondissement and an arms dealer near the Place de la Bastille, but "We don't have time," I say. We ran out a long time ago.

We pull up outside his address, the chicest little doctor's office in Paris, and I can hear the death silence from the street. The shutters are drawn. The lock on the front door has been busted apart.

"We should be armed," Eva says, but it is too late—I am already walking inside.

There is no clerk behind the front desk. There are no patients in the waiting room as I pass through, then down the hall, toward Mas's office.

I find the first body there.

It does not belong to Mas. It belongs to an assassin, laid out across the narrow hall. I take his gun, toss it to Eva.

"Feel better now?" I ask. I do. It is amazing how quickly tragedy can lift, become something else.

The next body belongs to another assassin, this one slumped against a wall, stunned and starry-eyed.

"Holy shit," Eva opines.

I shake my head and almost smile, almost hope.

I step over another body just as I hear his voice. He is on the phone. He is talking to his wife.

". . . I'm fine, I promise. I just want you to stay with the police, okay? I'm just waiting for the officers to arrive, and then I'm getting in a cab. I canceled all my appointments. I'm *fine*; I just want to make sure that you . . ."

I walk into the exam room. I am very lucky that Mas is expecting the cops and not more assassins. He actually smiles when he sees me. His face is spattered with blood.

"I'll be home soon," he tells Giselle. "I promise." He ends the call. "You fucking prick," he says to me.

"I did text you." I hop onto the exam table.

"You said some*one* was coming to kill me."

"I meant a singular entity. Not a singular assassin. I could have explained that if you had just *called me back*." I try not to smirk. I am so happy he is still alive. I am even happy he is still an asshole. "You told me you didn't want my help. *If I'm on fire*, you said."

He stalks across the room and neatly slaps me across the face. I do deserve it.

Eva steps in. "I'm impressed. I thought I was with the killer brother."

"I did three tours of duty," Mas says. "You want to see some real action? Try war."

"I was sure you were dead," I tell Mas. I was sure. I am always *so sure* of the worst possible outcome.

"Have a little faith in me," he says. "That one did catch me off guard." He points at a fourth body, a sniper jammed into a vent, dead arm dangling. Mas shakes his head, then glares at me. "I thought you said you were taking care of this."

"I'm so sorry."

"Right, well. Did you ever consider that maybe you're the one who needs me to protect you?"

"I would say that's a pretty accurate assessment," I admit.

The door buzzer sounds. "I'm glad you're here," Mas tells me, resting a hand on my shoulder and directing me toward the door. "Because now you can explain all this to the cops."

77

Eva

ITS CLEAR THIS IS NOT JONATHAN'S FIRST TIME LYING TO THE cops. He knows all the little tricks.

He thanks them profusely. He compliments them. He asks about their weapons. He is in awe of them.

"It must be *so hard* to be a cop!" he says in perfectly fluent French.

"Any idea what these men wanted?" an officer asks Mas. Mas is even better with cops. They like him immediately because he was in the army.

"My guess is drugs," Mas tells them. Four men, four handguns and two assault rifles, just to get high. The sad thing is, it's believable.

"You handled yourself very well," another officer says.

"I did what I had to do," Mas says. The cops *love* that, because it's practically a cop mantra. Mas has been sitting in a chair, being examined by a medical team, but now he stands. "If everything is in order for now, I need to get back to my wife."

"You had some officers deployed to your residence—is that correct?" the shorter officer says.

"Yes," Mas says.

"Why?"

Mas looks at Jonathan. "I told him to," Jonathan says. "His wife is pregnant, and we just wanted her to feel safe."

"All right," the officer says.

"Anything else?" Mas says.

"Not at the moment," he says. "Go see your wife. I'm sure she is very worried."

"Thank you," Mas says.

Outside, the cab is waiting to take us to Mas's apartment. I have to admit, it's nice to know that we don't have to face this alone.

MAS'S WIFE, GISELLE, IS MORE FURIOUS THAN WORRIED. SHE MEETS us at the door to their extremely chic, extremely large apartment in Pigalle.

"What were you fucking thinking?" she asks Mas as we filter through the door. She says "fucking" in English, but the rest is in French. "You send the police here. You tell me nothing. And now you tell me that four people tried to kill you? Why you? What makes you so special?" Mas is too overwhelmed to answer, so she rounds on Jonathan. "And *you*. I'm sure this has something to do with you," she says in English.

Mas opens his mouth, but Jonathan speaks first. "I'm an assassin. Was."

This stops her in her tracks. "What?"

"Sorry—that's the glamorous way of putting it," he says. "I was a contract killer. I killed people for money."

She hits Mas on the shoulder. "And you never told me this?"

"I never invited him over for dinner either," Mas says. "We were estranged."

She looks between them. "I think I liked that better. What changed?"

"I quit," Jonathan says. "Mas was trying to help me get out. I'm sorry. I didn't think—"

"You enlisted my husband to help you get out of the contract-killing business, and you didn't think it would be dangerous?"

"I have a fairly warped sense of danger," he admits.

"And what about you?" Giselle turns to me and I automatically cringe. Not because I'm afraid of her but because I want her to like me.

"Also a contract killer. Currently in the process of transitioning to a new field."

"My god." She shakes her head in annoyance.

We are all crammed into the hallway with the door closed. It's all very awkward. Giselle glares at Mas until finally she relents and embraces him. The anger leaves her face for a moment, and I can see the fear.

"You smell like blood," she tells him.

"I'm sorry," he says.

She holds his face in her hands and stares persistently at him, as if to assure herself that he's still there. Then she pulls away and gestures us into the apartment. "This is ridiculous," she says. "We can't just stand in the hallway."

We follow her into a sitting room with hand-painted wallpaper and tufted chairs.

"Your apartment is beautiful," I say.

"Thank you. I designed it myself." She offers me half a smile at full warmth, and I imagine a world in which I come here again. Every Sunday for brunch. I imagine us as friends. Family, even.

Giselle takes a seat. We all follow her lead except Jonathan, who stays perched by the door, watching.

"Who exactly is trying to kill you?" Giselle asks me.

"That's where it gets a little unclear," I say. "It's a forum on the dark web. People post jobs with money attached. Enterprising techies engage people like us to commit murder for money."

"It's just like you always say, my love," Mas tells her. "The internet is destroying society."

"What is the forum called?" Giselle asks.

"Hire-a-Hitman," I say. "I know—it's cringey."

"Get my laptop," she tells Mas.

Mas jumps up to fetch it. "Giselle is the head of cybersecurity for the EU. If anyone can find this thing, she can. She's kind of a genius." He hands her the laptop.

"Kind of?" She makes a face. "Now"—she looks from me to Jonathan—"tell me everything you know about this forum, and I bet you I'll find it. Then we'll see who is 'kind of.'"

SIX HOURS LATER, I'M STILL SITTING NEXT TO GISELLE WHILE SHE types furiously. Mas and Jonathan have left to make more coffee. They've been gone awhile. I hope they're talking.

Jonathan has been distant since last night. It's weird how you can feel someone has left you even when you're still with them. They're just gone, even when they're right there. For the first time I think that even if we do get out of this, we might not stay together. We might just go our separate ways.

"Can I ask you a personal question?" Giselle asks, fingers flying.

"Anything." If this goes right, I might owe her my life.

And I like her. She's smart and she's funny. In another life, we might have been friends. We might have been the wives of two brothers.

"Why do you do this?" she asks. "I mean, why *did* you?"

I open my mouth, ready to tell her the same old story. Childhood trauma. Buried in chaos. Because I was good at it. Because I didn't feel like I belonged. Because I didn't think I had a choice. "Because I was afraid," I say instead. "All the time." I exhale. "Plus, it was pretty badass."

She shakes her head, but a smile tickles her lips.

78

Jonathan

MAS AND I WENT INTO THE KITCHEN TO MAKE COFFEE, AND now we are both staring off into space. I am perched on the countertop, watching the world outside the window.

Paris is exactly the same as it always is: too gray, too dirty, too busy. That is something I have always loved about Paris. No matter what I do—who I kill, who I hurt, who hurts me—the city stays the same. You bleed, you suffer, you die and Paris just sighs, *I've seen it all before.*

"I'm really sorry," I tell Mas for the umpteenth time. "I should have told you what my plan was, so you could have told me how stupid it was."

"Story of our lives," he says, scooping another spoonful of coffee into the machine. "It's fine. We can't go back. You're here now."

"As soon as Giselle tracks these people down, I will kill them. And we can all live happily ever after. Separately."

He jams more coffee into the slot and starts the machine. "I don't think separately works."

"What?"

He sighs, rubs the back of his neck. He wanders toward me,

first gazing out the window, then turning to face me. "What do you want, Jonathan?"

"What do you mean?"

"In life. If you could have anything, what would you want?"

"I can't have *anything*."

"Really?" He puts his hands on his hips. "Because you seem to have gotten pretty much whatever you wanted. Money. Success—albeit in a pretty niche field. You've gotten away with murder—literally—how many times? Do you really think it's that impossible for you to have something simple? To have what everyone else has?"

"I don't know."

We sit together in silence as the coffee machine burbles and steams. I realize I have not been in a kitchen—been in a *home*—with Mas since we were children. Back then, I never could have imagined a scene like this. I knew where Europe was, but not that I could go there. I could not have pictured this four-thousand-dollar coffee machine, these custom countertops and the view outside the window—so leafy, so chic, so fucking picturesque that it could break your heart if you let it all in, if you let yourself be a part of it.

I have kept myself in a cage for so many years that even when I see beauty, I see it through bars. I am the prisoner and the prison. I am the solution to all of my problems and yet I *cannot* set myself free.

The coffee machine beeps as Giselle and Eva enter the kitchen.

"She really is a genius," Eva says, hovering just inside the door.

"You found the forum?" I ask.

"No." Giselle smiles, resting her head on Mas's shoulder. "I found the administrator."

XIII

———

DEATH

79

Eva

WE DON'T TAKE A TRAIN THIS TIME. OR A CAR. OR EVEN a taxi. We can walk to where this all started—to where this will end. The address is disconcertingly near Les Puces.

We wait until well after midnight, when the streets are mostly clear, when the city is mostly silent, waiting. We arm ourselves before we leave. Nothing fancy—two matching Glocks stowed under our jackets. The streets are not completely deserted, but they are empty enough for us to feel like they belong a little to us.

Jonathan is quiet. I try to convince myself it's because he was scared about Mas. That he's still in shock. That when all of this is over, he will go back to normal—but what is normal?

I've spent seven days with Jonathan. We've been to four countries and killed three people. You might think it's impossible to really get to know someone in that amount of time, but knowing him isn't the problem. I knew him from the start, because he's just like me.

We love hard, but we fear harder. We scare easy. We run, and we never look back.

"What are you thinking?" I ask him.

"I don't know . . . ," he says as we walk through dim, charmed streets.

I feel inside me this swelling urge to leave first, to run first, to break his heart *first*. Like that would turn losing into winning.

"I can't believe you're doing this," I say.

He almost doesn't take the bait. Almost. "Doing what?"

"Like you don't know."

He makes a groan-like sound.

"What, so you're just not gonna say anything? You're being a prick." He flinches.

"Oh. Okay. We're doing this now?"

"Well, we're headed toward certain death, so I don't know how we can possibly fit it in later."

He scoffs. "I have a lot going on right now."

"No shit. Me, too. Up until last night, I thought we were both in the same situation. Contract killers. Trying to leave the business. Everyone wants us dead. Sound familiar?"

"I think we should do this later." Jonathan lengthens his stride.

"You're gonna break up with me, aren't you? Just tell me, so I can break up with you first."

He cocks his head. "If I tell you, then wouldn't I be breaking up with you first?"

"Fine. I break up with you. Preemptively."

"Okay."

"*Okay*? That's your response. After everything we've been through?"

"We're hunting down a person who has facilitated hundreds of murders across Europe, possibly the globe."

"And you think that's more important?"

His face cracks. "Don't make me laugh."

"Jonathan," I say. "If we make it out alive, what then?"

He sighs, and I can tell he's as lost as he ever was. "That's the thing about the future," he says. "It hasn't happened yet."

"Don't you want me anymore?"

He rests a hand on my good arm. "I want you alive."

"Well, I want more than that." I shove his hand off, storm around the corner.

Jonathan starts to follow me, but then he stops in his tracks. "Oh *shit*."

"What 'oh shit'?" I search the tired streets but don't notice anything amiss.

"I've been here before."

"What? When?"

He looks at me. I've missed his eyes so much that I step back in surprise. "After we met on the train, I tried to find you. Your name wasn't on the passenger list, so I tracked down every person in our car, in case one of them would lead me to you."

"The American. The one who didn't leave." The one who watched me open the suitcase.

Jonathan takes a step forward, then stops again. "His name is Bruce. He taught me in a fencing class. He *hates* me. He lives in a penthouse—three penthouses actually, one on top of another—at the corner of Rue du Parc."

"Lucky guy." I wait for Jonathan to say more, but he doesn't.

We told Mas and Giselle that we were just going to look around. We swore this was reconnaissance. We pretended we would be right back. I don't think any of us believed it.

The thing is, we don't have an easy out. Jonathan and I gave our lives to someone, and now they get to decide what happens to them.

"There's no way we can just walk in and kill him, is there?" I ask.

"It seems unlikely."

"Do you think he knows we're here, right now?"

"Maybe."

I scan the streets, looking for direction, a sign, anything. But I have been an assassin long enough to know there is never a foolproof plan. There is never a job that goes completely right. Murder is unpredictable, any way you slice it. The one thing I have, the one thing I have relied on, the one thing that has gotten me *here* alive, is my ability to do things without thinking.

I cross to a trash can. I slip my Glock out from under my jacket, wipe my prints and drop the gun into the bin. Jonathan watches me. I start toward Rue du Parc.

"Where are you going?" he asks.

I spin around, walk backward a few steps. "Forward." I spin away from him and walk faster.

Not to be dramatic, but I don't want to go back to the life I had before. I can't go back, so the only way is forward.

To my death, maybe. But at least I have a destination.

I HAVE NO IDEA WHAT TO EXPECT AS I APPROACH THE TALL GLASS doors with my hands where the guards can see them.

A doorman steps out and holds one of the doors open for me. I did not expect anything, but I *really* did not expect that.

Jonathan is right behind me, hovering over me, like he could save either of us if things went wrong.

We step into the building. It's classically French. It has a leafy courtyard, with marble fountains gurgling. It smells like dust and lavender and it looks ancient and it makes you feel insignificant and romantic at the same time.

A guard stands at the door, pointing a gun at our heads. Another guard pats us down in the entryway. He finds a knife around Jonathan's ankle.

"I completely forgot I had that," Jonathan says.

The security guard sighs and says, "Empty your pockets."

Jonathan hands over fistfuls of pills, a multitool and a switchblade. The guard finds nothing on me, because I am an actual badass.

"He's waiting for you." The guard leads us to an old-fashioned wrought iron elevator inside a metal cage.

An elevator operator waits inside. The guard follows us in, keeping his gun trained on us.

"He doesn't want us dead," I say as the elevator rattles beneath us. "At least not yet."

"He probably wants to watch us die," Jonathan hums under his breath. "To make sure it happens this time."

The door pings open on an ordinary penthouse—not ordinary, maybe. Don't get me wrong; it's big and it's expensive and it's impressive. But it could belong to anyone. A real estate magnate, an oil baron, old money or new. There is nothing in the textured rugs or the floor-to-ceiling windows that screams *Murder-for-Hire Empire.*

The guard directs us into a great room with a low view across Paris: the point of the glass Louvre Pyramid, the Eiffel Tower and the Arc de Triomphe. The sun is just starting to bleach the sky. I have this sudden memory of my first day in Paris—I guess because this might be my last—how I walked along the Seine and observed all the pieces of Paris laid out like toys. I was a tourist, and life was a game.

Bruce enters the room. I recognize him immediately, but he looks stronger, sharper, more dangerous. Probably because I know he's a villain.

"How nice of you to stop by," he says in English. "Do you want a drink?"

"I'll hold off until we establish whether you want us dead," I say.

He laughs boldly. "What I like about you, Annika, is that you're such a joker. I think people in peril are just so much more humorous than other people. You really have to suffer, I think, to be truly funny."

"Thank you for contributing to my sense of humor."

He blinks at me. "Exceptional," he says, like I'm his pet. I guess I was. He turns to Jonathan. "Do *you* want a drink? Frank, is it? No, that's not right. It's Ethan. Don't look surprised. I know your real name. I know everything about you, now that you led me to your brother."

"I'm good on the drink," Jonathan says.

Bruce wanders to a drink cart and makes himself a martini. He's very clearly living in a fantasy world where he is James Bond. I know because I used to live in one, too. Underneath his facade is probably a very damaged, troubled person, but that doesn't really inspire sympathy when someone wants to kill you.

I scan the room—force of habit. I find all the escape routes, the best positions and the weapons. There are weapons everywhere: an umbrella stand full of swords, a rackful of guns, antique sabers mounted to a wall. They are so immaculate that I think he must never use them, but I've been wrong about that before. There are also four armed guards, one in each corner of the room, pointing guns at Jonathan and me.

"You can call me Bruce," he says. "That's not my real name, of course, but it's so much more fun pretending, isn't it?"

"Are you planning to kill us?" Jonathan asks. "Because if you are, I don't want to die having small talk."

"You see what I mean?" Bruce says to me. "Funny." He lifts his martini and takes a sip. Then he walks along the glass wall, observing the city below. "We met on the train, you may remember. That was a bit of a fuckup. Neither of you was supposed to be on that train. Neither was I. I was in Florence to keep an eye on you, Ethan. You'd had too many close calls and your performance was under review. It was completely by chance—or should we call it fate?—that Annika showed up to bury her living boyfriend."

My heart drops. "You know about Andrew?"

"Of course I know," Bruce says. "Don't worry. He's not dead. Yet. I *did* want him dead. He turned against the network—you remember. He went to the police—not that they believed him, of course. But you get enough people saying crazy things, it starts to sound rational.

"Lucky for me, getting shot off that bridge woke Andrew up. He ran away to Brazil. A year in the Pantanal and he was begging to come back. He works for me now, in a different department. He knows who I am and where I am, but he never told you, did he? But he told me that you stopped by, and all about your plan to fake your deaths." God, my ex really sucks.

"What do you want?" I ask.

"That is such a good question," he says. "It is a very important one, don't you think? It determines who you'll be in a way nothing else does. Whether you'll be satisfied with the world everyone else lives in. Or whether you *want* more.

"I'm a lot like you." He addresses Jonathan—no surprise. He clearly doesn't see me as a threat, which makes me want to kill him even more. As he speaks, I let my eyes wander, analyzing the room: the elevator, the stairwell, every door and window.

"I was always treated like a freak," he continues. "Even though there was nothing evidently wrong with me, people could tell I was different." I used to think it was funny that the villains in movies always took a moment to monologue their origin stories,

347

but it's clear that Bruce has been *dying* to have this moment, to tell someone *everything*. It's no fun being the bad guy behind a curtain. "There are benefits to being an outsider. You see things from a distance." I startle, thinking he's caught me calculating the distance from the axe on the wall to the elevator—but of course he hasn't. Women are the true outsiders.

"And there's a certain degree of detachment, and that detachment allows you to separate yourself from consequences, from devastation—even devastation you caused." I hate that I kind of understand what he's saying. There's nothing worse than a villain who's a little like you.

"I came from a good family—by 'good' I mean 'rich'—and I used my family's wealth to create more wealth. It was easy making money but it wasn't fun. For something to be fun, it has to be dangerous. I was searching for just the right opportunity. The opportunity to have *more*." He gestures across the window, as if he owns all of Paris.

"Did you order the hit on me?" Jonathan asks, getting straight to the point.

Bruce shrugs. "You were getting sloppy. I've been in this business for years; you see a lot of people crack up. Better safe than sorry.

"I could have had you identified as a defector, but I don't know if I have a man on my payroll who could take you out. I like efficiency, and after what I saw on that sleeper train I knew you liked this one, so I contacted Laura directly with the job. But as you know, Annika proved inefficient. I should never have trusted a woman." Ick. "The situation got a little out of control, but I think, ultimately, we can come together and make sure that everyone walks away happy."

"You said 'walk,'" I point out. *Walk*, as in not in a body bag.

348

"We don't want you dead. You've made us a lot of money. You've made yourselves a lot of money."

"You sent your assassins after us," I point out. Jonathan says nothing. I don't know what he's thinking. "You killed Laura," I say, because somebody should.

"We've all made mistakes," Bruce says. "Both of you have killed a lot of people."

"What made you change your mind?" I ask. "I mean, yesterday—even hours ago—you wanted us dead."

He's still looking at Jonathan, who is suspiciously silent. "Can you tell her what has changed, Ethan?" Bruce slips his phone out of his pocket and holds it up. Fuck. Maybe both of my exes suck.

"I told him I want to go back to the job." Jonathan was texting furiously on the train, calling someone over and over. It wasn't Mas. It was Alfie's old number. It was Bruce.

I can't believe Jonathan offered to go back without even telling me—except he did kind of warn me last night in Bordeaux. I thought I had convinced him. I thought we were in this together, but I was wrong. He doesn't want to change. He doesn't want me.

I turn to Bruce. "He offered to join you and you still went through with the assassination attempt on his brother?"

Bruce sips his martini, then answers me. "It's hard to call these things off at the last minute. We sent ten men to kill Mas. Not all of them got the message in time."

Jonathan steps forward. "I want to go back, but she doesn't have to."

"That is fine with me." Bruce shrugs. "We can make a deal. Everyone you love will be safe as long as you are ours."

"I thought we were in this together," I tell Jonathan.

"Can we talk privately?" Jonathan asks Bruce. "I mean, with the illusion of privacy?"

I can't imagine he will let us go off alone together, but he seems completely confident in his control of the situation. I can't exactly blame him. We've always been his pawns.

"Sure." He gestures to one of his guards. "Take them into the Louis XIV room." The guard starts toward a door. "No," Bruce corrects. "All of you."

All four guards lead us into the adjoining room, guns still trained at our temples.

IT'S HARD TO HAVE A PERSONAL CONVERSATION IN FRONT OF A FIR-ing squad, but as usual, I have to do what I have to do. I can see why Bruce chose this room—there are no weapons on the walls or anywhere else. The decor actually reminds me of our hotel room in Versailles; it looks like it has a floral communicable disease.

Jonathan is avoiding my eyes, choosing instead to watch the city below through a tall, narrow window. He was the one who requested a private audience with me, and yet he seems to have nothing to say.

I honestly hoped that he had a plan. That he thought we could take out the four men with guns trained on our heads, but he knows as well as I do that we can't. Maybe if we were armed, or had the benefit of distraction, or the playground of the city. But we're trapped in a flowery French room, and even if we could escape these four men, we could never get out of this building alive.

Most importantly, Jonathan doesn't want to leave.

I approach him at the window. "I understand why you're doing this," I say.

"No, you don't." He keeps his eyes fixed on the street below.

"Um. Yes, I do." My gaze flits over the armed guards. I wish I could kill them, just so they wouldn't be listening. I lower my voice. "You want to protect me."

"No, I don't." Jonathan exhales, then turns to face me. His face is cold; it's an expression I remember. I've seen it a few times: It's his kill face. The one he makes when he's about to take your life. "You don't need me to protect you. You're stronger than I am. That's why I'm doing this. Not to protect you. To protect me."

"I don't understand," I say, but I think I do.

"Bruce is right. I'm not like everybody else. I don't want to be. I want more."

"More *what*?"

He shrugs. I guess because he doesn't want to admit: more blood, more danger, more death. What he said last night was a little true, even if I don't want to admit it. There's no place for us on the other side of all this. There's no place where we would fit or make sense. He couldn't hold a job; I wouldn't want one.

Where would we live? How would we pay for it? What would we do when we woke up to another nightmare? When we felt that terror and had no way to escape it?

We would turn on ourselves. We would turn on each other.

I know that and I *knew* it. From the very first day on the train, when I thought we should hook up and walk away. He knew it when he said we should have sex and separate. We could pretend for only so long before we had to admit that the biggest lie that we ever told ourselves was that we could be together.

"Eva," he says gently. "I don't choose you. I choose this."

I open my mouth to protest but find myself saying, "I understand. I wish I didn't, but I do."

He shudders a little, but he doesn't argue. He doesn't try to stop me when I walk away.

A single guard escorts me out of Bruce's penthouse. He doesn't even keep his gun trained on me. It hangs limply at his side while he checks his phone in the elevator. That is how little he considers me a threat.

I could take him so easily. I could use his gun to blow his brains out. I could go back. But then what? Even I can't take out three armed guards and a supervillain. And Jonathan doesn't want me to.

The elevator falls. I watch Paris drop out from under me, crashing like my heart.

80

Jonathan

I WAS NEVER AFRAID OF GETTING HURT. I KNEW I DESERVED IT; I might even like it. I was afraid of hurting someone else, of killing the person I was supposed to love—by accident or on purpose.

As I watch Eva walk away, I can see how strong she is. I realize I could never break her. It makes me love her even more.

The armed guards return me to Bruce, who is pouring himself another martini. Eva's escort returns without her.

"You sure you don't want that drink now?" Bruce asks me.

"I'm good." I wait.

"Well, I'm not one for small talk either, so I will be direct." He pulls a sword from an umbrella stand. "You know I'm not going to let you come back, right?"

"Yes."

He indicates another sword. I do not pick it up right away. There are four guards with guns pointed at my head. There is no way I can survive, but that does not mean I cannot win.

"Ever since we fought in that class," he says, "I have been thinking—*obsessively*: Did he let me win? I need to know the answer." I do not pick up the sword. I can see his irritation. "You know I'm not going to let her walk away either, right?" he says, trying to get a rise out of me.

"Yes."

"Come on!" he says in French. He gestures to the sword. "I am going to kill you, and then I *personally* am going to track her down and slaughter her. No more hiring hit men. I can do your job better than you. I am going to gut your brother and his wife, and every other reason you have for living I am going to terminate. Do you understand? *Come on!*"

I do not pick up the sword. I do not take my mark. I do not salute him.

He rolls his eyes. "Whatever."

He charges me.

I grab the sword.

I parry his attack, he boxes me against the wall and, when we are inches apart, when I can see the bottomless pit where his soul should be, I tell him:

"Of fucking course I let you win."

81

Eva

MORE PEOPLE ARE ON THE STREET. MORE CARS ARE ON THE road. My world is ending but this world could swallow me up.

I stop at the end of the pavement.

I feel my phone in my hand, my eyes on the screen, before I realize what I am about to do. I was about to call Sherri—Laura. Instinctively, my hand went to my phone. My mind went to her. Like I haven't quite caught up with everything I've lost in the past few days. With everything I'm still losing.

I can't believe Jonathan chose to stay, except that I can actually, totally understand it. Because I'm here now with nothing. No way forward. My past is the only open road, drawing me like a magnet to the only home I've ever known: to the house where death lives.

I lost my family. I lost my best friend. Now I am walking away from the man who could be the love of my life. I'm starting to notice a pattern. It's as if I'm programmed to repeat the trauma from my youth again and again. I can't tell if the world is conspiring or if I'm conspiring against me.

But I know that I don't want to be stuck in this loop forever. I don't want this to be who I am. I want to take the good things I've learned: I want to be brave and strong and dangerous. But I don't want to be abandoned anymore. I don't want to be too late.

I know that Jonathan's plan won't end well. I know that if he keeps killing, then somehow, someday soon, he'll wind up dead. I don't want to lose him. I can't. I have to break the cycle now or I'll never ever leave it.

I look at Laura's alias on my phone screen. I feel the tears before I even know I'm crying. What would she say, if I could speak to her? What would she tell me to do?

She would tell me she believed in me. She would tell me to avenge her death. She would tell me to break the glass ceiling with a bullet to that monster's chest.

I don't care what Jonathan wants. *I* want that fucker dead. I don't need anyone's permission. I don't need to ask nicely. I'm my own handler now and this is the biggest job of my life and I am going to murder this cycle of death.

My eyes fall on the trash can where I dropped my Glock. I once believed that all I really needed was a Glock and a prayer. Maybe I still believe that.

And suddenly, the gun is in my hand.

And suddenly, I'm running back.

I don't know what I'm going to do when I get there, but I always work better when I trust my gut.

82

Jonathan

BRUCE AND I HAVE BEEN FENCING FOR FIVE MINUTES WHEN IT dawns on me that I am fighting for shit. People have been calling me sloppy for a while now, but this is the first time that I feel it. Bruce cuts my forearm. He knicks my neck. I am late on a block three, four times in a row.

When they called me sloppy, I assumed they meant I was reckless. Now that I feel it myself, I know that is not it. They did not think I was dangerous because I was deranged. They thought I was a liability because I was weak.

"I thought you were better than this," Bruce says. He is annoyed. Hell, so am I.

I do not think I can beat him. I used to be so angry. I was consumed with rage. It was my secret weapon. It was the thing that made me powerful, but when I reach for it now, I cannot find it.

I thought life was horrible, and then I met her.

I thought the world was a dark place, but how could it be, when she was always in it?

Maybe everything I thought about the world was wrong.

Maybe I saw only one side. Maybe I do not know the world at all. Maybe, by surrounding myself with death, I have never truly lived. Until her. Until now. Until I fell in love.

Loving her is making me soft. It is making me kind and careful and fucking thoughtful. Love has made me a better person, and a worse murderer.

Love is going to get me killed, like I always feared it would.

"It's her, isn't it?" he says, reading my mind. "She took away your power. I'm a little disappointed." His sword slices through the air. "I wanted to fight you at your peak."

"Then why did you send her?"

He backs away for a moment. He shakes out his hands, then darts forward again, striking harder. "You may not know me, but I have known you for years. I have seen you kill dozens of people; some I have watched with my own eyes. You were a monster once, you know. I think even I was afraid of you." He drives me back until I hit an eighteenth-century writing desk. He forces me back against it. Our swords shake with tension as I hold him at bay. "It seems I should not have been."

Beyond the window, the sky is a brilliant, unholy blue.

I should be happy that I am going to die like this: surrounded by antiques, with an excellent view of Paris, at the hands of a maniac. I have seen so many deaths, so I know this is a good one. I could have died anywhere: on the street, asleep, in the hospital, on that train, before I met her.

I should be happy, but I do not want to die. I do not want to be anyplace where she is not. I want to be old. I want to be boring. I want to be with her.

An alarm pierces the air. The guards jump to attention. They scan the room but no one appears. She must be downstairs. She must be coming back. Shit.

Bruce has me trapped against the desk. I can smell the stink of my own sweat, mixed with my blood from where he cut me. My muscles are quivering from fatigue.

Even if I manage to throw him off, even if I stab him, he will not die right away. And in the meantime, I will be shot by the firing squad that still has four guns pointed at my head.

It is not what I want, but at least if he is dead, she might live.

I struggle to reposition myself, but Bruce does not budge. I need to throw him off balance, but I am trapped.

"You've built quite the business model." I grunt. "You must be responsible for hundreds of deaths. But I wonder, have you ever killed anyone with your own hands?"

I can feel his rage bubble. "I would tell you to ask me again tomorrow," he says, "but you won't be here."

I loosen my grip, as if finally giving up. Bruce tips forward, caught off balance. I unleash the last of my rage, the last of my fury, the last of my hope.

I trip him up and I force him back. I stab him.

A guard yells, and then I feel the shot:

Bang!

And then I hear the firing squad:

Bang! Bang! Bang! Bang!

Sometimes it happens that fast.

83

Eva

I KICK THE DOOR OPEN BEFORE THE DOORMAN CAN GET IT FOR me. I zero in on the security guards first. They don't expect me, so the first one is easy. The second one shoots me.

The bullet just grazes my shoulder because I know to duck and roll after the first kill in a three-way shoot-out. I take cover behind an enormous imperial Ming vase because, if it's authentic, it's worth more than either of our lives.

He blows the vase apart, so I guess I know it's a fake. I get a shot in while the debris is still flying.

I spot the doorman creeping toward a box on the wall that has to be some kind of alarm. I could take out the doorman, but he's unarmed. And he's too far away to stop without risking myself.

Security guard number two is taking aim at me again, so I duck and roll (in the same direction, because the opposite is too predictable). I shoot the alarm on the off chance that it will disarm the system.

It doesn't. A horrible sound pierces the air. The guard cringes bodily at the sound, so his shot misses. Mine doesn't. He's down. The doorman knows when to make an exit.

The elevator operator is headed out the same way until I cock a gun at his head and say, nicely, "Top floor, please."

The elevator rockets up beneath my feet. The city falls away. I hate to admit it, but I feel fucking good. I missed this—sin, that it is.

The elevator snaps to a stop. The operator doesn't move to open the grate and I don't encourage him. We are still inside the wrought iron cage when I see Bruce pin Jonathan against a desk. I could've guessed their new arrangement wouldn't work out, but I thought it would last longer than five minutes.

I'm guessing this was Jonathan's plan—to get me out of harm's way so he could take down Bruce—but he should have learned by now that he can't do these things alone. He needs me, and it's okay to need someone. It's maybe the only thing that keeps you human.

Three of the guards are pointing their guns at Jonathan's head; the other is speaking into an alarm system on the wall, trying to make contact with the guys downstairs. Thanks to the wailing alarm, no one has heard me. No one has seen me yet.

I lift my gun and take aim.

I can see Jonathan shaking with the effort of holding Bruce off. If I shoot now, the bullet might go through Bruce and hit Jonathan. I need them to separate.

I try to be patient, try to wait for my shot, but Jonathan's flagging and it's only a matter of time before the guards notice me. Bruce has the upper hand. If I don't shoot now, I might be too late. Jonathan would want me to take the shot—I know he would, because I would want the same thing.

Sweat beads along my hairline. Goose bumps dapple my flesh. My heart is racing so fast. If Bruce kills Jonathan I'll lose my distraction, and I won't stand a chance against him and his guards. I need to shoot now. I need to kill him now.

The guard at the wall gives up on the alarm system. He seems to realize that the downstairs guards are gone, which can mean only one thing.

His eyes go straight to the elevator, to me. His jaw drops.

Meanwhile, Jonathan starts to lose his grip on his sword. Bruce leans in. My finger is contracting on the trigger when, suddenly, Jonathan feints and throws Bruce off.

Bruce staggers back as the guard yells in French, "The elevator!"

Bruce spots me through the grate. He looks confused, as if he can't understand why I—an assassin—would be pointing a gun at his head. Story of my fucking life.

Bang!

The four armed guards turn toward me and open fire, giving Jonathan an out.

Bang! Bang! Bang! Bang!

I take cover in the corner of the elevator. The operator panics and presses every button in sight. Sparks fly as the elevator drops.

We screech to a stop at the next floor down.

"We need to go back up," I direct.

The elevator operator shoots me a fearful look. He forces the cage open and makes a run for it. Fine. His job is the definition of "extraneous."

I search for some kind of override, but he's pressed too many buttons. The elevator doors start to shut. I pull the emergency stop.

I see the elevator operator racing toward a stairwell. I abandon the elevator and follow him. He runs faster, poor thing, but once we reach the stairwell, I head up as he goes down.

I left Jonathan with four armed guards carrying assault rifles. Even if I did kill Bruce, that leaves Jonathan with a sword at a gun party.

I need to get back there—fast.

84

Jonathan

THE SKY IS STILL BLUE.

Bruce is dead. The armed guards are shooting at the elevator shaft. I always know when to make an exit. I race toward the stairwell, slip inside the door before anyone remembers me.

I hear someone coming up the stairs. My knees give out. I catch myself on the banister. My heart is hammering in my chest.

I think I am going to die, and then I see her.

85

Eva

I RUN UP THE STAIRS AND KISS HIM. HE SMELLS LIKE SWEAT AND blood. He wobbles a little on his feet, leaning on me for balance.

"Let's get the fuck out of here," I say.

We charge down the stairs. I can hear sirens on the street, heading toward us. The chaos seems to have scared everyone off. The ground floor is deserted. The firing squad does not seem to be following us.

Jonathan and I hurry through a very cute French garden, where I wipe and dump my gun. We pass through a garden gate and land on the back side of the Avenue de la Campagne.

I thread my fingers through his. We charge down the alleyway. We keep our eyes on the busy streets beyond. We try to get as much distance from the scene as possible. The police sail by along the main road. We both exhale a sigh of relief.

"Now," I say, still struggling to catch my breath. My heart and my veins are electric with adrenaline. "We don't have to get into this now, but I just want to confirm—while it's still fresh in our minds—that I killed him."

"Beg your pardon? I stabbed him."

"Again, I don't want to argue right now, but you stabbed him in the stomach. I mean, maybe he would have gone septic in the hospital, but—"

"I took out multiple organs."

"I shot him. In the head. It was a kill shot."

"He was already as good as dead." Jonathan staggers a little, clearly exhausted.

"You know, I didn't want to bring this up," I say, "but you also thought you killed Andrew."

"You are so . . ." He lists against the wall of a building. I try to help him, and when I pull my hand away from his waist, I realize it's covered in blood.

"Oh my God, you've been shot."

"There was a firing squad," he says, sliding down the wall toward the ground. I can see the adrenaline leaving him. His face is flat white.

"Oh my God." I pull up his shirt. He's peppered with gunshot wounds. Worse, the blood is pumping. They hit an artery.

"Don't worry," he says, slightly slurring. "S'nothing. I've died four times." His head drops back against the wall. "It feels different this time."

I take his phone from his coat pocket. "Don't worry. I'm calling Mas."

I find Mas's number in recent calls and let the phone ring as I struggle to make a tourniquet big enough. My hands are shaking. I can't hear the sirens anymore, but I almost wish the police would find us, wish we could be caught, so someone could save us.

"I just want you to know—," he starts.

"Shut up! Don't say anything." I'm afraid that if he does, it will really be over.

"I just want you to know," he repeats, "that I should have chosen you."

"You did choose me."

"I mean, before all this. I should have chosen you instead of murder. Maybe then we wouldn't—"

"No! I didn't want to believe it, but maybe every bad thing brought us here. Maybe we had to— Jonathan, are you listening?"

He exhales. It sounds suspiciously like a death rattle. Then his head falls forward, so he's staring at the ground.

XIV

_____

HAPPILY EVER AFTER

Six Months Later

86

Eva

I AM STALKING DOWN THE HALLWAY OF AN OFFICE IN MUNICH. I have a Glock in my hand and a prayer in my heart as I execute my plan.

I catch my reflection in the tall glass windows. I went full-on assassin with my makeup today—a dark eye, bloodred lips. I feel like myself, more than ever before. I am so many things: a killer, a lover, a villain, a hero.

Through the windows, I see the long green expanse of the Englischer Garten. People sunbathe in the nude on the Schönfeldwiese lawn, sip tea in the Japanese teahouse or neck between the columns of the Monopteros. It's all very romantic. I map my escape through the garden as I creep toward my target.

I can hear my mark through the door. He's on the phone, shouting angrily. He's about to get a lot more upset.

On any job there is a time for subtlety and a time for panache. I have mastered the art of surprise, but sometimes I just have fun with it.

I kick in the door. I point my gun at my mark's head. I smile.

LATER, I CALL JONATHAN AS I HEAD TOWARD A CAB RANK.

"How did it go?" he asks.

"Great. I think I scared the living shit out of him." I am tracking down everyone in the network, with help from Giselle. I check up on them, make sure they're not up to no good. It gives me something to do. "How was the auction?"

Jonathan and Mas drove to Strasbourg for an estate sale. Jonathan was looking for new weapons for the antiques market stall he's been running.

"You won't believe this," he says, "but I won a pair of flintlock pistols that were allegedly used by Catherine the Great."

"Cool. How much did they cost?"

"You won't believe that either."

Jonathan doesn't accompany me on my missions. I started going alone while he was recovering from his multiple gunshot wounds. Once he was relatively healed, I could tell his heart wasn't in it. I think it's healthy that we each have our own thing.

Home is a very small apartment in Montmartre. With a courtyard, and neighbors who think we're weird. We have dinner with Mas and Giselle every Sunday. They had their baby, a girl called Carmela. I still hold my breath every time I hold her; some things are truly scary.

"I'm hopping on the next flight," I tell Jonathan, "but I might not be back in time for dinner."

"I think you should take the train," he says.

"Then I *definitely* won't be back for dinner."

"Just go to the train station."

The crowd is thick when I arrive at Munich Central Station. The world is filled with people living the most extraordinary, ordinary lives.

As I'm coming down the stairs I see him on the floor, in a suit that's been dry-cleaned too many times, with his hands in his pockets, gazing up at me.

When I reach the floor, he's gone. He's vanished into the crowd. I have to find him again.

I used to think that if I left the agency, my adventures would stop. My life would end. But I was wrong. And I was right.

My old life has ended. My new life is only just beginning.

Acknowledgments

Massive thanks to my agent, Sarah Bedingfield, for enthusiastic early support.

Big thanks to my editorial team, Jen Monroe and Candice Coote, as well as the rest of the crew at Berkley, especially Loren Jaggers.

Huge thanks to my friends and fellow Berkley authors: Lauren Accardo, Nekesa Afia, Olivia Blacke, Elizabeth Everett, Sarah Grunder Ruiz, Ali Hazelwood, Libby Hubscher, Amanda Jayatissa, Melissa Larsen, Amy Lea, Lyn Liao Butler, Mia P. Manansala, Tori Anne Martin, Lynn Painter, Freya Sampson and Sarah Zachrich Jeng. Thank you for holding my hand through it all.